D0236435

Pier Pressure

*Other Five Star Titles
by Dorothy Francis:*

Conch Shell Murder

Pier Pressure

A Keely Moreno mystery

Dorothy Francis

Five Star • Waterville, Maine

This novel is a work of fiction. Names, characters, places and incidents are either the product of the author's imagination, or, if real, used fictitiously.

First Edition
First Printing: January 2005

Published in 2005 in conjunction with Tekno Books and Ed Gorman.

Set in 11 pt. Plantin.

Printed in the United States on permanent paper.

Library of Congress Cataloging-in-Publication Data

Francis, Dorothy Brenner.
    Pier pressure : a Keely Moreno mystery / by Dorothy Francis.
        p. cm.
    ISBN 1-59414-271-8 (hc : alk. paper)
        1. Reflexology (Therapy)—Fiction.   2. Key West (Fla.)—
    Fiction.   3. Divorced women—Fiction.   4. Abused wives—
    Fiction.   I. Title.
    PS3556.R327P54 2005
    813'.54—dc22   2004057546

Dedication

For Dee Stuart my writing mentor and long-time friend

And

For Judith Pulse who introduced me to foot reflexology

Acknowledgments

My thanks to the many people who have helped make this book possible and especially to:

Maureen Moran, my agent
Ed Gorman, every writer's friend
John Helfers, my editor at Tekno
Mary P. Smith, my editor at Five Star

Also special thanks to Detective Jeremy Linsenmeyer, Marshalltown, IA, and to Sheriff Richard Roth, Monroe County, FL who provided information on police procedure. Any errors that may have slipped in are my own.

Chapter 1

The one thing my foot reflexology courses didn't teach me was how to deal with a corpse. That Sunday had started out in a rush as I gathered my supplies for an early morning appointment.

My name is Keely Moreno and I'm the only professional foot reflexologist in Key West—or maybe in all of the Florida Keys. Four years ago I earned my certificate from St. Petersburg's *International Institute of Reflexology*. I've worked hard to set up my private practice here on Duval Street. Many people are interested in new concepts of disease prevention, healing, and healthful living, and today as I glanced at the golden foot hanging above my sign, I smiled. ALTERNATIVE HEALING. KEELY MORENO. FOOT REFLEXOLOGIST. I have a thriving business.

Parking in Key West is the pits, so right now I don't own a car. I walk or ride my bike. I stood loading my bicycle basket with a small battery-operated footbath, deep-piled towels, and the scented oils I use for Margaux Ashford's treatment when Gram called to me from the doorway of her specialty shop next door to my office. CELIA HERNANDEZ SUNDRIES. That's what the sign above her doorway says. Gram operates a coffee bar and sells specialty coffees and hard-to-find gourmet items for local restaurants, food hounds, and coffee lovers.

"Keely. Keely. Please to stop one momento."

"Coming, Gram. Give me a sec." I took time to tuck the tape recorder I use to record patients' comments into my shirt pocket, slip my cell phone into my pants pocket.

9

Gram could see I'd dressed in my work-a-day khaki jump-suit and was preparing to leave. I tried to act as if I had an eternity of time, but I was running late for my seven o'clock standing appointment with Margaux. Why was Gram being so impervious to my time schedule? Why was she delaying me? I didn't want to be short with her, but neither did I want to be late for my appointment. Propping my bike on its kickstand, I stepped into her shop.

Although she pretends to be unaware of it, Gram's one of Key West's colorful tourist attractions. She dresses in a scarlet caftan and head bandeau, and her golden hoop earrings and sandals make her look like a make-believe pirate. Gram celebrated her seventy-second birthday last week, but she keeps her age a top secret, along with the fact that she wears earplugs at night so she can sleep in spite of Duval Street racket.

"Good morning, Gram. What's the good news?"

I planted a kiss on her cheek and inhaled the fragrance of freshly-ground coffee beans. Behind the serving counter with its high bar stools, a cappuccino machine dominated one corner of her shop, and an espresso machine the other. Gallon-size glass jars bearing coffee beans sat on floor-to-ceiling shelves. I grew up in this shop, living with Gram in an upper apartment after my mother's death. I still remember the pungent scent of hickory nut coffee beans and the sweet taste of French vanilla cappuccino.

Gram barely smiled at me. "Keely, you see Jude Cardell this morning?"

My shoulders slumped. I hated thinking of my ex so early in the day. In fact, I hated thinking of Jude at all, at any time, on any day.

"No, Gram. I didn't see Jude. Why do you ask?"

"Because I see him. It be almost hour ago. He walk past

your office. He no stop, but he look in. I think he up to trouble. Trouble for you."

"It's a public sidewalk, Gram. No law against people walking by. My window drapery's still drawn. Jude could look forever and see nothing."

I kept my voice light because I didn't want Gram to know how much Jude still frightened me. Some things in my life are private. Private and scary. After five years, I still hear his threat. *I'll see you dead.* His words replay in my mind. *I'll see you dead. I'll see you dead.* I worry. What real protection can a restraining order be?

"Jude hide his dark side well," Gram said. "People see him, say Mr. Nice Guy. I see him, I say *el Diablo.* You watch out for that one, Keely. You watch out."

"I'll do that, Gram. Jude impresses people as a nice business person working his way up at the *Hubble & Hubble* law firm, but he doesn't fool the Ashfords or me. We know Jude for what he is."

I wished I felt as confident as I sounded to Gram. I watch my back. Now and then I imagine I see Jude's hulking form lurking near, but I don't tell Gram that.

I'd never told Gram that Jude had deliberately inflicted my back injury. Oh, she knew I'd seen lots of doctors. She knew that when they couldn't relieve my pain they'd suggested spinal cord surgery. Scary idea. I'd stalled them off. Later, when I read an ad in the Miami *Herald* about foot reflexology as an alternative to surgery, I decided to give it a try. So Jude did one good thing. The pain he inflicted on me eventually led to establishing my career—to becoming a foot reflexologist.

"Keely, where you go? Why you so loaded down?"

Gram's voice snapped me from my thoughts, reminding me that I should be hurrying, but she didn't fool me by changing the subject. She knew about my early appointment. She was making small talk, to delay me. She disliked Margaux and maybe she thought Margaux would fire me if I failed to arrive promptly.

"I'm going to Margaux Ashford's. It's Sunday, Gram. You know the drill." I love Gram, so in spite of running late, I didn't hurry away.

Gram scowled. Few people in Key West smile at hearing Margaux's name.

"Before you go, help please. Lift new bag of beans to countertop? It be cruise ship day. I prepare for many customers."

Sometimes we locals resent thousands of cruise ship passengers making our sidewalks impassable. Then we remember the tinkle of our cash registers, and we smile.

"Sure, Gram. Where's the bag?"

"Behind counter. Hate begging help. Simple chores I once do with ease."

"No problem, Gram. No problem." I hoisted the heavy jute bag to the counter near the coffee grinder, pulled the drawstring to open it, and smooched her a kiss.

"See ya later, Gram." I mounted my bike and pedaled toward the Ashford home, lost in my thoughts.

Usually, I don't make house calls, but when Margaux Ashford requested that extra service, I agreed to give early-morning treatments for her back problems in the privacy of her home. In spite of Key West's live-and-let-live attitude, I still hear snide comments about Margaux's May/December marriage to Beau Ashford, twenty years her junior.

"She's tadpoling," one woman snickered.

"I might tadpole, too, if I had her bod," an older lady responded.

At sixty-nine, Margaux's a woman other women love to

hate. Not only has she inherited family money, but she also maintains the sleek and svelte body of a forty-year-old, a youthful hairdo that distracts the eye from a few wrinkles, and an agile way of moving that belies her age. In addition to all that, her editorial career is at high peak.

Margaux and her former husband and business manager, Otto Koffan, moved to Key West in semi-retirement a few years ago. Margaux had fallen in love with the island after visiting here several times as a guest speaker at the *Key West Literary Seminar*. Otto shared her enthusiasm for moving to this island in the sun the locals call Paradise.

Margaux's current husband, Beau Ashford, lost his wife to cancer several years ago and he eased his grief by taking a deep interest in and financially helping sponsor the *Key West Literary Seminar*. Now, in addition to serving on the boards of a local bank and the community college, Beau writes a respected weekly column for Key West's *Citizen* concerning historical events of this area.

Margaux persuaded Beau to submit a collection of his columns for book publication to her publisher and she offered to edit the manuscript. For weeks they worked closely together. Their association eventually led to Margaux's divorce from Otto, her marriage to Beau, and then to Otto's on-the-rebound marriage to Shandy Mertz, a cocktail waitress at *The Wharf*.

Now, three years later, some of the city's gossips still mention Beau's name in shocked or disgusted tones. Personally, I think they're green with envy because Margaux not only shares Beau's bed, but also enjoys a successful career working at home as an editor for HarperCollins in New York.

Margaux has been one of my top-notch customers for several years, and I make no judgments about her private life, or Beau's. Margaux feels that it detracts from her youthful image to be seen patronizing my shop, so I humor her. On Sunday mornings, I bike to the old house on Grinnell Street where she and Beau live.

This early February morning is typical of a winter Sunday in Key West. On Duval Street, beer cans, sandwich wrappers, and soda bottles lay like malevolent snacks in a dip of spilled well drinks and upchucked beer. The orange-jacketed street cleaners worked with a minimum of enthusiasm.

Turning onto Simonton Street because less clutter threatened my bike tires, I rode through the almost-deserted streets. I enjoyed these few minutes before the island came to life complete with boom box noise, tourist RVs almost wider than the narrow streets, and people frantically seeking quarters for the parking meters that allowed only fifteen minutes per coin.

I pedaled a bit faster. Margaux told me that Beau would be at Key Colony Beach today helping with a fishing derby, and she invited me to stay for brunch following her treatment. I love their home. After his first wife's death, Beau leased *Ashford Mansion*, the mansion he had shared with her in Old Town, to his twins, Jass and Punt, and moved to a different residential area. This morning, night-blooming jasmine still scented the air, and bougainvillea vines climbed the palm trees to the balconies of old-time Conch houses where they spilled over, dropping pink and purple petals onto the sidewalks below. At Truman Avenue I turned left and pedaled to Grinnell then headed toward the ocean. The Ashford home sat squeezed between two similar Conch houses, separated from its near neighbors by living privacy fences comprised of palms, seagrapes, and crotons.

On this crowded island, building contractors have only one way to go—up.

Beau and Margaux liked neither the sleek high-rise

condos near the airport nor those on the other side of the island with a Gulf-side view. Instead, they had chosen this old home decorated a century ago with gingerbread trim hand-carved by Conch sailors whiling away spare hours during long voyages. Like many of Key West's wealthy families, the Ashfords had made no changes to their home's exterior, but a Miami decorator had helped them modernize the interior.

I chained and locked my bicycle to a palm tree inside the white picket fence and entry gate. It's never smart to leave an unattended bicycle unlocked—not even on Sunday morning. Hoisting the portable footbath and lotions from my bike basket, I headed for the front door. Dwarf hibiscus plants in large clay pots lined the sidewalk and porch steps. Scarlet. Yellow. Orange. Pink. White. They subtly advertised Jass's career and business, her hibiscus greenhouse. I picked up a lavender blossom that had fallen on the porch steps and tucked it in the top buttonhole on my jumpsuit as I waited for Margaux to answer my knock.

All remained quiet. Then, through the window to the right of the doorway, I saw Margaux sitting in an armchair. A copy of *Southern Living* had fallen to the floor near her feet. At first I thought she sat sleeping. Then hairs rose on my nape. Her head lolled slightly to one side. Surely she had heard my steps on the porch. I frowned as I rapped again and my mouth went dry as my sense of foreboding increased.

"Margaux," I called as I tried the door. "It's me, Keely. Margaux?"

The door swung open and I stepped over the threshold. I had a horrible feeling I hadn't caught Margaux napping. Heart attack? Stroke? Perhaps sudden illness or a seizure had prevented her from reaching the phone to call for help. I stepped from the hallway into the living room and gasped.

Blood drenched her white robe and had dripped onto the chair, the carpet.

Then I saw more blood oozing from the bullet hole in her head.

Chapter 2

In a reflex action, I rushed to Margaux's side. Maybe she was still alive. Maybe I could help her, save her. I'd taken CPR training last year. Maybe. Maybe. But even as those frantic thoughts raced through my mind, I knew in my gut that Margaux was dead. Now the stench of blood and death that I hadn't noticed at first made me want to run, but shock and nausea held me to the spot. I'd read many times about the unforgettable odor of death. Now I experienced it first-hand. My knees wobbled as I forced myself to stand motionless before her, frozen now by fear and the ever-rising urge to vomit. I grabbed a deep breath, clamped my hand over my mouth and nose, and somehow managed to swallow.

In the distance, bells pealed like a threnody from the Catholic Church. Closer at hand, a dog howled, a car horn honked, and brakes squealed—ordinary sounds, intruding on the early Sunday stillness. A breeze set nearby palm branches in motion, reminding me of gentle rain. Move. Move. My mind ordered my body into motion. Taking care to avoid stepping in the blood that stained the carpet, I bent to touch it. Damp. I jerked my hand back. What had I expected? I wiped my finger on the leg of my jumpsuit, leaving a rust-colored stain.

Then I stepped closer to Margaux. I didn't want to touch her. No. No. The idea repelled me, and my mind recoiled from the thought. But I had to touch her, didn't I? Yes. I had to make sure she was beyond help.

My teeth chattered and my whole body trembled as I reached for her left wrist that lay on the folds of her blood-stained robe. Maybe I'd feel a pulse. Maybe a rescue unit could save her if I acted quickly. Maybe her life at this very moment depended on my swift action, my clear thinking. Maybe. Maybe.

Murder? Suicide? Thoughts jumbled in my mind. Who would want to murder Margaux? I could think of nobody. Suicide? My mind screamed the word. No! Margaux Ashford had no reason to commit suicide. She had everything going for her. Everything. She had it all. When I touched her wrist, I thought her skin felt cold, but my own icy fingers made me doubt my sense of touch. I moved silently, carefully, gently as I pressed my fingers on the underside of her wrist, steadying her arm with my thumb on top of her wrist. No pulse beat. None. Or maybe my shaking had caused me to miss it.

Changing the position of my fingers, I tried again, waiting for the faint beat that would indicate life. Nothing. I straightened up and backed away from—the body. I felt sure Margaux was dead. She had been my customer, not a dear friend, but in that moment I felt a closeness to her and I felt horrified at her violent death. Although I was well practiced at holding back and hiding tears, I felt dampness on my cheeks. I wiped my face with the palms of my hands and the tears stopped as suddenly as they had started.

I backed off another step. What if someone had shot Margaux and fled from the scene? Or worse yet, what if a killer still lurked nearby? This old house offered a plethora of nook-and-cranny hiding places. I could be the next victim! Common sense jogged my fear and told me to get the heck away from this house, to run for my life.

Let someone else find Margaux's body. Anyone else. Someone who knew how to deal with that sort of thing. I could gather my reflexology gear, stow it in my bike basket, and pedal back to Duval Street before anyone knew I had been here. This neighborhood still slept. Nobody would be the wiser. Then my shoulders slumped. I couldn't live with myself if I ran away. Besides, too many people knew of my Sunday morning schedule, my appointments with Margaux. Gram. Beau's kids. And Beau, of course. But more important, *I knew*. I'd have to live with my decision forever.

Fate had thrown me into this situation up to my eyebrows and I had to deal with it. Reluctantly I eased my cell phone from my pocket. Somehow I stopped my fingers from trembling long enough to key in nine-one-one.

"Police dispatcher," a cool voice flowed across the wire as if from a great distance. "Who's speaking, please?"

"Keely Moreno here." My throat felt stiff as a steel pipe, and my stress-frazzled voice threatened to fail. The line hummed as I cleared my throat. "I'm calling to report a—a body. A dead body. Please send help quickly."

"Where are you, Miss Moreno?" the dispatcher asked, her voice still unflustered and sea-water cool.

"I'm at the Beau Ashford home on Grinnell Street. I'm not sure of the exact address. Shall I step outside and look at the house number?"

"No, Miss Moreno. Our people know the Ashford house. Everyone knows it by sight. Please keep calm and stay where you are. Our rescue unit's on its way and will arrive in a very few minutes. You may need to supply some details."

"Thank you." I wanted to say something more that would keep our conversation alive and going. I wanted her to talk me through the agonizing moments until help arrived. She was my lifeline, but I could think of nothing more to say. I clicked the power switch, jammed the phone back into my pocket, and paced the room while I waited for the police, the ambulance, the fire truck. Would they arrive with sirens wailing? Maybe I should call Jass, Beau's daughter and my close friend, and tell her what I'd found. Over the telephone? Would that be the kind thing to do? Forget that. Jass was probably still in Miami keeping tabs on her annual entry in the Hibiscus Show. She'd learn the news soon enough.

I backed off from calling Jass's twin, too. Who knew where or with whom Punt might be sleeping? Nor could I bear waiting another minute in the Ashford home. I forced myself to move calmly as I stepped onto the front porch, walked down the five steps, and into the yard. Why was I counting the steps so carefully? For once I understood people like Shandy Koffan who had a compulsive need to count things—everything. I walked through the yard, out the gate, and into the street. In spite of what the dispatcher had said, I planned to flag down the rescue unit, to make sure the driver didn't accidentally pass by the Ashford house.

I had only been standing at the curbing for a few moments when I caught a glimpse of Jude walking away from me on the other side of the street. What was he doing in this neighborhood? Jude lived on Key Haven, several miles from here, closer to Boca Chica than to Grinnell Street. Was he returning to the scene of the crime? I knew that was an unfair thought. Maybe I had discovered no crime other than suicide. Much as I hated to admit it, Jude had a right to walk anywhere he chose to walk—anywhere except near me. Right now his presence rattled me, and I ducked behind a palm tree, fearing he might turn and see me at any moment, but maybe I had been mistaken. Maybe the man wasn't Jude at all. Finding Margaux's body had shaken me. I peeked from behind the palm for another look.

No. There was no mistaking Jude's bulky form, his shiny bald head, and his pale skin. Pale skin's hard to come by in Key West. Why had I ever fallen for Jude Cardell? I had my reasons at the time, but that question often haunted my worst nightmares as I remembered a broken jaw, bruised breasts, and frequent cigarette burns on many hidden and tender body spots that Jude knew would never meet the public eye.

Jude was handsome in a way, with broad cheekbones, a Roman nose, and eyes the color of aquamarines. But since our divorce he'd shaved his head. I wondered what the dignified attorneys at *Hubble & Hubble* thought of that. But in Key West, anything goes. Jude reminded me of a giant toadstool, a fungus grown secretly and stealthily in some dank cave. A scary and unsavory fungus.

I thought of the pistol in my office desk drawer. I hated guns. Nikko had bought it for me at the time of my divorce. Nikko's the retired cop who lives in an apartment above my office, and Gram and I know him well. Although he accompanied me to the practice range and supervised my extensive target training, the gun still frightens me. I hate its coldness in my hand, the pungent odor of the spent bullets. I've never used it off the practice range, but somehow, I wished I had it with me now.

Sirens wailing in the distance jerked my attention to the present long before the police car arrived. Wailing sirens are a frightening sound in Key West, although they are frequently an intrusion. Drivers know they're supposed to pull over, stop, and give the emergency vehicle the right of way, but many times a narrow street offers no safe space to do that. Out on Highway 1, pulling over may splash a driver into the sea. On the narrow city streets, pulling over could cause an accident, but no traffic clogged Grinnell Street yet this morning.

The police car arrived, carrying two uniformed officers. Then the ambulance pulled to the curb. Then the fire truck. After that another police car joined the fray, bringing men in suits and ties. Slamming car doors created a cacophony of sound. For a few moments, neighbors peeked from behind louvers and shades before they ventured into their yards to see the action coming down at the Ashfords'. One woman in a polka-dot housecoat and pink hair rollers made a pretense of sweeping her porch steps and front walk. A man leaned on his fence, openly ogling the scene.

I jumped, startled, as a plainclothes detective approached me and flashed his ID. Detective Jonathan Curry. His compact frame loomed over me, intimidated me, but his steel gray eyes carried more power than his height. They bored like laser beams, burning into my brain, threatening to illumine any secrets I might try to hide. I fought a rising panic along with a deep sensation of aloneness. What if I couldn't breathe? What if my words clogged in my throat? I straightened my back and raised my chin. Sometimes that gave me a feeling of needed height. Not this time.

"You Keely Moreno?"

"Yes, sir."

Detective Curry pulled a dog-eared notepad and a ballpoint from his jacket pocket without taking his gaze from my face. "You're the one who reported the body?"

"Yes, sir."

"Where is it?"

"Inside the house, sir, but I saw it first through the porch window before I reached the door."

"You knocked on the door?" His ballpoint flew across the page.

"Yes, sir."

"Nobody answered?"

"Right. Nobody answered." *How could she answer when she's dead?* I wanted to scream at him, but I choked the words back along with the sarcastic thought.

"Come with me, please," Detective Curry ordered.

Although I hated the idea of going back inside that house, I tagged after him up the five steps and through the open doorway. Several more police officers arrived and followed us, their footsteps sounding hollow against the wooden stairs.

I recognized Joe Rankin, the barrel-chested cop who had befriended me after Mom's death and who knew all about my problems with Jude. He's now one of my patients and we nodded to each other. I also knew Dr. Wantize, the pudgy medical examiner, and Kurt Worthington, a stringbean of a man who worked as police photographer. In a matter of a few moments, the police officers outside got the go-ahead from someone to stretch yellow tape around the Ashford property. CRIME SCENE DO NOT CROSS. I shuddered as I read the black letters from where I stood near the door. Did the tape mean the police suspected murder? Or was suicide a crime, too?

Dr. Wantize examined Margaux's body, doing the stethoscope thing to check for heartbeat, forcing her eyelids open with his thumb, and shining a bright light onto her sightless pupils. Detective Curry stepped between me and Margaux's body, and for a few moments I couldn't tell what the policemen were doing. I didn't really want to know. When Curry stepped aside to talk with Joe Rankin, I saw another cop place paper bags around Margaux's hands like mittens, securing them at her wrists. I could hardly bear to look, nor could I bear to look away as Dr. Wantize worked with thermometers, vials of liquid, and Handi-Wipes. At last, he shook his head and nodded toward Detective Curry.

"Been dead seven or eight hours, that's my guess. That puts the time of death around ten to midnight last night. Hard to tell exactly, but I'm guessing that's a close estimate."

Detective Curry nodded and scrawled an entry on his notepad. "Suicide? Murder? Your opinion?"

"That's your bailiwick, Jon. I'll give you the pertinent facts. You make the call."

"With your help and advice," Curry said. "Looks like this could be a tough one. No suicide note?"

"Not in this area," Wantize replied. "Don't know about other rooms."

"My men'll check the rest of the house."

Kurt Worthington's flashbulb left dizzying circles before my eyes as he snapped many pics of the room and of Margaux's body, before replacing his camera in its case and slinging the strap over his shoulder.

"All through, Detective," he said at last.

The ambulance crew lumbered inside with a stretcher. Working quickly for such big men, they lifted Margaux's body onto the narrow plank and I saw a gun fall to the floor, saw another cop pick it up and drop it into an evidence bag before they covered her with a blanket, and carried her to the ambulance. The growing crowd waiting outside the crime scene tape called muted questions to the crew, but received few answers.

"No comment," one officer called out.

"Stand back, please," another officer ordered. "Give the ambulance crew room."

"Where are they taking her?" I asked. "Hospital? Funeral Home?" I looked away from the scene in the street.

"Morgue." Detective Curry's voice sounded like a pair of scissors, clipping the word from a string of inner thoughts. Then he gave me his full attention once more. "Who found the body?" he asked.

"I did, sir." He'd asked me that before, but I didn't remind him of that. Was he checking my memory? Did he think I might forget? Or change my story? I'd had enough interaction with the police during my marriage and divorce

24

from Jude to know first-hand what he might be thinking.

"Your full name, please."

"Keely Moreno."

He wrote it down as if hearing it for the first time. "Address?"

"Duval Street." When he insisted, I gave the exact address of my business.

"Did you touch anything in the house?"

"Yes, sir. I touched Margaux's . . . hand. Her left hand."

He lowered his notepad. "Why did you do that?" His probing gaze bored into me. "Didn't you realize you might be contaminating the crime scene?" His laser beam stare carried an accusation.

"I found Margaux Ashford, my client, unresponsive, sir. I needed to see if she was still alive, to see if I, or perhaps doctors, could help her."

Detective Curry's ballpoint scratched on his notepad, refusing to write. He jammed it back into his pocket and pulled out a fresh one. After testing it and finding it worthy, he continued his questions.

". . . *anything you say may be used against you.*" The words from mystery novels and TV movies replayed through my mind and again my teeth began to chatter, although the day had grown warmer.

"Suppose you tell me your story from the beginning," Detective Curry said. "What time did you discover the body and what were you doing here at this time of the day? You had legitimate business at seven A.M.?"

"Are you going to read me my rights?" Again, the feeling of being utterly alone washed over me, threatening to drag me into some deep abyss I would rather avoid. If Detective Curry let me make one telephone call, I'd call Beau. No. Wrong. Beau was out of town. I'd call Nikko. A retired cop would know about a situation like this one. "Do I need a lawyer?"

"You're not under arrest, Miss Moreno. My gut feeling is that you happened to show up at the wrong place at the wrong time. Right now, I'm asking informal questions to help me figure out what happened here last night. You don't have to answer on the spot, of course. If you'd feel more at ease, I'll take you to police headquarters for formal questioning."

At ease! Hah! I didn't have to answer his informal questions. Double Hah! But I knew if I refused to answer here and now I'd look guilty. Of murder? Of helping Margaux commit suicide? Some choice he offered me. Some fat choice I had. I tried to imagine what Nikko or Beau would tell me to do, but I sensed the detective's growing impatience. And I began to talk.

Chapter 3

"I told you that Margaux Ashford is—was my patient, my reflexology patient. We have—had a standing appointment for her foot reflexology treatment every Sunday morning at seven. I arrived a bit late this morning due to some delays at my office, but my watch said only a few minutes past seven when I arrived and knocked on her front door."

"Foot reflexology treatment?" Detective Curry lifted his ballpoint and waited. "She had a problem with her feet? Explain, please."

Did he write in shorthand? Did he plan to record every word I said? I began to talk faster, hoping to confuse him and hoping he'd have trouble keeping up.

"I'm a certified foot reflexologist with an office on Duval Street." I began my information dump, the explanation I gave to new patients or potential patients who showed interest in alternative approaches to healing. Only for prospective patients, I talked much more slowly and punctuated my words with frequent smiles. Now I kept a solemn face and used my memorized speech to stall for time, to give myself more moments to think. Could I speed-talk and think about something else at the same time? I hoped so, but as long as I talked about reflexology I wasn't talking about Margaux's death.

"Reflexology's an ancient form of pressure therapy. The Egyptians knew about it thousands of years ago. It involves applying focused pressure to certain known reflex points located in the foot. These points correspond to certain areas in the body. The therapy results in increased blood circulation to the affected body areas, relaxation in those areas, and a release of tensions. Reflexology has stopped pain for many people."

I half expected Detective Curry to laugh or to question my explanation that obviously covered territory brand new to him. Since he did neither, he rose a bit in my estimation.

"So you came here on legitimate business," he said.

"Yes, sir."

"Are you aware that the person finding a dead body is of special interest to the police?"

"Yes." I could think of nothing else to say. Did he intend to accuse me of murder? Of assisting a suicide? I began to feel trapped, suffocated by my own breath and voice. And my feeling of aloneness penetrated more deeply into my being. I added fear of the police and their questions to my fear of Jude Cardell.

"How long had Mrs. Ashford been calling on your services?" Pen poised once more, Detective Curry gazed into my eyes.

"For a couple of years—more or less. I have an accurate record of each of her visits on tape as well as on my office computer." I didn't tell him I had the tape recorder in my pocket. In his case, I considered it a don't-ask-don't-tell situation, but all my patients know I record our conversations during a work session. "If you'd like to see my records concerning Margaux Ashford, I'll print them out for you."

"That may be necessary for the courtroom later, but not right now. I'll take your word that you have her records."

The courtroom? Could he hear my mind shouting those words? Was he threatening me? I clamped my jaws together to keep my teeth from chattering as I pictured twelve jurors staring at me from a jury box while a black-robed judge banged a gavel for attention in the courtroom.

"Your reflexology treatments must have given Mrs. Ashford relief, right?"

"Yes, of course. That's why she booked the standing appointment."

"Do you ever treat patients with shoulder and back pain?" He dropped his pad and ballpoint back into his pocket.

"Of course," I replied. A trick question? I wondered. Why would he ask that?

"Are you taking new patients? I mean, if you could fit me in, I'd like to have you see what you can do for my shoulders. Doctors haven't seemed to help me any. Foot reflexology's a new healing concept to me, but I'm willing to try it. Is it painful?"

"Very little pain involved." It amused me that this big guy, this formidable detective, might be afraid of a little pain.

"I like to play tennis and golf, but here lately . . ."

I hesitated. Would a detective investigating a suicide or a murder spend time asking questions about my reflexology business? About making an appointment? Something about his quick questions and his seemingly quick acceptance of reflexology as an alternative treatment put me on guard.

He came here to investigate a death, didn't he? Did he really have shoulder and back problems, or did he just want to see my office, see if I had a legitimate business? My mind swirled with questions I couldn't answer. Police detectives didn't have to make appointments to investigate, did they? Nothing could stop this man from coming to my office at any time with a search warrant or with more questions. Or nothing would keep him from coming to my office to make an appointment. I decided to take him at his word—at least for the time being. He wanted a reflexology treatment and I seldom turn down the chance to work with a new and needy patient.

"Yes, I can give you a time slot, but I'll have to check my appointment calendar at the office."

"Fine," he said. "I'd like to go there with you now. My men will finish taking care of the crime scene and notifying the next of kin."

Now I felt almost sure that he wanted to check out my place of business. I considered telling him that Margaux had no next of kin except Beau, that she had been born in a Greek village where her family had all been killed by raiding Albanians many years ago. That she had escaped by playing dead until the raiders left. I kept quiet. Why should I be of help? Let this detective do his own detecting into Margaux's past.

"Do you care to ride along with me?" he asked. "Or do you prefer to go on ahead and let me follow you there?"

I nodded toward the reflexology equipment I'd laid on the entryway table when I stepped into the house.

"I travel by bicycle. After I've loaded my equipment into my bike basket, you're welcome to follow me to my office. Or if that's too slow for you, you can meet me there. Duval Street. My office's next to my grandmother's coffee shop. Celia Hernandez Sundries."

"I know the place," he said. "I'll meet you there. I've enjoyed your grandmother's espresso for years. Can't say that I've ever noticed your office, though."

I had many mixed feelings about having Detective Curry visit my office right now. I'd left it very early, before I'd had a chance to straighten it up, make it presentable for visitors, and I've never been noted for my housekeeping skills. I had no choice. He followed me out the door.

Detective Curry helped me off the porch and down the steps with my reflexology gear, assisted me in loading it onto my bicycle, and then watched while I pedaled toward Duval Street. At least he didn't seem to think I might try to escape via bicycle. Of course, he beat me to my office. When I arrived, he already sat perched on a high stool at Gram's coffee bar sipping espresso.

Unspoken questions leaped at me from Gram's dark eyes, but she said nothing. I wondered if Curry had told her about Margaux, but I didn't want to ask. Plenty of time to talk to Gram about Margaux later, and I preferred to do it privately.

Since Detective Curry already knew Gram, they needed no introduction. He thanked her for her hospitality, set his coffee cup down, and we walked directly to my workplace. As I bent slightly to unlock the door, the ring on my necklace swung into his view.

"An interesting ring," Detective Curry commented. "It has the rosy glow of Cuban gold. Is it a family piece?"

"Yes, my mother's wedding band." I didn't go into the details about Mom's death and I hated being asked about them, but I felt his questions coming.

"Your mother lives in Key West, too?" he asked.

I opened the door, pushed my bicycle inside, then propped it on its kickstand, before I answered his question. "No, sir. My mother's dead. Her murderer's doing life without chance of parole in a prison up north."

"Did this happen recently?"

"I was fifteen when she died. One crazed druggie went on a binge and snuffed out one worthwhile life. Maybe you remember the case. It made big news headlines at the time." I wished I hadn't said so much. Didn't want him to think I was playing for sympathy or feeling sorry for myself, but when conversation turns to my mother, my feelings run strong and deep.

"Must have happened before I moved to the Keys," he said. "I apologize for touching on sad memories."

"Sad memories, yes, but I like remembering those good

days when Mom was alive. Long before my birth, Gram sent Mom as a baby from Havana to Miami on the Pedro Pan airlift."

"I'm not aware of that airlift." He paused barely inside the doorway.

"You may recall reading a bit about it. It took place around nineteen fifty-nine or nineteen sixty. The organizers both in Cuba and Miami kept it very hush-hush at the time, but now I see articles about it in the papers every so often. Beau Ashford wrote a column about it last month."

"No, I don't remember that airlift. I lived abroad then—with the military. But I'm interested. Tell me a little about it."

Again, I suspected Detective Curry had ulterior motives for delving into more details concerning the Pedro Pan airlift, but I preferred that subject to the subject of my mother's death or finding Margaux's body. I wanted to keep him listening. I wanted to be the one talking—talking about anything except a dead body.

My office held the mixed fragrances of peppermint, sage, lemon—some of the soaps and herbs I used in oils and lotions. I led Detective Curry to a chair beside my cluttered desk.

"Please make yourself comfortable. I'll be right with you."

I wheeled my bike back behind the partition that separated my office from my apartment. When I returned, Curry sat eyeing my desk, so I made a hurried pretense of straightening it, tossing a faded blossom from a crystal dish into my wastebasket, quickly replacing it with the blossom in my buttonhole. Then I shoved some unopened mail into my top drawer, slid a reflexology magazine to a desk corner. After that brief flurry of activity, I opened the privacy curtain for more light, but I placed a CLOSED sign in the window while sweat beaded under my bangs.

"You're closing right now?" Curry asked. "Don't let my presence stop your daily business."

"I'm closing out of respect for Margaux Ashford," I said. "I'll call today's clients in a few minutes." Even as I settled into the swivel chair behind my teakwood desk and began talking, I still had the feeling that Detective Curry remained in charge.

"You were telling me about the Pedro Pan airlift," Curry said.

"When Castro and his guerrillas ousted President Batista from Cuba, some Cuban citizens in Havana, along with Catholic charities in Miami, organized a secret airlift to whisk kids out of Cuba. Castro was closing schools and churches and confiscating privately-owned property. If the kids had no relatives in America, parents sent them to Catholic orphanages until they themselves could escape Cuba and reunite with them.

"Mother spent a year in an orphanage before Gram's family managed to reach Miami by rowboat and claim her. My grandparents rowed ninety miles between Havana and Key West through shark-infested waters. Since then, our family has called Key West home. Mom married, but I never knew my father. He died when I was a baby. Then years later, Mom died at the hand of a killer. That's my story—all twenty-seven years of it."

I wished I had a longer story. The prospect of showing this detective around my office unnerved me. I suspected that in his mind he was accusing me of either murdering Margaux or of having some part in her suicide. *You know the person finding the body is always of special interest to the police.* His words replayed in my mind. Could he search my office without my permission? Didn't such searching require a warrant of some kind? What if he saw the gun in my desk drawer? Would he take it? Could he pick up whatever he wanted without my permission just because I found Margaux's body?

Scary questions raced through my mind and I wanted to get this man out of my office and on his way to wherever detectives go once they're through making body finders nervous. But I could see getting rid of him wasn't going to be that easy. He settled more comfortably into his chair, eyeing my account book and my calendar that lay on my desk beside the computer.

Did he really want an appointment? Or was he playing it cool—trying to put me at ease so I would reveal something incriminating?

Chapter 4

I had recently painted my office walls white and now the sun shining through the front picture window highlighted the whole room. Detective Curry studied the floor-to-ceiling shelves that held a few books, a stack of clean towels, colorful bottles, and jars of lotions. When his eye fell on my adjustable patient's chair, he rose and studied it carefully.

"This's where your patient sits during treatment?"

I joined him standing beside the chair. "Yes." I pushed a lever on the velvet-covered recliner that brought the footrest up to waist height and lowered the headrest. "This chair will accommodate a three-hundred-and-fifty-pound person and it's quite comfortable. It places the client's feet at a height that makes it easy for me to do my work."

Curry ran his hand over the soft fabric of the chair before he turned away.

"I place a pillow under the patient's head in case he doesn't enjoy having his feet higher than his head."

"I can see how a pillow might be needed."

With another glance around, Curry's eye caught my temporary living quarters only partially hidden behind a folding partition. He walked to the back of the office.

"You live in this office space, too?" His gaze took in my tiny living area, dining table, kitchen, bedroom. I wondered if he'd check out the bathroom to be sure I wasn't hiding more dead bodies.

"I used to live here full time, but now I'm only in the apartment one month of the year."

His gaze formed a question, but I said nothing until he

asked. "Why only one month of the year? This's the address you gave me. Where do you live the other eleven months?"

"I house-sit for a couple from North Dakota who rent a vacation place in an old established neighborhood on Georgia Street. They bought an ancient house they intend to modernize, but they only come down during March, so the modernizing is progressing very slowly. I sublet the house from them for the rest of the year. I'm pleased with the low rental price they offer, and they're pleased to have someone occupying their place—keeping it looking lived-in. It's a good deal for both of us. Rentals are hard to come by in Key West and I enjoy getting away from the busyness of Duval."

"I can understand that."

Detective Curry walked back toward the chair beside my desk, and I tried to distract him before he sat again. I still doubted he had come here purely for health reasons, so I gave him the hard sell—something I seldom do with potential customers whose business I value. "If you want to schedule a reflexology treatment today, I'll check my calendar for openings."

"Please do. The doc is talking about rotor-cuff surgery." He sighed. "I'd like to avoid that, if at all possible. What free times do you have? What's your work schedule like?"

Maybe he was for real after all. Or maybe he was, as Gram would say, catching two 'cuda on one bait shrimp—casing me out as a murder suspect and arranging for a treatment at the same time. The more hours he spent here getting treatments, the more opportunity he'd have to study my activities.

"Usually, I see only four clients a day. Each treatment lasts an hour or a bit more for the first one, and it's strenuous work."

"For your hands?"

"Yes—for my hands." I didn't try to tell him about the

drain on my body, on my soul, as energy flowed from my body into that of my patient. Few people understood that. "I like an hour's rest between sessions." I flipped over several pages of my appointment book. "When are you free? What hours are best for you?"

"Do you offer evening appointments?"

"No. My regular times are nine, eleven, one, and three and I take Wednesday afternoons off."

"When's your next free time?"

"How about next Saturday at three?"

Detective Curry checked a pocket calendar. "That would work out fine for me." He jotted the time and date onto his book, and I also gave him a business card with the time penciled on the back. Somehow I knew he'd remember his appointment. So would I.

"I'll see you then." I moved toward the door, subtly trying to urge him to do likewise. But he had more questions.

"Have you taken foot reflexology treatments that have helped you, Miss Moreno?"

"Yes, of course. I found it hard to believe that foot manipulations could relieve back pain as well as prevent future stress. But it's true. I won't say reflexology healed me. It wasn't a quick fix and the treatments didn't work overnight."

"But they did make your back feel more comfortable?"

"Yes. After a few weeks of treatments I could move about pain-free. I've felt fine now for several years. I wanted to pass this means of relief to others, so I earned my reflexology certificate and opened this office. Today people from all walks of life come to me to ease their aches, pains, and stress, and it pleases me to have found a way to help them and to earn enough to support myself, my boat, and my backcountry fishing habit."

"I'm looking forward to my appointment," he said as at last he left my office.

Once he drove out of sight, I drew the muslin drapery across the front window, re-enforcing the CLOSED sign. For a moment I sighed and sat down at my desk. But when I closed my eyes, hoping for a few minutes of solitude, the image of Margaux's body replayed on the screen of my mind along with the image of Jude walking down the street in that neighborhood where he didn't belong. The morning's happenings had left me drained of all energy, yet I almost welcomed talking to Gram when she tapped on my door.

"What's up, Keely?" Her earrings bobbed and her caftan swished as the sweet scent of cinnamon-flavored coffee wafted into the room with her. I closed the door quickly. "News announcer break into program." Gram's eyes grew wide. "He say Margaux Ashford dead. No more details. You know she dead? You find her? That be why detective here?"

"Right." I gave Gram all the details I had, knowing she wouldn't be satisfied until I did. But I didn't mention seeing Jude Cardell. Gram hated facing the fact that Jude still lived on planet earth, let alone right here in Key West. She thought he should have stayed in Miami where we had moved shortly after our marriage. I thought so, too, and I still shuddered at the thought of him. Jude's former violence warned me that in spite of all the judge's reassurances, the court's restraining order might be no more valuable than the paper it was written on.

Following our divorce, my counselor had pointed out that Jude's personality matched that of an abuser. Jude had wined and dined me and rushed me into marriage. I was so in love, or thought I was in love, that I let him manipulate me into doing whatever he wanted. His wish became my order. Then, once we were married and although I didn't want to leave

Key West, he insisted on moving to Miami, saying there were more job opportunities for him in a big city.

The counselor said his insistence on moving followed the abuser pattern—take the woman away from family and friends. That makes it much easier to control her. And control is the name of the abuser's game. In Miami, the wining and dining stopped and Jude's insane jealousy started. He accused me of having affairs with everyone from our next-door neighbor to the greengrocer at the Winn-Dixie. Although we could have used another income, Jude didn't want me to find a job: too many men in the workforce for me to flirt with.

"Police many time suspect person finding body."

Gram's words snapped me from my unpleasant memories of Jude and back to my unpleasant memories of Margaux's body and Detective Curry's questions.

"I know. You needn't remind me. The police have already made it clear that they consider me a suspect. Of course, Detective Curry also mentioned the possibility of suicide."

"Rotten deal for you to find body, Keely. Margaux spell trouble right from get-go. Lots of people think that, too. Who you suppose did her in?"

"You're jumping to conclusions, Gram. I saw no signs of a forced entry into the house. The door stood unlocked. I knocked and it swung open. It wasn't even tightly closed."

"Then a friend do it to her. If door be unlocked—means she let someone in. Someone she knew. Why would such snooty woman do suicide?" Gram lifted her nose into the air, mimicking her idea of snooty. "She think herself above death. She no do the community such a grand service as suicide."

"Gram! Back off. Beau loved her. Our literary community respected her. I considered her a good client."

"Carumba!" Gram voiced her pent-up feelings and left my office as quickly as she had arrived.

I jumped, startled as my talking wall clock announced twelve o'clock. Bad news travels fast. Shandy Koffan hadn't arrived for her nine o'clock. Surely she must have known my office would be closed. Had the news blurb told who found the body? I should have asked Gram that question. Out of courtesy, I called Consuela to cancel her one o'clock and she answered immediately. I held the receiver at a distance to protect my eardrums.

"Of course I've heard about Margaux." Consuela always spoke in mega-decibels although I had assured her many times that I wasn't hard of hearing. I held the receiver even farther from my ear. "Please expect no tears from me, Keely Moreno. None at all. Not even one little tear. That woman meant nothing to me—nothing but humiliations and put-downs."

"I didn't call you seeking tears, Consuela. I merely called to formally cancel your appointment for this afternoon. I'm just not up to giving treatments right now, and I'm closing my office today in respect for Margaux and the Ashford family. I'll be able to give you a make-up time tomorrow, Monday, at eleven."

"I dislike Monday appointments. You know that. I've told you that many times."

"Okay, if Monday doesn't suit you, we'll probably have to wait until Thursday."

"Why? Why not on Tuesday? Or Wednesday?"

"Because Margaux's memorial service may be scheduled for Tuesday or Wednesday, and I'm usually closed on Wednesday afternoons. Under the circumstances, I'd appreciate it if you'd come on Monday."

"What if I have a raging migraine this afternoon?"

"If that happens, you call me. I can give evening appointments, but only in an emergency. In the meantime, take care in what you say about Margaux. A closed mouth gathers no foot. Anything you say could be used against you if the police begin searching for a killer."

"I'm no killer. Surely the police can see that."

"What the police hear may be more important than what they see."

"The fact that Margaux's dead, changes not my opinion of her. I prefer to say exactly what I feel. Do you object?"

I sighed. "Say what you please, Consuela."

"The world would be a better place if everyone spoke honest feelings. Everyone knows Margaux and I had no great love for each other."

I held the receiver even farther from my ear. "Take care, Consuela, and do call me if you need me." I hung up quickly, and I smiled, imagining her still talking to a dead phone line.

Now I called Shandy and rescheduled her for tomorrow morning. After that I faced making the call I dreaded—the one to Jass. She planned to return from Miami in time for her three o'clock time slot because she couldn't bear waiting around at the show headquarters until they announced the winners. Although I didn't expect her to keep her appointment today, I had to call her.

Jass and I had been close friends since childhood, but even so, I could only guess at her down-deep feelings about Margaux, a stepmother old enough to be her grandmother. Today Jass would be keyed up over her entry in the Miami hibiscus extravaganza due to open tomorrow morning. Shandy helps her in the greenhouse, and the two of them had spent Saturday preparing entries for the show. Jass planned to drive the plants to Miami in pre-dawn hours this morning, and the winners wouldn't be announced until late this afternoon. What could I say to Jass at this point?

I jumped when my phone rang at the same instant I had

picked it up to make my call. "Keely Moreno speaking."

"Jass here, Keely."

I expected to hear tears in her voice, but I heard none. Her tone sounded precise and matter-of-fact.

"Detective Curry just called on me, but now he's gone. Keely, we need to talk."

"I was about to call you, Jass. I'm so sorry for your loss."

"Thank you. I'm sorry you had to be the one to find her body. That must have been a terrible experience."

"Yes." I could think of nothing more to say.

"I could show up for my three o'clock appointment, but out of respect for Dad, I'd rather not be seen out and about today. Margaux's death has left me shaken. Could you come here? Not for a treatment, but just to talk."

"Of course, Jass. I've been talking to the police, then to Gram. And Consuela. I'm really sorry about Margaux and . . . you have my heartfelt sympathy." What else could I say? But Jass made it easy for me.

"Thanks, Keely. I accept your sympathy, but my concern right now goes out to Dad. He's not here. I don't know exactly where he is. Keely, no matter what I or others thought of Margaux, Dad loved her. I'd hate for him to hear of her death over radio or TV."

"He hasn't returned from the fishing tournament?"

"No. It's not over until late this afternoon and it might take him a couple of hours to drive down from Key Colony Beach in the Sunday traffic. Punt's been trying to reach him on his cell phone, but so far—no answer. Maybe Dad doesn't have it turned on."

"I'll come right over."

"Use our secret back entrance, okay? Reporters are thick as fire ants in front of the house, but I haven't seen any out back."

"I'll be there in a few minutes." I hung up and started to push my bike off its kickstand, then I stopped. My uneasiness at Detective Curry's presence and questions had left perspiration stains on my jumpsuit, and my hair and my skin seemed to carry the stench of death. I took time to shower and shampoo and change into a fresh outfit before I let myself out the back door that led into the alley behind my office.

After a short ride through bumper-to bumper traffic to South Street, I saw *Ashford Mansion* almost immediately because its three stories plus the widow's walk rose high. It towered above the surrounding homes. With all its gingerbread trim and the wrap-around verandas on each floor, it reminded me of a white layered cake and I could imagine a miniature bride and groom standing on the widow's walk like the topping on a traditional wedding cake.

I wondered if the house ever reminded Jass of a wedding cake—or of the wedding she had to cancel when Scott Murdock died in Afghanistan. Enough of those sad thoughts! The land surrounding *Ashford Mansion* had been in the family since the days when galleons plied the seas between the New World and Spain. Sea captains shipped supplies from Barcelona to the New World colonists and then carried gold and silver back to Barcelona from mines in Bogota. Right now I preferred to think about the past and try to forget the present. But no way.

No neighboring homes encroached on *Ashford Mansion,* and a scarlet-blossomed hibiscus hedge surrounded the property. Jass had drowned her sorrow at losing her fiancé by burying herself in the study of horticulture at an eastern university. Over the years, she had manicured the family's private grounds until they formed a hidden garden secreted beneath palms and seagrape trees. Beds of scarlet poinsettias and golden alamanda plants shone like bright jewels near a greenhouse that held most of Jass's experimental hibiscus plants.

A few of her dwarf plants sat on the lawn outside the greenhouse. Her current and ongoing interest lay in propagating dwarf plants that would remain small and not revert to their natural large growth after only a year or so. She also did in-depth experiments with blossom color, but those plants were locked for safekeeping inside the greenhouse.

Consuela lived in an apartment one block from *Ashford Mansion,* and each morning, while the first Mrs. Ashford lived, Consuela had arrived to make and serve breakfast for the family in the solarium. Once the breakfast hour ended, Consuela devoted the rest of the day to her writing. When Beau remarried, he and Margaux moved into the house on Grinnell, and Consuela had to find a new job.

Thinking of Consuela and her writing made me worry about her outspoken views and her feeling toward Margaux. I couldn't help but wonder if those feelings had gotten out of hand last night. Did Consuela know how to use a gun?

Chapter 5

I saw Jass standing in the front doorway, dwarfed by the towering Ashford home. She stood diminished by the height of the wrap-round verandas, the widow's walk. As usual, she wore a green A-line skirt and a T-shirt. Plump, red-haired, and freckled, Jass had a smile that made total strangers feel at ease immediately. Locals called her Miss Hibiscus. Sometimes I teased her, saying she wore green to match her thumb. If a stalk had even a bit of life in it, Jass could make it grow and flourish.

I followed her request to use the rear entrance. *Ashford Mansion* reminded me of happier times. Jass and her twin brother, Punt, had been my close friends all through high school, and Beau's generosity enabled me to take reflexology training. Beau had been my father figure following my mother's death. I've repaid my financial obligations, and my friendship with the Ashfords has grown throughout the years.

Riding on past the mansion, I turned right and then took a second quick right. Behind the house, I dismounted and walked my bike down a lane almost too narrow to be called an alley. An untamed growth of Brazilian pepper and thatch palm almost blocked the secret entry we'd used as kids. Branches caught in my hair and scratched my arms as I pushed my bike through that growth and then through a small break in the well-manicured hibiscus hedge. After propping my bike against a palm near the greenhouse, I brushed twigs and leaves from my hair and clothes before approaching the house.

Jass's VW convertible sat in the carport beside Punt's vintage Karmann Ghia. I looked up, half expecting to see Punt watching me from the catwalk surrounding his apartment. But he never appeared.

"Come in, Keely," Jass called to me as she opened the kitchen door then paused at the back stairway leading to family quarters on the second floor. I gave her a warm hug.

"I'm sorry for your loss, Jass. Please tell me if there's any way I can help you." I peered into the first-floor parlor, glad to see no visitors present.

"Let me ask you the same thing. I know you've been through a bad scene and I'm so glad you've come over. Let's go upstairs."

Jass had turned the first-floor parlor and three bedrooms into commercial display rooms for her hibiscus business. In addition to her plants, she'd decorated the rooms in antiques salvaged from ill-fated sailing galleons. She loved to tell customers the story behind each antique, from the astrolabe the ancient mariners used to determine direction to the elegant china on the shelves behind her plants.

"Are we alone?" I asked. I wondered if she had invited Punt or Shandy to join us. Since Shandy helped Jass in the greenhouse, they'd spent a lot of time together this past weekend getting ready for the Miami show. Punt came and went as he chose, but right now I hoped to talk to Jass alone.

"Yes. We're alone—at least for the time being." She led the way into the second-floor living room, a green setting that pointed up her coloring and her personality. My sandals sank into the soft carpeting that made a sea-colored background for the white wicker couch, coffee table, and armchairs. "Sit, Keely. Make yourself comfortable."

I sat on the couch and Jass joined me. For a moment neither of us said anything. I tried to blot out the horror of the morning by concentrating on the fragrance of gardenia that permeated the room. Early for gardenias to be blooming. I looked around, trying to locate the plant, but Jass cut through my pretense.

"I'm scared, Keely." She leaned toward me and began twisting a strand of hair that had slipped from her long pony-tail. "We need to find out who murdered Margaux, and we need to find out quickly."

"Hold on one minute." I leaned back and studied her. "Who said murder? The police?"

"No. Not the police. And that worries me. Detective Jona-than Curry stopped by here briefly just a few minutes ago. So far he has given me little information."

"He must have come straight here after he left my place. He asked me a million questions."

"Maybe you shouldn't tell him too much. Maybe you need a lawyer."

"He said I didn't. Said the questions were informal."

"That's probably what they always tell a suspect."

"A suspect? You think I'm a suspect?"

"Of course I don't think that, but the police may."

"Did Curry say that?"

"No. Not at all, and I've heard nothing else from the police. I've only caught a few of their veiled releases to the media, but you know Key West. The powers that be at the police station as well as at city hall and at the newspapers try to keep bad news very hush-hush."

"Yeah. Merchants don't want the tourists to think crime ever touches Key West. Spoils the paradise image."

"Punt says he heard the police are suggesting suicide, but I know Margaux didn't take her own life. Punt agrees. You know that, too, don't you, Keely? Know that Margaux wasn't suicidal?"

"That'd be my guess, but nobody can say that for sure. You can't know what's inside another person's mind."

"I think the police are calling her death a suicide, thinking that call will protect Dad—and maybe eliminate a tough murder investigation."

"You don't think Beau had anything to do with Margaux's death, do you?" I stood and began pacing. "Jass, I simply can't imagine such a thing."

"No, of course not, but when a killer murders a married woman, the husband's the first and sometimes the chief suspect."

I thought about that for a moment before I nodded in agreement. "In this town, Margaux is—was an outsider. New Yorkers sometimes have a brisk attitude that rubs our laid-back locals the wrong way."

"Dad's a Conch, born and raised right here on the rock. Key Westers look out for their own."

I smiled. "Once Beau told me he hadn't been north of the Boca Chica Bridge for over a month. I think he was bragging."

"He probably only crossed the bridge then because circumstances forced him to. Dad's a Conch, born and bred."

"You think the police might shade the facts if it'd help Beau?" I hadn't thought of that possibility and hated thinking of it now.

"Dad's a community-minded philanthropist. Face it. The police might tend to latch onto the easy way out of a gritty situation. A call of suicide would not only protect a respected city benefactor, but it'd also eliminate the need for a costly and character-smearing investigation."

"You're right. The police might be tempted to take the easy way out."

"I don't want to see that happen. I'd hate to see Dad—or you—face a murder investigation, Keely. We have to find out who shot Margaux. Even if her death goes down as a suicide, the gossip will flourish forever."

"Key West's usually a live-and-let-live sort of island."

"Not always. Who would people blame for unhappiness great enough to cause a woman to take her own life?"

"Her husband, I suppose."

"Right. Gossips would whisper about it for years. I can't let that happen to Dad."

"I understand, and you're probably right about the gossips." Jass brought the situation into sharp focus. My stomach muscles tensed and I scowled. I hadn't seriously thought of myself being investigated for murder because I found the body. Detective Curry had said his questions were informal ones, and I had believed him—sort of. Nor had I thought of Beau being investigated. This opened new territory of thinking for me. Who could I trust?

"Jass, if the police go after Beau, and if enough influential people don't want to see him take the rap, maybe I'll be their scapegoat."

"Such things happen. We need to face that possibility. Sometimes juries accidentally convict innocent people of crimes they didn't commit."

"I read several months ago about college journalism students up north doing in-depth DNA investigating as a class project. They discovered several convicts innocent—men convicted of capital crimes and waiting on death row, men who had rotted in prison for years. Our judicial system scares me."

"We have to stop a suicide call, Keely, even if it means in-depth investigations of people we know and love. We have to act quickly. I've read that if the police make no arrest within forty-eight hours of a murder, the case can drag on for weeks, months, or even years. The villain may never be found."

"I suppose you have a bright idea as to how we'll find

Margaux's killer—if there is one."

"We'll have to do some private detecting on our own."

As I sat down, Jass walked to a white wicker desk, pulled out ballpoint and paper, then returned to sit next to me on the couch cushions. "Let's make a list of the people who had both motive and opportunity for shooting Margaux. Those are the people the police may overlook."

At first I wanted to tell Jass she'd been reading too many detective novels, but deep down I suspected she might be right. Why should the police do a big deal investigation if it could be avoided with one word—suicide?

"You may have a workable idea, Jass. Do you remember a murder case a few years ago? I think the victim's name was Alexa Chitting."

"Sounds familiar."

"The police had been sure a street person had murdered her during a robbery. When the family hired a private detective to investigate, they were able to prove murder."

"Help me make a list, Keely."

When I could get my mind to focus, I thought about my own plight. In Margaux's case, a verdict of suicide would certainly make my life easier. If the police called Margaux's death murder, I'd be high on their suspect list. Once they finished investigating Beau, they'd start in on me. *The person who finds the body is always of special interest to the police.*

"What do you say, Keely? Are you going to help me?"

"What does Punt think of all this?" I asked.

"Why not ask Punt in person?"

Punt had entered the room so quietly it startled me to see him there. His head almost touched the top of the arched doorway near the back stairway and his six-foot frame looked rangy but totally at ease. For once he wasn't wearing his mirrored sunglasses. I hated the sinister look they gave him. He wore his usual cutoffs and a blue tank top that matched his eyes. He'd pulled his long auburn hair into a neat ponytail much like Jass's and a leather thong held it in place. People call Punt the black sheep of the family. Maybe they're right, but I'm not into name-calling.

"Hi, Punt," Jass called. "I think we need your help."

In spite of all the gossipy talk against Punt, I still liked him and in a way I felt sorry for him, felt sorry for anyone who felt so unhappy he had to turn to drugs to solve his problems. Punt and I had dated a lot in high school. He reigned as the school's top jock football hero until he started doing drugs and got kicked off the team. That's when I'd dropped him, too. Reluctantly. Plenty of girls tried to save him from himself, but druggies seldom want to be saved. I had slightly more respect for him now than I had then, although he'd merely graduated from recovered druggie to local beach bum.

If Punt had ever worked a day in his life, he kept it a secret. Why should he work when he could draw on Dad's generosity and Mama's trust fund? I couldn't respect that. Punt watched the world through his mirrored shades, but his laid-back actions belied his love of speed—in cars, boats, and maybe women, too. I'd seen him tooling around town with several different barmaids who reminded me of Playboy bunnies seeking the warmth of the Keys—or Punt's bed. Punt was like a warning sign, cautioning everyone to keep their distance.

"Where've you been?" Jass asked him before he could ask what sort of help we needed.

"At Dad's on Grinnell. I wanted to see the death scene up close and personal. I hear the police are still talking suicide."

"We can't let them do that, Punt." Jass stood and paced. "You understand that, don't you? We can't let it happen."

"How can we stop them? We can't dictate to the police.

51

They might listen to you and Dad, but no way are they going to give me the time of day. I've seen them from the wrong side of the desk too many times."

"We've gotta convince them that someone murdered Margaux. That's what Keely and I were talking about. Dad and Keely might be suspects, but we know they're innocent. Help us, please. We're making a list of likely suspects." Jass sat again and picked up her pen and paper.

"Ha!" Punt flopped onto an easy chair across from the coffee table. "Margaux had few close friends in Key West. Your list could be a long one."

"Okay. So we know few people beside Dad really liked her," Jass said. "We'll need to narrow our list of suspects to those who had strong motive and adequate opportunity. That's pure logic."

"You and I and Beau might be the first three to head the list," Punt said. "Keely will make four."

"Rats," I blurted. "Just because I found her body? No fair. I liked Margaux. She may not have been my favorite person, but I had no reason to murder her."

Punt exchanged a knowing look with Jass, kicked off his sandals, and propped his feet on the coffee table. "If Keely's going to work with us, we'd better tell her."

"Count me in," I said. "Tell me what?"

Chapter 6

"We need to discuss Margaux's will," Jass said, "and you need to know its contents. The family hasn't read it in its complete form—too wordy and complicated. Harley Hubble drew it up for Margaux and she wanted the family as well as Otto Koffan to know of its existence, if not its complete contents. Her lawyer read her major bequests to us in her presence. He scheduled an in-depth reading of the will later."

"Why did she need a will?" I asked. "Was she ill?"

"No," Punt snorted. "She was *old*. Old people make wills."

"Be real, Punt. Her age played no part in her need to draw up a will. Most smart people have wills—at least those do who want their assets to go to people they love and respect rather than to the government, who'll divvy them according to federal and state laws."

"So she had a will," I said. "Works for me. What did it say, in general, of course?"

"Margaux wanted to bond with us, with her newly acquired family," Jass said. "I can understand that. The age difference between her and Dad. The gossip. She knew their marriage caused whispers and raised eyebrows."

"Big time," Punt said. "Really big time."

"She worried that Punt and I couldn't, or wouldn't, tolerate so much negative attention, so to try to win us over, she bequeathed us each a small fortune."

"Didn't hurt my feelings any," Punt said.

"I'd heard Margaux rolled in dough even before she married Beau," I said. "That true?"

"Right." Punt grinned. "Family money. My very favorite kind. She managed to whisk it out of Greece and she settled in New York. She was one smart babe. I'm guessing her looks turned heads—the right heads. She made connections, made it big in commercial real estate as well as in the elite literary field."

"We won't know the exact stipulations of the will until the formal reading with lawyers present," Jass said. "We know who inherits, but not how much."

"If we know who inherits, I guess we could make a list of suspects based on that information," I said.

"Just remember you're in her will," Punt said, "and it couldn't happen to a nicer person." Punt smiled at me—a genuine smile, not one of his smirky grins that meant so little to anyone. I began to remember the neat kid I knew in high school.

Sometimes Punt and I accidentally found ourselves fishing on the same backcountry flats. As good sportsmen and good fishermen, we kept our distance from each other. Recently, I watched him boat his tackle during a run of bonefish while he released a pelican that had become entangled in monofilament line. Only a true sportsman would have taken the time to do that. A bonefish catch makes big-time bragging material for any fisherman.

"Maybe with Margaux's bequest you'll be able to close up shop, Keely," Jass said, breaking into my thoughts.

"No way. I like my work, my office. Anyway, I'm not counting my javelinas before they're caught. That's an old saying of Gram's—comes straight from Havana."

"Well," Punt said, "no matter how you feel about Margaux's will, if the police cry murder, you'll be suspect along with the rest of us. We'll have to come up with some good alibis."

"Like the truth," Jass said.

"I can think of some suspects," I said. "Shandy Koffan, for instance. If Otto inherits, Shandy'll get a trickle-down benefit, too. Maybe she's bitter at seeing Margaux living on easy street while she's still sporting spike heels and black mesh stockings and toting cocktails. As Otto's wife, she'd several reasons to be pleased at Margaux's death."

"Could be," Punt agreed.

"Maybe," Jass said. "But Shandy's worked for me part-time in my greenhouse for months—even before her marriage to Otto. She loves plants almost as much as I do. I've never heard her badmouth Margaux."

"And what about Nikko?" Punt asked as Jass added Shandy's name to our list.

"Nikko's in her will, too?" I asked.

"No," Punt said, "but the studs around Smathers Beach say he's in her bed now and then."

"Punt!" Jass scowled. "What's *that* supposed to mean?"

"What's an affair usually mean?" Punt asked. "Margaux enjoyed Nikko's Greek cooking? Wise up, sis. Nikko's built like a giant-size fireplug and that burly type appeals to lots of women."

I'd never thought of Nikko as anything but my good friend and Gram's good friend, and Punt's description of him and his activities left me speechless.

"I don't see Margaux as Nikko's first extra-curricular activity either," Punt added. "Maybe he got tired of her. Maybe she demanded more than he could deliver. Or maybe she wanted out of the relationship and Nikko hated losing face—especially to an older woman. There're lots of reasons for a relationship to go on the rocks, but the rocks are usually in the bed."

I couldn't imagine Nikko and Margaux involved in an

affair, but I don't hang around Smathers listening to the beach-bum gossip.

"Murder seems a drastic way to end a relationship," I said. "I admire Nikko. He helped me when I felt desperate and needed protection from Jude. He helps Gram. I hate having to consider him a murder suspect."

"Maybe he'll have a foolproof alibi," Punt said. "For my own sake, I hope he does."

"Your own sake?" Jass asked. "What's your sudden interest in Nikko?"

Punt hesitated, then he shook his head and replied. "Guess I can't keep it a secret much longer—especially in view of Margaux's death. For several weeks Nikko and I have been formulating business plans, plans that have nothing to do with his private life. I know Dad would like to see me gainfully employed." Punt hesitated again before he continued. "Well, I approached Nikko. He didn't approach me. It was my idea. He could have vetoed it, but he didn't. I suggested that the two of us form a private detective agency here in Key West."

"Be real," Jass said. "What do you know about being a private detective?"

"Not much—yet. But Nikko has a P.I. license valid in Florida and he's promised to teach me the ropes, to help me earn my own license. The general plan is for me to work for him as his assistant while I learn."

"Sounds like pie in the sky to me," Jass said.

"Give me a break, Sis. I'm beginning to realize I need some goals in life, but I don't think I could settle down to a desk job."

"You used to paint," Jass said. "Maybe you could take some lessons, paint some local scenes, and open an art gallery. Or maybe you could open a gallery and feature the works of other artists."

"I'm not about to have an art attack," Punt said with a sigh. "I find the idea of being a P.I. both appealing and exciting. I want to give it a try and I want the whole thing to be a surprise to Dad. The way today's scene is coming down, Nikko and I may have found our first case to solve. But we need time to find office space, to get a work plan going. If the idea doesn't fly, then Dad needs to know nothing about it."

"I won't breathe a word," Jass promised.

"I'd appreciate that."

I didn't enter into their conversation that had threatened to escalate into a full-blown argument. "Let's get on with our list of suspects. I've already mentioned Shandy. And let's don't forget Consuela. Whenever Margaux's name comes up, Consuela shimmies her hips and shouts, *Someday I'm going to keel her.*"

"Everyone knows that's an idle threat," Jass said. "Consuela's a loudmouth. People don't take her threats seriously."

Punt shrugged. "Consuela may make idle threats, but any verbal threat against Margaux could merit police attention now that she's dead."

"I've read Consuela's book," Jass said, "the one that's been published. I thought it rather good and I think it was mean-spirited of Margaux to call it sentimental and inaccurate and to refuse to look at Consuela's new manuscript—her work in progress."

"Even if Margaux considered the story sentimental and poorly researched, she could have helped Consuela revise it, make it better," I said. "Consuela can be a pain, but most of us have learned to tolerate her."

"She and Margaux butted heads every time they met," Punt said. "The sophisticated New Yorker meets the Cuban bombshell—and pow. Too bad they couldn't find a common meeting ground."

"We all need foolproof alibis." Jass stared into the distance as she changed the subject. "We know Dad attended the fishing tournament . . ."

"We know Dad *said* he planned to attend the weekend fishing tournament," Punt said. "None of us actually saw him there."

"You surely don't suspect Dad." Jass stood and glared at Punt. "You'll be suspecting me next."

"I'm going to suspect everyone until I know all the facts," Punt said, "and don't forget the possibility that Margaux might have been done in by a street person."

"A total stranger?" I asked. "You've got to be kidding. How can we check out every street person in Key West? Why would a street person have motive?"

"Maybe we're getting too deep into this suspect stuff," Jass said.

"Yeah, right. Maybe we are," I said. "Remember, we're not detectives. We've no authority. We can't go up to people and ask them where they were from ten until midnight last night."

"I think we *can* do that," Jass said. "Maybe we can't approach and question street people, but Keely, think about this. You talk to most of these suspects on a weekly basis as your regular customers. Surely working in a little conversation about Margaux's death would be easy enough. It'll be the subject *du jour* for weeks to come."

"Maybe so." I shook my head in doubt. "Her death will be the talk of the Keys . . . but . . ."

"Right," Jass said. "You could begin a conversation by 're-membering' where you were and the designated time. You could even talk a bit, reluctantly of course, about discovering

Margaux's body. Then you could subtly ask your customer where he was and how he heard the news."

"That might work, I suppose," I said. "Most of the suspects are my steady customers. Even Nikko took treatments to help me get started when my office was new, but once I became established he cut his appointments to once a month. I'll have to check my calendar, but I'm fairly sure he has an appointment soon."

"I could talk to Nikko, too," Jass said. "I've been eating at *The Wharf* a lot since they've been planning my hibiscus show there on Thursday. Even if my special blossom doesn't win first place in today's Miami competition, the manager at *The Wharf* is going on with the show anyway. Good advertising for both of us, he says. Anyway, when I eat there, I usually stop by the kitchen to compliment Nikko on his cooking."

"Gram talks to Nikko a lot when he visits her shop to pick up supplies," I said. "She could quiz him, too. In fact, I'm sure she'd like to. Gram's curious and she wants to keep on top of things."

Punt had stayed out of this conversation, but now the way he cleared his throat demanded our attention. "Don't forget that Nikko's my detective partner," Punt said.

"That doesn't place him above suspicion," Jass said.

"There's another suspect we've forgotten to mention, women." Punt stood and began pacing.

"Who's that?" Jass asked.

Punt waited a few moments before answering. "Don't forget Jude Cardell."

"Jude?" Jass and I spoke in unison.

"Yes, Jude. Jude's a law clerk and secretary at *Hubble & Hubble*. He had access to Margaux's will. No doubt he read it with great interest. Can't think of anyone in this town who wouldn't have read that will had the opportunity presented itself. Don't forget that at one time Jude threatened Keely's life."

"I prefer to think of that as another idle threat—like Consuela's," Jass said.

"I try to forget both Jude and his threat, Punt. Help me forget. Don't be bringing Jude's name up now."

"You can forget his threat, but that doesn't make it go away. Jude threatened you. Witnesses heard him. I'm one of them, and I'm willing to testify against him in court should it become necessary."

"Okay, okay," Jass said, "but . . ."

"Jude's not dumb, and he's dangerous. Since he probably knew Keely would inherit from Margaux's will, he could have shot Margaux for pure meanness, knowing Keely would find her body and likely take a lot of heat from the police. Maybe face a murder rap. Jude's already on the police blotter as an abuser. He knows the drill when it comes to police interrogations."

"Hold on one minute," I blurted. "How could he have known I'd find the body?"

"By following you," Punt said. "I hope you don't think that restraining order means anything. In his mind, Jude'll never let you off the hook. I think he moved back to Key West just to torment you."

"I agree with that," Jass said.

"Gram thinks so, too."

"After watching your place and following you a few Sunday mornings, Jude would have figured out your standing appointment with Margaux," Punt said. "He could have known that Beau would be out of town last night. Lots of people were talking about the tournament, and Margaux told friends that Beau was involved in it. What a perfect time for Jude to act!"

"Like everyone else, he knows the person finding a body would get special attention from the police." Jass sighed.

"You may be right." I could barely whisper the words, they frightened me so.

Again, Jass began to pace. "Which one of us is going to find out if Jude has an alibi? Which one of us is going to check out that alibi—if there is one? He's dangerous. I want no part of him."

"I plan never to go near him," I said. "That's for sure."

"If we can get the police to call Margaux's death a homicide, maybe the police will check out his alibi," Punt said. "It wouldn't break my heart to see Jude on the hot seat."

I wondered what Punt had against Jude. Most people who didn't know Jude well liked him, from what I've heard. He hid his dark side.

"Keely, where were you late Saturday night?" Jass looked me in the eye. "We've all got to come clean."

Both Punt and Jass stared at me, and my stomach felt like a kettle of boiling water as my sudden resentment rose. Heat flushed my face and my voice croaked as I tried to answer Jass.

"Calm down," Jass said. "We know you're innocent, but we need to know you've a strong alibi. We need to hear it."

A few deep breaths helped me find the grace and dignity to answer. "That's the problem, Jass. I have no alibi—at least none that'd hold up in court. I stayed home alone all evening—reading, watching TV, sleeping. Saturday night's seldom a big-event night in my life. What were you two doing?"

"I've a good alibi," Jass said. "I'd been in Miami all day taking care of the details, the paperwork involved in entering the hibiscus show. I felt exhausted by the time I got home, but nervous energy kept me wired."

"So get to the point," Punt said. "What'd you do?"

"In the early part of the evening I worked in my green-house writing out orders for fertilizers and soil additives. Then around nine o'clock I went with June Bishop to the late movie, a double feature. We were inside the theater all the time and I'm sure June will vouch for me. What about you, Punt?"

"I hung out at *Sloppy Joe's* from eight-thirty until after midnight. About ten, one of the guys in the band invited me to sit in for a while. Shim Latner lent me his guitar. I played until the band left the stand around one o'clock. After that we jammed until three or so. Then I came home and went to bed. Jass, since you were up late, maybe you heard me come in."

"Afraid not." Jass sighed. "We'll trust each other. We wouldn't be holding this conversation if we were guilty, and there's another thing we have to consider quickly. Margaux stipulated plans for her memorial service in her will."

"Didn't know people could do that," I said. "Why would anyone want to?"

"Margaux thought she could do anything her little heart desired," Punt said. "She liked to see people dance to do her bidding, and she knew her memorial service would be her last chance to make the calls."

"So what about this service?" I asked. "What did she want? A fanfare? A drum and bugle corps? A Duval Street parade?"

"None of that," Jass said. "Within forty-eight hours of her death, she wanted her body cremated, a memorial service to be attended by invitation only, and a burial at sea to be held on the same day."

"What if there's a small craft advisory?" Punt asked. "I suppose we'll have to dump her ashes into a bait bucket and store it 'til the seas calm. Could take days. I've seen it blow hard for a week in February."

"Be real, Punt. Be an optimist. The long-range weather forecast predicts winds at five to ten for the next four days. That takes us through Wednesday, but we still have to act quickly. If the police call Margaux's death a suicide and her body is cremated, most evidence of foul play will have been destroyed."

Before Punt or I could agree or disagree, we heard a car pull up in the driveway. Beau had arrived.

Chapter 7

Jass jumped up and hurried toward the foyer that led to the front stairway. Punt followed her down the winding steps to the hibiscus display room below. From a vantage spot near the stairway, I watched Beau through a leaded glass window as he rapped with the brass knocker and then opened the door and stepped inside. I wished I could avoid meeting him right now, avoid being drawn into the grief and anger he must be feeling, but I saw no way out. Jass, with Punt following, rushed to greet him.

With his tall, muscular body, Beau could have been the poster boy for state-of-the-art scuba gear and swim trunks. Even now in his black silk shirt and cream-colored shorts, his dark hair along with his tanned skin and his sea-blue eyes reminded me of a lithe Neptune rising from the sea. I could believe the rumor that two local salvage companies were after him to sign contracts with them, to dive again and help locate *The Esponisa*, another sunken galleon.

At the foot of the steps, Beau pulled both Jass and Punt to him in a warm embrace, then followed them upstairs to the sitting room. Perhaps this tragedy would help Beau and Punt forget some of the problems that separated them.

"Keely." Beau didn't seem astonished to see me in the sitting room, and when he stepped toward me, I clasped his hand in both of mine.

It didn't surprise me to feel him shaking. Or was I the one shaking? "I'm so sorry, Beau. You have my heartfelt sympathy."

"Dad, where have you been?" Jass asked.

Beau hesitated a moment as if trying to get things straight in his mind. "I've been trying to get home," he said at last. "Heavy Sunday afternoon traffic, as always. And since I didn't know about . . . the emergency, I kept in my lane and resisted the urge to pass the line of traffic ahead of me. I encountered a long delay on Seven-Mile Bridge. Some guy's Town Car had an alternator problem and when he got that patched up, he ran out of gas. Local, too, not a tourist."

"Let me make you some coffee," Jass said. "You must be exhausted. We've tried and tried to reach you on your cell phone."

"I turned it off because the traffic claimed my full attention. A ringing phone distracts me. I can't carry on a phone conversation and drive at the same time. I'm sorry I caused you to worry. Had I known . . ."

Beau shook his head as he slumped onto the couch, propped his elbows on his knees, and dropped his head into his hands. "I didn't hear the news about Margaux until a police car began following me with lights flashing and siren wailing. Somehow I found a place to pull off the highway and the patrolman gave me the news. I stopped by the house, then a detective asked me to go to the morgue to . . . identify the body." Beau's voice dropped to a bare whisper, but he lifted his head and faced us.

"You've had a rough time, Dad," Jass said, standing near the back stairway. "You too, Keely. Excuse me while I bring us some snacks."

"I really must be going." I tried to ease toward the back stairway, but Beau beckoned me toward the couch, then seemed at a loss for words. In a strained silence, we heard Jass downstairs readying coffee mugs and silverware as she moved about in the kitchen, and soon the aroma of brewing coffee wafted to us.

"Keely," Beau said at last. "I'm so sorry you had to be the one to . . . to be first on the scene of the tragedy. The patrolman told me you handled the situation well—as well as a situation like that could be handled. I appreciate your quick thinking, your concern, your calling nine-one-one."

"I hear the police are saying Margaux's death's a suicide," I said.

"They haven't decided for sure. I can't imagine such a thing. The police searched the house and the detectives asked me to do another search while they watched. We found no suicide note, yet I felt the police were holding information from me."

"We think someone murdered Margaux," Punt said. "What do you think about that, Dad?"

"The police asked me to stay in town." Beau shook his head. "As if I might catch a quick flight out of the country or something. I don't know what to expect. I don't know what the police are thinking."

"In case they're thinking murder, Jass and Keely and I have been drawing up a list of suspects," Punt said.

At that moment, Jass came up the stairs carrying a tray with coffee mugs and cookies.

"Help yourselves, everyone," she invited, then she handed Beau a mug and a napkin.

"Women always think food can make a bad situation better," Punt said as he helped himself to a cookie.

"Maybe it can," Jass insisted.

"I really must go," I said. "You three need some time alone, and I need to get home." I stood. "If I can be of help, let me know. If I don't hear from you, I'll get in touch tomorrow."

"Talk to people," Punt said. "Let's carry out the plan we discussed."

"What plan was that?" Beau wrapped his hands around the coffee mug as if to warm them.

"Please excuse me." I moved toward the stairs. "Jass and Punt can share our thoughts with you when you've rested and feel more like listening."

"Let me drive you home," Punt swallowed his cookie and stood beside me.

"Thanks, Punt, but no thanks. I rode my bike, remember? I'll need it for transportation to work tomorrow morning."

Jass followed me downstairs, opened the back door, then snapped on a dim porch light. It surprised me that darkness had fallen.

"Take care, Keely. I'll call you tomorrow morning. You'll be at your shop, won't you?"

"Yes. I closed for today, but I'll open tomorrow as usual. I can't talk to the suspects if I close the office."

"Do take special care, Keely."

"I will. You get back upstairs to your family. I'll be fine."

Night's like a black quilt that drops quickly over the Keys. There's almost no twilight between sunset and dark. At about five in the afternoon, or sometimes even sooner, the tourists begin drifting toward *Mallory Dock* to view the sunset and to watch the buskers who perform their sunset-ritual acts. Before I opened my reflexology office, I used to make a living of sorts by selling Key lime cookies and palm frond hats at the dock, but tonight that seemed ages ago. Now, even at this distance, the trade wind carried the eerie sound, the lonesome sound, of a bagpipe. I imagined the player dressed in plaid kilt and tam as he blew into his cumbersome instrument, summoning people to view the evening's entertainment.

Jass turned on the lights that outlined the widow's walk on the roof. From this cattycorner angle in the yard I saw five lights gleaming from each of two sides on the high porch.

Nine of them were white and one glowed a bright green. I wondered if Beau knew the green light shone in memory of Jass's mother.

In the tropics and near-tropics people sometimes say they've seen the flash of a green light at sunset—right at the instant the sun slips over the horizon and into the sea. Nobody has assigned meaning to this light, and personally, I've never noticed it, nor have I spent a lot of time looking. Gram claims to have seen the oddity twice as a girl in Havana.

Jass insists that both she and her mother saw the green flash from a cruise ship in the Bahamas. So, in the whimsical notion that her mother may be watching from above, Jass included one green bulb in the lights outlining the widow's walk. Every now and then someone writes a human interest article about the green flash and the lights on *Ashford Mansion*.

Right now none of the lights helped me find my bicycle. I felt sure I'd left it leaning against a palm tree right inside the hibiscus hedge at the back of the property, but I couldn't find it. What had possessed me to make me forget to lock it? Squinting at the ground, I walked the whole length of the hedge. Then I moved a few feet closer to the house and walked the same distance again. No bicycle. My fault for failing to chain it to the palm tree, but I didn't think anyone had seen me push through the thicket into this private backyard. Damn! I needed that bike.

I hated my choices at this point. I could walk on home. Neither my shop nor my apartment were beyond walking distance. On an island only two miles wide, almost everything lies within walking distance. Yes, I could hoof it. I hated to intrude on the Ashfords right now by asking for a ride.

A few minutes later, I told myself my need for my bike tomorrow morning made my decision to call Jass realistic. To my own need, I added the fact that Gram sometimes had errands for me that required wheels. Deep down, however, I knew the events of the day had rattled me, shaken me more than I cared to admit. I hated the idea of walking alone on Key West tonight. Pulling out my cell phone, I keyed in Jass's private number.

"Keely?" Of course Jass sounded surprised to be hearing from me again so soon.

"My bike's disappeared. Ask Punt if I can still take him up on his offer of a ride."

"You sure you looked carefully? We seldom have trespassers."

"I'll take another look, but . . ."

"Never mind, Keely. Punt's on his way down. He'll take a look around and then drive you home if the two of you can't find your bike."

"Thanks a bunch, Jass. Hate to bother you."

"No bother at all."

By the time I shoved the cell phone back into my pocket, Punt stepped outside. I won't say he hurried. Punt seldom hurries, but he did act concerned. Together we paced across the backyard as I had done before, and then we retraced our steps and covered the same territory again.

"Strange," Punt said. "Better call the police and report the bike missing. No way you can collect any insurance unless you've reported the theft."

"Think I'll wait and report it tomorrow. Don't want any more talk with the police. I've had the full course for today and I'm sure you have, too."

"Yeah," Punt agreed. "Tomorrow's soon enough. I don't mind driving you home. Glad to escape the planning session upstairs, and there's nothing anyone can do right now to relieve Dad's grief. Anyway, he'd rather listen to Jass than to me."

"Planning session?" I ignored the veiled allusion to the rift between Punt and his dad.

"Yeah. Dad and Jass are already planning Margaux's memorial, deciding who to include in such a private service. I wanted to tell them to include me out, but I suppose that's wishful thinking."

I hoped the invitation list wouldn't include my name either, yet I knew it would. It wasn't that I disliked Margaux or disliked celebrating her life, but I hated funerals and memorial services—especially those for victims of violence such as Margaux . . . and my mother. I didn't share my feelings with Punt, nor did he share his with me. We both slid into his Karmann Ghia and when he turned the corner into the early evening traffic, I touched his arm and pointed.

"There, Punt! Look! Right there on the sidewalk dead ahead of us! Well . . . he's behind us now. We've passed him. Slow down. That kid's riding my bicycle."

Punt braked the car. "You sure? Bikes tend to look a lot alike. Especially after dark."

"I'm sure. Those baskets are my trademark. You don't see many bikes with green baskets that glow in the dark mounted on each side of the rear wheel."

Punt pulled the convertible into a vacant driveway, opened his door, and yelled at the blond-haired kid on the bike who looked to be no more than eleven or twelve. Even though the night had grown chilly, the kid was barefoot and he wore only a tank top and cut-offs.

"Hey, Buddy," Punt called out, and I joined him on the sidewalk as we jogged toward the boy. "Where'd you get that bike?"

For a moment the boy looked as if he might drop the bike and run, but after a second or two, he turned and pushed the bike toward us.

Punt said no more. Towering above the kid, he stared down at him with a gaze cold enough to freeze ice.

"Gee, mister. I didn't steal the bike. A guy on the street gave it to me. Really. That's pure truth. I'm no thief."

"What guy?" Punt and I both looked up and down the street, seeing nobody in sight in either direction. The boy's lower lip trembled as he followed our gaze and shrugged. "A big guy came riding up to me on the bike and said, 'Hey kid, you want a neat bike?' "

"We're supposed to believe a story like that?" Punt asked. "Tell us the truth and give the bike back. That's all we want. The bike back."

"But that's exactly how it came down." The boy glared at us and stamped a bare foot against the concrete. "I'm late getting home from Mallory and I knew Mom would skin me alive. So I had speeded up from walking to jogging when this big guy appeared from nowhere, gliding along sort of slow-like on this here bike."

The boy hesitated and I prompted him. "Then what happened?"

"He offered me the bike. He shoved it at me and disappeared, jogging off toward Highway 1. He didn't even hang around to see if I wanted it. But I guess he knew I would. Who'd turn down a free bike?"

"What'd he look like?" I stepped closer to the bike and gave it the once-over, seeing no damage. "Can you describe him?"

"Beer belly." The kid grinned. "Big guy. And tall. Wore jeans and a black hooded sweatshirt. If he hadn't been so nice to me, I'd have been scared of him, that's for sure."

"Probably a thousand people on Key West tonight would fit that description," Punt said. "Give us the bike and get on home. Don't borrow any more bikes—at least not tonight."

The boy thrust the bike at Punt and turned to leave. We watched him take a few steps, then he stopped and turned back toward us.

"One thing about the guy looked different," he called. "He seemed young, young as my dad maybe, but bald. When his hood fell back and he walked under a street light, the beam sort of bounced off his head. Maybe he has cancer or something. A kid in my class has cancer and the doctors shaved his head. Maybe . . ."

"Run on, kid," Punt said. "We believe you." Then he turned to me. "Jude! I told you you couldn't trust a restraining order."

"I believe you, Punt. It's only a worthless piece of paper."

I didn't tell Punt that I'd seen Jude walking on Grinnell Street that morning and that Gram had seen him walking past my shop. Had Jude been following me all day? My scalp tingled at the thought of him following me, furtively watching me turn into Jass's backyard, waiting until dark to skulk off with my bicycle. For all I knew, Jude might still be lurking nearby, waiting to catch me walking home alone in the dark.

"Sometime I'd like to know how Jude Cardell talked you into marrying him. I know it's none of my business, but after high school you wouldn't give me the time of day, yet that bastard . . ."

I didn't remind Punt that after high school he came on as a druggie, in and out of jail and making headlines in the newspaper's daily *Crime Report* on a regular basis.

"Well, now what?" Punt looked at the bulky bike and we both knew it wouldn't fit into the Karmann Ghia. We walked back toward our driveway parking place.

"I can ride it home, Punt."

"No way will I let you even consider riding it home with Jude in the neighborhood." Punt thought for a moment.

"Tell you what. You drive the car going slowly, and I'll pedal along behind you."

"No way. That won't do. I don't ride at night—no lights, too dangerous."

Once we reached the car, Punt backed from the driveway and onto the street. He got out, helped me into the driver's seat, and handed me the keys. "Let's go. I'll hang on and you can pull me. Your house or your office?"

I sighed in resignation. "My house. Georgia Street, and be careful." I wished I were spending the night at my office. At least Gram and Nikko were nearby on Duval, and several other merchants lived in apartments above their shops. However I had promised Mr. and Mrs. Moore to look after their home. Georgia Street lay in a safe part of town, but up-north snowbirds owned many of the houses—people who only came to the Keys when cold chased them from the northland.

When I stopped the car in front of my place, Punt took my hand in his and squeezed it so tightly I felt my ring cut into my finger.

"I'm walking you to the door, chaining your bike to the porch rail, and seeing you inside, Keely. Then I'll circle this block for awhile. Anything strange happens, you give me a buzz." He jotted his cell phone number on a scrap of paper he pulled from his glove compartment.

"Thanks for your help and your concern, Punt. I appreciate."

At the door, he waited until I unlocked it and snapped on the porch light as well as an inside lamp.

"Take care, Keely." He paused for a moment, then turned and walked back to his car.

Chapter 8

I entered the house with the eerie feeling that someone lurked inside waiting for me. Hiding. Waiting. Ready to pounce. My heart thumped like a steel drum and I wiped my clammy hands down the sides of my jumpsuit. The drapery at the front picture window hung open and I started to close it. No point in letting anyone outside peer in at me. On second thought, I dropped the pull cord and left the drapery alone. If Punt circled the block as promised, he'd be able to see inside, see if anyone or anything threatened me.

At the time I agreed to house-sit for the Moore family, I'd liked the place—the backyard pool, the floor plan, the Florida decor. A shotgun house, Gram called it. A person could shoot a bullet down the central hallway, hitting nothing but the back entryway. The bedrooms, the living-dining room, and the kitchen all opened off that central hallway. Mrs. Moore had left the scarred pine floors bare and had covered the worst spots with throw rugs.

Since she and her husband planned to remodel the place, they had bought a minimum of furniture. The sea-blue cushions she'd flung here and there for accent color contrasted nicely with the varying shades of tropical foliage growing in old clay pots. Each room of the home looked like a page from *House Beautiful*—the *before* page. Mrs. Moore tried to explain and to show me pictures of how she imagined the *after* page would look following the remodeling. I didn't envy her all that work, or if she planned to hire help, I didn't envy her that chore either. Key West has plenty of willing handymen— unless the sun's shining and it's a good fishing day.

Tonight my fear of Jude Cardell erased any beauty the old house might have had from my mind. Walking slowly to the first bedroom on my left, I snapped on the light before I entered and took a careful look around. Then, stepping inside the room, I peered into the closet, under the bed. Nothing. I felt like an old maid taking needless precautions to avoid some nonexistent intruder, but I couldn't help myself. I picked up and carried a knife from the kitchen as I checked out the second bedroom and then the rooms that opened on the right side of the central hallway. Nothing unusual. I slipped the knife back into a utility drawer. I breathed easier as I drew the drapery across the front window, feeling sure Punt had gone home by now.

I sat in a spot where I could see both the back door and the front door as I called Gram. I doubted she'd put her ear plugs in for the night. She'd be thinking about me, worrying about me. She answered on the first ring.

I told her about the kid and the bike, but I never mentioned Jude. Some things Gram handles poorly, and Jude's one of them. Even though I tried to make light of the bicycle's near-theft, Gram heard the strain in my voice.

"Why you no sleep at my place tonight, Keely? You be safe here. Cops keep Duval safe."

"I'm fine right here, Gram." I didn't tell her about the murder suspect list Jass, Punt, and I had drawn up, knowing that, too, would worry her. "Beau arrived home from the fishing tournament and talked with us for awhile. Of course he was almost down and out with grief. He really looked terrible."

"Dumb to grieve over that phony biddy," Gram snapped.

"His wife, Gram. His wife. He loved her."

"Tell me again, you be okay."

"I'm okay and I'll see you bright and early in the morning

as usual." I breathed easier after I ended our conversation. Usually Gram showed a live-and-let-live attitude toward people, but never toward Margaux.

How long had it been since I'd eaten? I could hardly remember. I smiled, thinking of Jass's irritation whenever I said I forgot to eat. Jass claimed she'd never forgotten a meal in her life, and she probably hadn't. This day seemed to have lasted a month. Breakfast. A few dishes in the sink reminded me of toast, orange juice, and Cheerios.

I'd grabbed a Heath bar from my desk drawer after Detective Curry left my office, and Jass had offered snacks at her house. My stomach growled. Although I'd rather have dropped right into bed, I forced myself to scramble a couple of eggs, shred lettuce for a salad. I checked my stoneware mushroom keeper. Forget mushrooms. Old age had left them restless. Toast. Hot tea instead of coffee. I wanted to sleep tonight.

The food soothed my stomach and a hot bath soothed my body. I always slept in the buff, hating the restriction of a gown or pajamas. Once in bed, I thought I'd sleep immediately, but no. I reached under my pillow to assure myself the small canister of pepper spray still lay there. I had slept with that bit of potential protection since my divorce. Nikko tried to persuade me to replace it with my gun, but guns made me nervous. Guns reminded me of Mom's death—and now of Margaux's.

As I lay tense and exhausted, my mind retraced the day's happenings. When I closed my eyes, the image of Margaux's body seemed imbedded on the back of my eyelids. Would I be accused of that murder? The thought chilled me. I knew Margaux hadn't committed suicide. I agreed with Jass that the guilty person must be found in order to protect the names of the innocent and in order to get a killer off the streets. *The person finding the body . . .*

When I opened my eyes and stared into the darkness, outdoor night sounds seemed amplified. In the distance I heard a car horn honk followed by the squeal of tires. Closer at hand the wind whispered through palm fronds. Then a thump outside told me something had hit the front door. Hard. Bolting upright and suppressing a scream, I slipped from bed.

Without turning on a light, I crept across the cool floor to the living room, pulled the drapery aside a crack, and peeked out. *Yeowl!* A neighborhood cat clung to the door screen for a few moments before jumping to the porch and darting away on cat business. I relaxed and returned to bed.

I still lay staring at the ceiling when someone knocked on the front door. *Don't answer it.* I lay still, listening. Who could it be at this hour? Jass? Beau? Punt? *Jude? Please, God, not Jude.*

If I didn't answer the knock, someone might try to break in. I had promised the Moores to protect their house. The next knock sounded louder, more demanding. I grabbed a robe, felt its cool silkiness glide over my body. Tuning no light on, I eased barefoot into the hallway and peeked through the security hole in the door.

Detective Curry and a woman stood on the porch. Plain clothes. They both wore gray suits and white shirts.

"One minute, please," I called. I fumbled with the security chain and then with the lock until I could open the door. "What is it, please?" A screen door stood between us, but I didn't open it or invite them in.

"We're sorry to bother you at this time." Detective Curry's steely eyes bored into me. "This's my partner, Detective Winslow. May we come in?"

I nodded to Detective Winslow as I opened the screen and let them enter. Detective Curry met my direct gaze while Detective Winslow's dark eyes inspected me from my clinging robe to my bare feet as if looking for incriminating flaws. Her head with its mane of tawny brown-gold hair barely reached Detective Curry's shoulder, and she moved with a cat-like grace. The word "tiger" leaped to mind.

"How may I help you?" I didn't invite them to sit down.

"We'd like you to accompany us to police headquarters," Detective Curry said.

"Why?" My reply sounded blunt and revealed my irritation, but I didn't care. "Do you have a warrant?" Was that a logical question? Seems like I'd heard it on TV shows.

"We have no warrant, Miss Moreno," Detective Curry said. "We just have a few more informal questions we'd like you to answer. Informal questions. It's your privilege to refuse to come with us or to answer queries, of course."

"Of course." I tried not to sneer. "May I get dressed?"

"Yes."

"Please have a seat. I'll be quick."

I tried to guess what strategy the detectives might be using. If they suspected me of murder, surely they'd hold off questioning me and alerting me to the direction of their investigation until they had developed a strong case against me. Surely they hadn't had time to develop such a case. On the other hand, they might believe that quick and early pressure might cause me to confess and save them lots of trouble.

They both sat on the couch, staring after me as I retreated to the bedroom and closed the door. My hands shook as I let the robe slide from my shoulders and pool into a puddle of crimson silk on the floor before I reached for my bra and panties. I wondered about the meaning of this visit. Detectives in the middle of the night? It reminded me of a Gestapo movie. Then a glance at my watch told me it was only a bit after nine o'clock. Maybe detective teams drew round-the-clock detail—our tax dollars at work.

What did one wear to the police station on a Sunday night? Now I bit on my tongue to quiet my chattering teeth, and I eased into my workday outfit—a khaki jumpsuit. They looked professional; I looked professional. When I returned to the living room, both detectives rose as if on signal.

They led the way out the front door, and I followed, pausing only long enough to lock the house again. Nobody spoke until we reached the gray Ford parked in front of the house.

"You'll ride in the passenger seat, please," Detective Curry said. Detective Winslow opened the car door for me, waited until I seated myself, then closed the door and crawled into the back seat behind me. Did they think I might try to escape if they let me ride in the back seat alone?

Detective Curry drove to Truman Avenue and then headed toward the newly-opened police headquarters near the fire station. Tonight artificial light cast a pink glow on the tall pillars at the entrance of the building. I gave only a glance at what appeared to be a small fountain with a brass plaque mounted on a pedestal. Who cared what the words on the plaque said!

Once we entered a small foyer inside the station, I glanced casually at the white benches against the wall next to the elevator. Tonight the benches were empty, but the lingering smell of stale cigarette smoke snapped me back to the problem at hand. The questioning. What more could they ask me? I had told them all I knew early this morning.

Detective Curry punched the elevator button and we slowly ascended to the offices above. I followed him, almost unseeing, into a large room, still light and bright with newly applied paint.

"Have you ever been fingerprinted?" Detective Curry asked.

"No." The one word seemed to be a complete answer to me.

"You've never been booked before?"

"No. Never."

"Do you mind if we take your fingerprints now?"

"No." The word came more slowly this time. Did I really have the right to protest? What would my protest tell them? I stuck to my reply—no, I didn't mind. At least not very much. What would it hurt to have a record of my prints at the police station?

Detective Winslow led me to a counter to wait while she slipped behind it and readied the fingerprinting equipment. White paper form with a blank square for eight fingers, two thumbs. Ink pad. She wrote my name and the date at the top of the form, then one by one, she pressed each of my fingers onto the ink pad and transferred a print onto the white page. After that she allowed me to clean my fingers on a bit of damp tissue.

"Do you mind if we take your picture?" Detective Curry asked.

"No." Was politeness dictating that he avoid calling the picture a mug shot?

Again, Detective Winslow did the job, positioning me against a plain backdrop, face to camera, then silhouette to camera. I tried not to imagine my photo hanging on a post office wall. After the fingerprinting and the photo sessions I followed Detective Curry into a small office barely large enough for his desk and chair, a four-drawer steel file cabinet, and a straight-backed chair for me. Detective Winslow stood guard at the doorway.

"Your name, please," Detective Curry asked.

I answered that question and several others that he'd already asked that morning. Then he cut to new material.

"Do you own a gun, Miss Moreno?"

"Yes, I do." I knew almost immediately I should have called a lawyer. Police have a way of making you say things you never intended to say, and they frequently lie to suspects. I've seen enough episodes of *NYPD Blue* and *Law and Order* to know that. I'd say lying is basic to police interrogations. I couldn't trust these detectives, but I didn't know what lawyer to call. If I phoned Beau, he'd suggest *Hubble & Hubble* and probably make the call for me, but that'd place Jude in an in-the-know position. No way.

"Is the gun registered in your name?"

"It is."

"What kind of a gun is it?"

"It's a .32 caliber pistol."

"When did you purchase this gun?"

"About four years ago. I'm not sure of the exact date, but I have that information in my office on Duval."

"Where did you buy this gun?"

"At a pawn shop in the Winn-Dixie Plaza on Big Pine Key."

"Why did you buy the gun?"

"For protection."

"Did anyone help you with this transaction?"

"Yes. Nikko Fotopoulos, a retired police officer. He taught me gun safety rules, and he also taught me to shoot on a practice range in Key West."

"Miss Moreno, the gun you have described for us, the gun you admit to owning, that gun is the weapon that we found in Margaux Ashford's hand this morning."

Somehow I didn't think they were lying to me now.

Chapter 9

Detective Curry's words stunned me. I couldn't get my breath. My lungs felt as if someone had tightened a steel band around them—a band that grew tighter by the second. This man who'd pretended to be my friend had led me into a trap with his questioning. No, that was wrong. He'd never said anything about friendship. That thinking had formed in my own mind because I'd allowed it to. He had merely signed up for a reflexology treatment. That made us business acquaintances, not friends. There's a big difference.

My face, which had burned only seconds ago, now felt like an icy mask. Never in my life had I ever fainted, but my head began to swim. Detective Winslow rushed to my side to hold me upright on the chair while Detective Curry brought me a Dixie cup of water. The room stabilized and I drank the water before I said anything.

"My statement concerning the death weapon startled you?" Curry asked.

I took a slow, deep breath that helped me regain some of my composure. "It startled me because it's a lie. It can't be true."

"How can you be so sure?" Curry asked.

"Because my gun's in the bottom of my desk drawer on Duval Street. You can check it out. It's there, right where I said it is."

"Then you won't object to coming along with us to your office and showing us the gun?"

"Of course not." This time I felt in charge of the situation and I stood, ready to accompany them to Duval Street. "You were very quick to verify my alleged ownership of that gun."

"It wasn't a long process this time," Detective Curry said. "Sometimes when the police find what they believe is a murder weapon they have to spend precious time determining who owned it. Your gun held an engraved number. It was purchased in the state of Florida. It took only a few minutes to make sure that you were the legal registered owner. Of course there's the possibility that someone else had possession of the gun at the time of the murder. And we'll have to determine for sure that the bullet that killed Margaux Ashford came from your gun. Before we place anyone under arrest, we'll have to determine who fired the gun. Those things will take longer. I told you this was informal questioning. We're merely trying to be sure that the gun found in Margaux Ashford's right hand is your gun. We appreciate your cooperation."

Detective Curry's words left me to consider how a gun registered to me, a gun I knew was in my desk drawer, could be connected with Margaux's murder. Again I rode in front while Detective Winslow sat directly behind me. Did she carry a gun? I supposed that she did, that all detectives carried guns. I wondered if she hated that part of being a detective or if she reveled in it. Traffic moved more quickly now and when we reached my office, we found a parking place within the block. Gram had closed her shop, but I could sense her watching from an upstairs window. Not much happened on our end of Duval that escaped Gram's ever-watchful eye.

I unlocked the door, snapped on the overhead light, and then stepped to my desk to punch the switch on the desk lamp. I have the type of desk drawers that automatically lock until someone opens the top drawer, and I opened that drawer.

"You leave your desk unlocked?" Curry asked.

"It was locked," I said. "You saw me open the top drawer and release the lock."

"But the top drawer was unlocked? It required no key to open it?"

"That's right. I keep nothing valuable in my desk."

"Nothing except your gun," Curry said.

Again, my face grew hot. I'd never considered the gun valuable, and suddenly I knew I'd been very careless with it. I hated the thing, but I knew that in Curry's eyes a gun probably held great value and I knew I should have been more careful with it.

"Show us your pistol, please," Curry demanded.

I yanked the bottom drawer open and shoved a box of envelopes aside. I pulled out part of a ream of paper and slapped it onto my desk blotter before I slid my hand beneath the envelope box. No gun. I yanked the envelopes out and tossed them beside the paper. My hands began to sweat as I forced my gaze to meet Curry's.

"It's gone. I can't believe it. The gun's gone."

"We have it at police headquarters," Curry said.

"Then why . . . why did you bring me here?" I demanded. "You could have shown it to me right there."

"Would you have recognized it? Many guns look similar to other guns. Could have picked it out of a group of weapons? Are you sure you would have recognized it as yours?"

"No. No, I'm not sure. I can't guess how it came into your possession." I lied. I could imagine how the gun got into Margaux's hand. Jude. Jude had to be at the bottom of this. I'd seen him on Grinnell Street. He'd threatened to see me dead. This was his way of carrying out that threat— to have me accused and convicted of Margaux's murder. When I spoke again, my voice came out a whisper. "Are . . .

are you going to arrest me?"

"No, not yet. I told you that this'd be an informal questioning. It remains that. We appreciate your cooperating with the authorities. There may be a good explanation as to why your gun isn't here . . . as to why Margaux Ashford clutched it in her hand this morning. We'll do our best to find that reason. And we'll make certain that this is the gun that fired the bullet which penetrated Margaux Ashford's head."

"I hope so, and I suggest you start your investigation by questioning Jude Cardell. I wonder where he was last night."

"Your ex." It was a statement, not a question so I didn't reply. "You think Jude broke into your office and took your gun, broke into the Ashford home, murdered Margaux Ashford?"

"I'm not sure what I believe."

Detective Curry offered his chair to Detective Winslow, then he stood behind her as he began questioning me again. "When was the last time you saw Margaux Ashford alive?"

"A week ago on Sunday morning. She had a regular house call appointment."

"When was the last time you saw the gun in your drawer, Keely?"

Now he used my first name. A trap, an attempt to establish false friendship? I wondered what his response might be if I started calling him Jon. Men in authority sometimes use the first name trick to try to diminish a woman's sense of importance. I didn't call him Jon. I tried to answer his question.

"I can't remember when I saw the gun last. As I told you, I never use it. I dislike the thought of using it. I only keep it around because Nikko and Gram insist."

"Who has access to that bottom drawer?" Curry asked.

"Me. I'm the only one."

"You and anyone who comes to your office for treatments. Isn't that right?"

"I've never known anyone to go poking through my private desk."

"But someone might if that someone needed a gun and knew one lay in your drawer. Isn't that right? All a person'd have to do would be to send you away on some errand that might seem perfectly legitimate. Or a phone call in your apartment might call you away. Or your grandmother might ask you to help her. Many things could entice you from your desk. Right?"

"Right." I couldn't argue. My mind rebelled at the thought of handcuffs around my wrists. This was America. People had to be proven guilty before . . . or did people have to prove themselves innocent? Our legal system scares me more and more every time I think of it. That thought replayed through my mind again as I stared at the floor, waiting for whatever would come next.

"Miss Moreno, may we dust your desk for fingerprints, especially the bottom drawer—fingerprints other than your own?"

"Yes, of course. Please do." I tried to imagine whose prints might be on that drawer other than my own. Any of my patients, I supposed, but certainly not Jude's. He wouldn't dare break into my office. Would he?

Detective Winslow went to the car for the fingerprint kit. After she returned with it, they dusted all the drawers, fronts, sides, edges, insides. It took many minutes before they had the evidence they wanted.

"We'll take these prints back to headquarters and check them out there."

Detective Winslow packed up the fingerprinting gear and Curry spoke again. "That'll be all for tonight, Miss Moreno.

We'll take you back to Georgia Street now if that's where you want to go."

"It is."

At my house, Detective Curry walked me to the door, waited until I stepped inside, and then rejoined Detective Winslow in the car. I watched them a long time before they drove away. The clock hands pointed to eleven, and I returned to bed feeling sure I'd lie awake until morning. I wanted to call Gram, Nikko, Jass. But no. No point in sounding an alarm.

Just when I began to relax and started to drift off, the phone rang. I bolted upright in bed then grabbed my cell phone. What now?

"Jass here, Keely. Hate to call so late, but I had to tell you. My hibiscus blossom won first place in Miami. The contest chairman just called. I did it. I won!"

The pride in her voice almost walked across the sound waves into my bedroom and I rejoiced with her. "Big congratulations, Jass! You're a winner. You deserve the honor. Can you get the news in tomorrow's *Citizen*?"

"Can't say about that, but people will know soon enough. Won't keep you now, but I had to tell you the news."

"I'd really have been bummed out if you hadn't called the minute you found out. Again congratulations!"

I lay there visualizing Jass's excitement, letting it blot out my worries about my gun and the police. Many minutes passed before I relaxed and felt myself drifting to sleep.

I didn't know how long I had slept before I opened my eyes and saw Jude standing beside my bed. Shorts. Tank top. Bald head. He reeked of booze and pot as he leaned closer to me. How had he managed to get in? I tried to scream, but no sound came. Punt had promised to patrol the area for a while. Had it been an empty promise? Where was Punt now? But no.

That had been a long time ago.

"How are you tonight, Kee Kee Keely?"

Jude had always called me Kee Kee Keely when he wanted his way in bed or when he wanted to beat me black and blue. His oily voice made me pull the sheet closer around my neck and shoulders as if mere cotton could protect me from his savagery.

"Get out!" I'd intended to shout, but the words came out a bare whisper.

"Have you missed me, Kee Kee Keely? Missed me enough to invite me back into your bed? Don't be afraid, Kee Kee Keely. I've come to give you a good time."

"You've gotta be kidding, Jude. Get out of here. Get out right now." My voice had returned and I heard myself shouting, raving. Jude laughed at me and jerked the sheet away, revealing my nakedness. Vulnerable. I lay there like a beached dolphin.

"Come on," Jude said. "Let's play a few of our sweet games for old times' sake." Jude pulled a padded Billy club from his waistband. "This has always been my favorite toy. It may leave a few bruises, but no open wounds that require docs and emergency rooms—and the bruises'll be hidden."

"Damn you, Jude Cardell! I have a restraining order. I'll report you to the law." My phone lay nowhere near. I tried to prop myself on an elbow, reach for the pepper spray under my pillow, but Jude grabbed my wrist and twisted my arm.

"Stop! Stop! Please stop!" I managed to wrest my arm away from him, leap to my feet, and run. I headed for the back door, but I knew I had no chance of escaping. I heard his feet pounding behind me. I ran into the guest bathroom, through the adjoining door into the guest bedroom. Jude's steps pounded behind me. Closer. Closer. I wanted to give up. If I exhausted myself running from him, I'd have no strength left to fight him once he overtook me. And I knew he'd overtake me sooner or later. In one final effort, I headed for the back door, and then I sank to the floor crying. If I ran into the yard he could throw me into the pool. I huddled near the door, totally exhausted and unable to muster the strength to scream for help. I knew then that Jude would hurt me for one simple reason—because he could. Nobody could stop him—especially not me.

The kicks and blows I expected didn't come and I awakened in a cold sweat with tears still running down my cheeks. I lay prone on the kitchen floor for a few moments until I felt sure I'd been dreaming. It had been weeks since that same terrorizing nightmare had plagued me, but the shrink had said it might haunt me now and then for a lifetime. Dragging to my feet, I took another warm shower and once more I returned to bed. This time I slept soundly and peacefully until I heard crowing roosters trying to wake up the dawn. Cock fighting's illegal in Key West, but roosters still crow.

Monday morning. Seven o'clock. I had two hours until my appointment with Shandy Koffan at my office. Who had pinpointed Shandy as a murder suspect with motive and opportunity? Punt? Jass? Maybe me? I couldn't remember, but I supposed Shandy could be the guilty one—the woman scorned. No. Wrong. The wife of the husband scorned. Circumstances around Margaux's death and thoughts of yesterday's happenings played through my mind like a VCR on fast forward as I tried to outline a workable plan for the day.

Would the police tell the media that the murder weapon belonged to me? I had to tell Beau, didn't I? And Jass. And Punt. And Gram and Nikko. How could this be happening to me? I felt like a fly caught in a spider's web. All I could do was wait and twist in the wind until the spider decided to eat me.

Chapter 10

At last I settled down enough to call Jass and Gram and tell them about being questioned at police headquarters, about my gun having been found in Margaux's hand, and that the police were checking to see if it was the death weapon. They believed me when I said the gun had been stolen from my desk, but what could they say? At least they knew the situation and I knew Jass would pass the news to Beau and Punt. Gram might keep the matter secret for awhile, but eventually she'd pass it on to Nikko. How I wished I hadn't ignored Nikko's advice to keep the gun under lock and key if I refused to carry it on my person!

I thought again about alibis. Would Detective Curry take my advice seriously and talk to Jude? I doubted that. Mentally, I scanned down our suspect list. I felt a need to get to work talking to suspects before the police called me in for more serious questioning that might require a lawyer and a response to the Miranda warning.

Punt. Could I trust him? I had to know that before I could continue with our plan of checking alibis. If Punt's alibi held up, maybe we could work together on investigating other alibis. Who'd check on Beau? Who besides the police? Even the police wouldn't rattle Beau's cage if Margaux's death went down on the books as a suicide.

Sloppy's was only a few blocks from my office. That's where Punt said he'd spent Saturday night and that's where I decided to go first—even before I stopped by my office and said hello to Gram. I pedaled through the damp morning air to the bar where a likeness of Hemingway hung above the entryway. Don't know what I expected to find so early in the morning. *Sloppy's* wouldn't open for several hours. I knew that, but I pounded on the closed door anyway.

No response. I pounded again.

"You got a problem, ma'am?" A motorcycle cop called to me from the curbing. "That place's closed. Maybe I can help. You leave something there last night?"

I started to reply, to make up a tale about a forgotten purse or car keys, when the door creaked open. An old Cuban leaning on a broom scowled at me.

"What you want?"

He waved at the bike cop and the cop rode away.

"You know Punt Ashford?" I asked.

"Everybody know Punt Ashford." He scowled and gave me a closer look. "What you want?"

"I want to know if Punt came here on Saturday night, Sunday morning." My shoulders sagged. How did I think a janitor could help me? Even if he came up with answers I wanted to hear, would anyone believe him? He didn't look like he'd ever been anywhere near a courtroom—or a bathtub.

"Why you want to know? You his woman?" He leered at me. "Punt Ashford be missing from your bed?"

I thought of a lot of smart and not-so-smart answers, but I forced a civil tone as I replied. "It's important to me and to his family to know if Punt patronized this bar on Saturday night."

The janitor held out his hand and grinned, sticking his tongue in the hole where two front teeth were missing. "What you pay?"

I hadn't expected this, but I dug deep into the pocket of my jumpsuit and came up with a ten and slapped it into his grimy hand. He shook his head, grinned, rubbed his thumb and two fingers together. I pulled out two ones and showed him the inside of my empty pocket. He scowled and pocketed the bills.

"Punt not here on Saturday night."

"You sure?"

"Lady, you doubt me, why you ask?"

"Think carefully."

"Okay. He be here for a short while. I be sure."

"Okay, so you're sure. What part of the night was he here?"

"Early part. Around eight or nine."

"Not later?"

"Lady, you doubt me, why you ask? He have coffee then he leave."

"You know a guitar man named Shim?"

"Never heard of no Shim. Worked here a long time. Know most everyone, but no Shim."

"Thanks."

He closed the door and I rode on toward my shop twelve dollars poorer. So much for Punt's alibi. He came to *Sloppy's* early on Saturday night, but he left. And Shim? A strange name. Had Punt made it up? If he had made it up, why? What was he hiding?

Punt's lying disappointed me, left an ache in my gut, but what had I expected? Maybe he'd been out with some woman—a woman he didn't want anyone to know about. Did he think I'd be interested in who he went out with? I wouldn't care about his women friends or his alibi if I wasn't almost sure to be in for serious questioning about Margaux's death. The truth concerning Punt's whereabouts last Saturday night could make a big difference in my life.

I pedaled on to my shop and chained and locked my bike to a utility pole near the back door. Stepping inside, I opened the drapery at the front window and turned the CLOSED sign to OPEN. Gram appeared at my door immediately, leaving three sleepy-eyed customers sipping espresso at her coffee bar.

"Good morning, Keely." Gram's caftan swished as she entered my office and thrust the *Citizen* into my hand. "Take a read. Better to know what be said about you."

The editor usually hides the bad news on page nine or ten, but Margaux's death made front page headlines above the fold. WIFE OF CIVIC LEADER FOUND DEAD. I scanned more specific details that filled the rest of two columns. Then I returned to the start and read each line carefully. My name leaped out as the finder of the body in the first two paragraphs, then the rest of the article gave a partial bio of Margaux's life in Greece, Key West, and New York City. The article left the murder/suicide question unresolved. Nor did it mention the gun found in her hand being registered in my name.

"Article bring you more business," Gram said. "Tourists come to peek at you. Be good advertising."

"Gram! Get real! A woman lies dead, a woman important to this island. It's no time to think of business and advertising. Whether or not people liked her, Margaux Ashford ranked as a community leader."

"She a bitch." Gram shrugged. "Good riddance. One other person agree."

"Who?" I stepped toward her. Did she have information I wasn't aware of?

"The person who shoot her. That person agree with me."

I sighed as I scanned the article again. The police had mentioned the possibility of suicide although no suicide note had yet been found. Did the police think Margaux stole my gun and then shot herself with it? Fat chance. The paper also mentioned the possibility of homicide, saying the case was still under investigation. I snapped on my desk radio and tuned to the local station so I'd be sure to hear any further announcements concerning the Ashford death. As I cleared my throat, I beckoned Gram to come closer.

"Gram, the Ashfords and I think someone murdered Margaux. We're going to do some investigating on our own to see if we can find the killer in case the police try to say suicide."

"Why you care? Why you try investigate?" Gram scowled and shook her finger at me. "Stay out of this, Keely. Bad business. Distance yourself."

"I can't stay out of it. Can't you see I'm already in it? I need to find the killer in order to protect myself. Punt and Jass will be investigating, too, and I hope you'll be willing to help us. You want the guilty person found and brought to justice, don't you?"

"Me help?" Gram gave a palms-up gesture. "Know nothing about this death. No way can help."

"Of course there's a way. An important way. You can listen. You're a sponge when it comes to listening."

"No like being called a sponge."

"Tap into the conversations of the people who drop into your shop for coffee. Listen to common street talk and tell us what people are saying about Margaux's death."

"Me think some say good riddance."

"Some people might discuss where they were last Saturday night when the shooting happened or perhaps where their friends were. If you hear anything that sounds the least bit important, tell me. If I'm not around, call Jass or Punt. Promise me that."

"Okay. Promise."

"Jass, Punt, and I have a list of suspects." I gave her the names, omitting Nikko and Jude. Gram would tend to protect Nikko because he's our good friend, and knowing Jude might be involved would scare her to death. I didn't want her to think I lived in danger from Jude—again.

"Here come your first appointment. Bottle blonde." Gram nodded toward the door and slipped outside without speaking to Shandy as Shandy entered my office.

Shandy frequently comes to me for a reflexology treatment, saying the treatments relieve her headaches. I often remind her that foot reflexology sometimes relieves only the symptoms, rather than the cause.

Gram's right. Shandy bleaches her hair, but in Key West bleached hair isn't worth a comment. It fits in with the patina of the island. It blends with the beach sand, and it goes well with the pink hibiscus blossom Shandy wears tucked behind her left ear. The hibiscus's a holdover from her job where the manager orders all waitresses to wear pink blossoms to match *The Wharf*'s décor.

"Good morning, Shandy. Great day, right?"

Shandy ducked her head in that shy way she had, and she spoke in a whispery little-girl voice that drove me crazy. I guessed the barflies at *The Wharf* liked it. She told me once that every night she makes megabucks in tips.

"Yeah," she said at last. "The tourists think it's a great day." Shandy sat on the patron's bench at the side of the lounge chair. "They're out in full force even this early in the morning. I had to park clear over on Whitehead Street. Counted twenty parking slots all filled before I found an empty."

I smiled at Shandy's compulsion for counting things. Once I watched her buy a bottle of aspirin, shake them into a dish, and count them to be sure there were a hundred as advertised. People who know her merely smile at her strange quirk. I think she knows this. It may be what makes her so shy. She told me once that she realizes counting's a strange habit, but she can't help doing it. I've known her for months, but even around me she ducks her head and looks at the ground when she speaks. She reminds me of one of the miniature Key deer up on Big Pine, on the alert and ready to run for cover if danger threatens.

"Lucky I had six quarters in my purse. I dropped them all into the meter. An hour and a half should give me enough time for a cappuccino when we're through here."

Did she intend to avoid talking about Margaux's death? I wondered if she knew the contents of Margaux's will. Would Otto have told her of the bequests? Maybe he wouldn't know the details himself until the lawyers read the will aloud to those who inherited. I suppressed a sigh. For all I knew Shandy might already be planning how to help Otto spend his new wealth.

While Shandy removed her sandals, I walked to the back of my apartment and filled the portable footbath with warm water and lemon-scented soap. That footbath has saved me mega grief. Most people'd be shocked if they had to touch some of the feet I've seen—calloused, misshapen, and just plain smelly. But Shandy had great feet, small, dainty, and always well manicured. I wondered if she did the manicure herself. She knew my office routine and she relaxed and wiggled her toes as I snapped on the footbath. We both inhaled the citrus scent while the water swished gently around her feet.

"Feels wonderful, Keely."

I had hoped Shandy would talk about Margaux's death, but since she hadn't, I decided to bring it up myself. Snapping the footbath off, I dried her feet with a fluffy towel and watched her pad to the lounger. When the chair mechanism lifted her feet to my working level, I gave her a pillow to raise her head so we could look at each other as we talked.

Moistening my hands with lavender-scented lotion, I began gently massaging her left foot. I felt her relax, but when I concentrated pressure on her toes, she let out a small gasp.

"Hurt?" I asked.

"Yes. What're you doing?"

"Breaking up those crystalline and calcium deposits so blood can circulate to the nerve endings in your sinuses and the pituitary gland. Those're places where lots of headaches begin." I felt her relax again as more crystals began to break up. While she lay relaxed I massaged the sides of her feet in a way that could relieve arm and shoulder problems, sciatic pain. Those areas, too, could cause headaches.

"Have you seen the paper this morning?" I asked.

"Hasn't everyone?" She sighed then tensed again as I returned to work more forcefully on her toes. "Don't expect me to be overwhelmed with grief, Keely. That woman left Otto a broken man with a shattered heart. She thought of nobody but herself and her svelte body, her fine clothes."

"I'm sure you've helped Otto's heart to mend." I massaged the inside of her foot, then applied a bit of pressure to her arch. She winced, but she didn't draw away from my touch.

"I've tried to help Otto, but the shrink has him on so many pills we can hardly keep track of them. Our kitchen table looks like a pharmacy. Pill bottles everywhere. Sheets of paper warning of so many side effects we have to use a magnifying glass to read all the small print. We hate the expense of it! Otto shells out big bucks for a bottle of pills, tries one, and when it gives him the runs, a sleepless night, or an upset stomach, he quits it. Won't swallow another. We flush them down. Same as flushing money."

"Surely some of the pills help him," I said.

"When one pill starts working, another one stops. So then the doc changes both prescriptions and we start working again from square one. I'm totally sick of the whole scene."

"That must be discouraging. I hope my treatments are being of some help to him."

"He thinks they are. That's the big thing—what he thinks. I worry about him, Keely. He won't tell me where he was at the time of Margaux's death. Don't you think that's strange?"

Chapter 11

Sandy's words about Otto's secrecy snapped my mind to full attention and I probed for more information.

"Maybe he's on so much medication he can't recall details. I can remember where I was, clearly enough. I'd stayed at home reading and watching TV. That doesn't give me an alibi though, not in the eyes of the police. No corroborating witnesses."

"Guess you should have had someone in bed with you." Shandy chuckled and I put a little extra pressure on her big toe.

"No fair! No fair!" She laughed and pulled her foot from my grip.

"You've got a big mouth," I teased. "Where were you on Saturday night? I suppose you have a perfect alibi."

"I reported for work, as usual, but I got off at ten. I suppose I should have hurried home to look in on Otto, but I didn't. Sometimes I get tired of asking him how he feels. I think it tends to make him concentrate on how *bad* he feels. He never remembers to ask me how I feel, but that's not important. Usually I feel fine. Tired, but okay—unless my head aches. Anyway on Saturday the moon and stars lit the night like a fairyland, and I took a long walk on White Street, ending up on the pier."

"Walking alone, or with somebody?"

"Alone. My alibi's like yours—nobody there to corroborate it, and it'd have been nice to have had someone to walk with. I don't expect to be called on to give an alibi. Do you?"

"One never knows." I avoided her direct question.

"Well, I suppose you might need an alibi since you found the body. That must have been an excruciating experience."

"Not one of my faves." I kept my voice light as I tried not to shudder.

"If anyone asks me for an alibi, all I can tell them's what I saw from the pier."

"You see something special? See our honorable mayor out skinny-dipping or skate boarding?"

"Nothing that interesting, but I counted those lights I could see on the widow's walk at *Ashford Mansion.* I counted them twice to make sure of the number. There're ten, and one of them's green. Did you know that? Seems very strange to me. Why'd there be just one green light? Maybe it's Jass's way of playing up her image as the lady in green—Miss Hibiscus."

"Guess I've never paid that much attention to the lights." I'm seldom good at prevaricating. I hoped Sandy believed me, but what did it matter? Everyone knew about the widow's walk lights. Writers had written them up in lots of tourist "must see" brochures. The widow's walk and its lights were hard to miss.

I gave my attention to Shandy's right foot, where I found more crystalline deposits. It didn't surprise me that she suffered from severe headaches, and it made me feel my work was worthwhile when she kept returning for more treatments, telling me she'd been headache-free for a week.

When I finished this treatment, I wiped Shandy's feet with a clean towel, then spent a few moments applying peppermint-scented lotion to her feet before I helped her from the lounger.

"Thanks much, Keely. One, two, three, four, five." She counted five ten-dollar bills into my hand then walked the few steps to Gram's place for a cappuccino.

I'd learned nothing of importance. Shandy had no alibi for Saturday, and if Otto had one, he refused to reveal it to his wife. That information intrigued me. Strange, but people on strong medicines sometimes did weird things. On the other hand, maybe Otto was hiding something. Maybe both of them were hiding something.

They both came to my office regularly. I suppose that at some time either of them could accidentally have seen my gun in the desk drawer. Either of them could have sent me to the back of my office or even to Gram's shop on some make-believe errand, and taken the gun in my absence. I hated being suspicious of my customers. My session with Shandy left me feeling shaky and unsure of myself—and of her.

For the next few minutes I did relaxing exercises with my hands. I'd developed a routine of squeezing a soft rubber ball to keep my fingers supple. Right now I needed more than that. I needed to feel my bare feet connect with earth, to feel myself drawing cosmic strength from the planet. Today, my schedule didn't allow for that luxury.

Coffee break time, but I seldom drank coffee until afternoon when I wanted a caffeine lift. I closed my eyes as I relaxed in a cushioned chair behind a privacy screen in my apartment, puzzling over my stolen bike, my horrible nightmare, Punt's flimsy alibi, and most of all thinking about the theft of my gun. Who hated me enough to try to make me look like a murderer? Only Jude, I thought. Only Jude. *I'll see you dead.*

I sat lost in my thoughts until I suddenly heard a news announcer break into a music program. I leaped to my feet, hurried to my desk, and turned the volume up as I stood staring at the radio.

"The police are now officially calling Margaux Ashford's death a homicide. The medical examiner and a team of detectives have ascertained that the victim had no powder burns on her hands that would indicate she had fired the gun. The gunshot to her head, delivered by persons unknown, was the sole cause of her death. Detective Curry has asked the public for information concerning anyone or any suspicious activities they may have seen around or near the Ashford home last Saturday night or early Sunday morning."

I hadn't realized I'd been holding my breath until I gasped for air. So far the announcer had mentioned nothing about the murder weapon belonging to me. Did they have a reason for withholding that information from the public? I hoped so. I certainly wasn't going to be the one to broadcast it.

The announcer had barely stopped speaking when my telephone rang and I heard Jass on the wire.

"You hear the news, Keely?"

"I just heard."

"Homicide." Jass spoke again before I could get a word in. "They said nothing about the gun having been registered to you. I think that's very strange, but maybe there's a reason. Maybe keeping it secret will help their investigation."

"Last night I asked if they were going to arrest me and they said not yet—whatever that may mean. I'm so sorry about this whole mess, Jass. So very sorry and so scared. What does Beau say? Have the police picked him up for questioning?"

"I don't know. I haven't seen him nor talked to him this morning. I tried to call him, but he must have taken his phone off the hook. All I got were busy signals."

"Can't blame him for that. Oh, lordy, Jass. Maybe his phone line's been tapped. Maybe mine, too. We're going to have to be careful what we say unless we're one-on-one."

"I suppose you're right about that, and I'm glad the police have made their decision. Of course, no good decision could be made. Either murder or suicide—both Dad and you are going to have to take a lot of publicity. We'll help each other. I'll let you go now, Keely. I wanted to be sure you knew the latest."

"Thanks, Jass. What do you suppose will happen next?"

"The memorial service, for one thing. The mortuary had to make some intricate changes in their plans, but we've managed to schedule the service for tomorrow afternoon at three. That meets the requirements of the will. I'm still telephoning a list of people Dad wants to invite."

"Can I help you?"

"Thanks, but no. I think verbal invitations should come directly from the family."

"Or the mortuary. How about that?"

"Dad says family and we'll go along with his wishes. He's helping, too. Thanks for being there, Keely."

Jass broke the connection as Consuela arrived for her appointment, necklaces and bangles jangling in a way that attracted attention to her outfit, which fit her like a coat of paint. Today she wore a yellow V-neck tank with a gold pelican pinned strategically to draw one's eye to her cleavage. Her tight slitted skirt matched the tank. She wore yellow sandals, and she wore yellow ribbons in her dark hair. Clearly, today was Consuela's yellow day.

Jass says that Consuela keeps scrapbooks on Cher and her activities and tries to match Cher's outlandish costumes and sultry voice. She may succeed with the clothes, but she's a total failure with the voice. Consuela only sounds loud loud loud.

"Consuela," I began, "I've my federal tax forms almost ready, and it'd help me a great deal if I had your last name."

"I refuse to tell you. Consuela's my only name."

"If the IRS checks me out in depth, I could end up facing an audit if I can't supply a customer's full name." I didn't know whether that was true or not, but I wanted Consuela's name for my own records. What kind of a business has no record of a steady client's complete name? I also asked her about it now to throw her a bit off guard. If she refused to answer that question, maybe she'd humor me by answering questions about her whereabouts at the time of Margaux's death.

"No use to ask my name, Keely. You know that by now. Famous people don't need last names. Cher. Avi. Madonna. Can you imagine any of those famous people supplying last names? It would ruin their public image. It would ruin my public image, too, even though I have yet to achieve my full potential as a writer."

Consuela's like a casino with lights dancing off her bright costumes and with brassy sound effects brought on by jangling jewelry. Even her voice is brassy. Many times the scent of jasmine or Chinese orchids precedes her entry into a room. Everyone knows when Consuela approaches. Now, she flopped onto the patron's bench, kicked off sandals with spiked heels high enough to compromise her center of gravity and also high enough to cause every male on Duval to do a double-take.

"Radio shout murder," she said as she waited for her footbath. "Radio can scream murder and it make me no difference. I continue to write. I continue working on my book for wee children."

"How can you be so unfeeling? The Ashfords are in mourning. They're planning a memorial service, a burial at sea. As a part-time employee, maybe there's something you could do to help them."

"I go to their door. I ask to help. Jass say I help most by leaving. So I keep silent at my home. I write."

I suppressed a grin. I could believe Jass's response. Jass

felt sorry for Consuela so she hired her on a part-time basis. Sometimes Consuela prepares snacks for people stopping in to see Jass's plants and she also helps Jass with cleaning. When she finishes her duties, she's free for the day. The arrangement suits them both.

"What're you working on now? I've read your first children's book and I thought kids would like both the storyline and the pictures."

"Margaux found the idea barely acceptable but she said yes, publishers welcomed tales written in English easy enough for Spanish-speaking readers. ESL readers, Margaux called them."

"English Second Language."

"Right. Margaux also say the book wouldn't have been published but for her. She say she did careful editing that turn my garbled English into something understandable."

Many times Margaux lacked tact when dealing with Consuela.

"Today, and for over a week now, I work on book in Spanish. No English second language; Spanish first language. There is market for such. Many Spanish-speak kids in American schools. They no understand English. They need Spanish words to comfort them while learn the English. I no need help to write Spanish."

"Maybe the Spanish speakers should concentrate more on learning English," I said. "Maybe if they had no choice but to read in English, they would learn more quickly."

"Where were you the night Margaux died?"

Consuela's sudden change of subject caught me off guard. I was the one supposed to be doing the alibi checkups. Had she somehow heard about the gun's registry?

"I was home asleep."

"You need to, as they say, get a life. Dull business, this

sleeping on a Saturday night. Saturday night music play. Wine flows."

"So where were you?"

"I danced the night away at *Two Friends*."

"Who were you dancing with?"

"Two partners. One before band intermission. Another one after. Smart cookies no tell."

"And smart cookies don't crumble. Remember that if the police come to you with questions."

Consuela jerked her foot from my grasp as I put pressure on the bottom of her big toe. I retrieved her foot and continued working. Her alibi would be hard to check out. If Consuela had been present at *Two Friends*, everyone would have been aware of it, but she could have slipped away between partners at the band intermission. Maybe slipped away long enough to shoot Margaux Ashford.

A little before noon, Consuela struggled from the contour chair without waiting for my consent. Had I hurt her? Did my mentioning the police upset her? Or was she angry because I wanted her last name? I tried to stop her, to talk to her, but she left in a huff. That happened frequently, but she always returned later to pay her bill.

Chapter 12

No use trying to stop Consuela! In her break-neck pace to leave my office, she almost bowled Punt over. For a moment I almost forgot my anger at Punt for lying to me about his alibi as I stepped outside to watch Consuela's departure.

"Whew!" Punt exclaimed, laughing. "I see Consuela's up to form." He looked at me through his mirrored shades, waiting for a reply or a reaction, and when I didn't respond, he shrugged. "Just stopping by to see if you heard the news. The police called the house before they released the murder verdict to the media. Radio ran it first, but I suppose it's made the TV stations by now."

"I don't know whether to be glad or sorry. Either way, it's dreadful news for your family."

"Perhaps for you, too. You'll probably be questioned, again and again, you know."

"Yes, but I can handle that." I tried to forget the grilling I went through at the time of my divorce. Sometimes the police have a hard time believing the innocent. "If I tell the truth, I won't be blamed."

"We'll all be there to back you up, Keely."

"Beau's going to need our support, too. Rotten scenes may happen all round us, Punt, but the most important things are the ones that happen in our minds. We can't let gossip or accusations or insinuating questions get us down."

"You're quite a philosopher," Punt said. "Have the police told you to stay in town?"

"Yes."

"Any more problems last night after I left you—I mean

beside the detectives giving you their seriously personal attention?"

I wasn't about to tell Punt about my scare when the cat jumped onto the screen or about the nightmare that returned to terrorize me. At first he had distracted me with his talk about the murder, but now my anger about his lying about his alibi boiled through my body. How dare he! How did he have the nerve to face me, let alone ask me questions? Somehow I kept my voice calm as I glared into the mirrors that hid his eyes.

"No problems last night, but plenty of them this morning."

"Consuela? What got into her?"

"Consuela's a minor problem. Punt, I hate it when people lie to me."

"Consuela lied to you? What about?"

"Not Consuela. You, Punt. You lied to me and you know what about. Did you think I wouldn't check on your alibi? Hah!"

Punt backed off a few steps, pushed his sunglasses to the top of his head, and looked me in the eye. If his astonished expression was a put-on, he must have taken acting lessons.

"Keely, be real! I didn't lie to you. Why would I do that?"

"You tell me!" I led the way farther into my office, so passers-by wouldn't hear us arguing. "I stopped by *Sloppy's* first thing this morning on my way to work. The clean-up guy said he worked there Saturday night. He said you had been there but that you left around eight or nine o'clock. He had no recollection of seeing you there late in the evening or sitting in with any band. None. Nada."

"You must have been talking to Peg Leg. He's the one lying to you, Keely, not me. He knows good and well he saw me there. We even talked a few minutes around midnight."

"Then why would he lie? It makes no sense. I tipped him, maybe not enough, but I gave him all the bills I had with me at the time. Even showed him my empty pockets."

"He's a sly one and he knows how to work people for tips," Punt said. "Also, he never thinks the tips are big enough. I think that's why he lied to you. Let's go to *Sloppy's* and talk to him right now, make him 'fess up. Then I'll take you to lunch."

"I want to hear the 'fess up part before I agree to lunch."

I wanted to believe Punt. We walked the few blocks to the bar, dodging tourists who seemed to think they owned the sidewalk, side-stepping salespeople handing out brochures about this afternoon's twenty-five-dollar dive trip to the reef, tonight's moonlit dinner sail around the harbor. Sometimes I have to try very hard to remember that if it weren't for the tourists, Key West would be like a dry watering hole. It scared me to think what might happen to this island's businesses if Americans once again had free access to Cuba's natural sand beaches.

Consuela and *Sloppy's* had a lot in common. You could hear them both from a great distance.

A jukebox blasted a rock rendition of *Bus Rider*, and tourists shouted at each other to make their words heard as they snarfed boiled shrimp steamed in beer and slurped Margaritas. Punt led the way through a maze of customers, some standing in clusters, and some seated at tables. At the back of the room near the stage, a drummer, a guitarist, and a keyboard man warmed up their instruments, checking the sound system, probably seeing how many amps they could up the volume.

"Hey, Peg Leg," Punt shouted and waved as he saw the janitor with broom and dustpan cleaning up shards of a Bud Lite bottle near the rear exit. The man limped toward us. I hadn't noticed the limp this morning, but then he'd stopped me at the door.

"What you want?"

Those seemed to be his favorite three words.

"Want you to tell this lady the truth about Saturday night. You know damn well I came in here, that I sat in with the band on their ten to midnight set. Why'd you lie to her?"

Peg Leg held out his hand palm up. Then he rubbed his thumb and fingers together. "You stiffed me."

"You expect a tip for lifting my guitar case from the stage to the floor?"

"Right. I expect. You stiff me." Peg Leg gave me a sly smile and I knew he'd lied to me to even the score with Punt. One bad turn deserves another.

Punt pulled out a twenty and dangled it low beside his left leg and out of Peg Leg's reach. "Okay you s.o.b., you tell this lady the truth, and be quick about it."

With his lowered gaze never leaving the twenty, Peg Leg spoke up. "Punt Ashford be here last Saturday night. He play guitar with boys in band. Ten to midnight, then they break up. Leave."

Punt raised the bill. Peg Leg grabbed it, pocketed it, limped away.

"Now do you believe me?" Punt asked.

"I believe, and I apologize for doubting you. But Peg Leg says you left here. Where did you go? You said you and some guys jammed until three."

"Went to Shim's place. He lives on Stock Island. A bunch of us jammed there until the wee hours—maybe even after three. But that was long past the med examiner's projected death time for Margaux. Let's forget it and have lunch."

"Deal. And I'll pay. My treat. I shouldn't have doubted you."

"Where would you like to go?"

I glanced at my watch. "Haven't a lot of time left, but . . ."

"Yes? I can see an idea brewing."

"We'd have time for a sandwich at *Two Friends,* and we could check on Consuela's alibi at the same time. She said she went dancing there on Saturday night."

"Someone will remember that, all right." Punt laughed. "That postage-stamp dance floor would hardly allow space enough for more than two people—especially if Consuela was one of them."

We hurried toward the patio restaurant where white lattice-work enclosed an open-air dining area apart from the bar, tiny bandstand, and dance floor hardly bigger than a dive flag. We both ordered grouper sandwiches plus iced tea, and an extra fiver encouraged the waiter to hurry.

"You work here on Saturday night?" I asked the waiter.

"No," he replied. "Lose something?"

"No, but we need to talk to someone who worked here on Saturday until midnight."

The waiter jerked his head toward the bar. "Bennie. Talk to him. He did the Saturday night scene."

Once our iced tea sat before us, we rose and threaded our way to the bar.

"You know Bennie?" I asked Punt.

"No. Don't think he's my kind of people."

"Bennie?" I stepped up to the bar and motioned to him, and when he came over, I shouted my question above the sound of Madonna begging Argentina not to cry for her. "Did you see Consuela here dancing on Saturday night?"

Bennie grinned and nodded. "Right. Everybody working that night saw her—and heard her!"

"She stay 'til closing time?"

"She came and went throughout the evening. That's Consuela."

"Did you know her partners?"

I offered Bennie a tip, but he refused the tip and refused to answer. Nice guy, Bennie. I pocketed my bill and we inched back to our table and ate our sandwiches.

"Guess Consuela has an alibi of sorts," I said. "But we'll have to track down her Saturday night dance partners. She could have left for a while and then returned. Some job, keeping track of Consuela."

"It may be possible," Punt said. "I'll work on it. See what I can do."

"Wish I had more time right now, Punt. I hate to rush through a meal, especially through a grouper sandwich, but I have to get back to my office—to work. I'm making another house call."

"Thought you didn't do much of that sort of thing. Who's the important patient this time?"

"Beau. He called early this morning. How could I turn him down? He looked so down and out last night."

"He's under big-time pressure right now." Punt gulped his iced tea. "I'm surprised he even found minutes for a treatment."

"I know I can relieve some of his stress. Of course, I said yes."

"You're an easy mark, Keely Moreno. Maybe I'd be interested in a few treatments if you came to my house."

"Don't count on it." I paid our tab and we hurried back to my office.

"Let me drive you to Dad's place," Punt offered.

"Not today, Punt. I'll ride my bike."

Punt shrugged. "Your call, but I stopped by your office for a reason. How soon are you free this afternoon?"

"Right after Beau's treatment. Why?"

"Let's work together on this alibi checking."

"Consuela's?"

Punt shook his head. "Later. I'd like to drive up to Key Colony Beach, talk to some people who were in charge of that fishing tournament."

"You doubt Beau's alibi? You think he might be guilty of . . ." I couldn't bring myself to say the words.

"No, I don't think Dad's guilty. No way, but I want to check out his alibi, in case the police do a rotten job. Now that they've officially called Margaux's death a homicide, I know they'll check on Dad's story. I want to collect my own primary source information for the family."

"Good idea, I suppose."

"Will you drive to Key Colony with me this afternoon? We'll do some investigating, have dinner. Sound okay?"

I wanted to say no. I'd put a mental block between me and the male inhabitants of my world, and I planned never to get involved with any man ever again. Men were on my no-no list—big time. Yet Punt's invitation tempted me more than I wanted to admit. It would be fun to have a night out—a night away from Key West and all the problems I faced here. I didn't try to fool myself into thinking Punt's interest in me went any further than checking Beau's alibi. I'd seen Punt scooping the loop with a variety of babes. He had cosmopolitan tastes.

"May I pick you up here a little after two?"

"Okay. Let's do it. I'll be ready."

As I watched Punt leave, I thought of Gram. Gram has some strange Cuban beliefs. For instance, she believes that two people never meet for the first time accidentally. She believes that they meet when they need each other. I've known Punt for years, but for some reason I felt that we were strangers meeting for the first time today. So where was the need? I disliked pursuing that line of thought too far.

I loaded my reflexology gear onto my bike and pedaled toward Grinnell Street, hating to admit that I wished I'd taken Punt up on his offer to drive me. I'd have felt safer ensconced in a car, even a convertible, than I felt riding my two-wheeler. Facing this appointment with Beau left me feeling more vulnerable than I cared to admit. I remembered seeing Jude yesterday morning. What'd he been doing in this Grinnell Street neighborhood? Lordy, had that only been yesterday? It seemed as if a month of Sundays had passed since I discovered Margaux's body.

Riding slowly, I delayed reaching Beau's house as long as possible. How could I bear to walk up those front steps again or walk through that doorway into the house? I chained my bike to a palm tree and lifted my supplies from the baskets. The yellow crime scene tape no longer outlined the property, and the trade wind blowing through the bougainvillea vines sent petals tumbling to the sidewalk—petals the color of blood.

Chapter 13

Remembering yesterday morning at the Ashford home, I steeled myself to avoid looking through the window beside the front entrance, but of course I couldn't keep from looking. I relaxed only slightly when I saw someone had drawn a shade across the window. The police? Beau?

I hesitated for a moment, and Beau opened the door before I could knock. His shoulders drooped and his shirt looked like the same one he'd worn yesterday. Dark circles under his eyes told me he'd had little sleep and probably little, if anything, to eat.

"Hello, Keely. Thanks much for coming to the house."

I started to say, "It's my pleasure," but that seemed wrong for the occasion. "Glad I can help you, Beau. I'm pleased that you called."

"Don't think I could have made it to your office. There's been a crowd nosing around here all day. Police. Reporters. Mortuary personnel. Jass. Punt. Everybody cleared out a while ago. Lunch time, I suppose."

Beau made the situation easier for me, perhaps easier for himself, too. Keeping his back to the chair where Margaux had been sitting, he urged me across the room toward the stairway, leading to the second floor.

Gold-framed paintings and photographs of Ashford ancestors lined the walls, the women looking prim-faced in their black dresses and lacy collars, the men looking macho in their sea captain garbs—billed caps, dark, brass-buttoned coats.

"I've set up an adjustable lounge chair in my den. Hope it'll work for us."

From the foyer in the upper hallway, he motioned me through a wide doorway and into a sunny room that overlooked the palms surrounding the backyard pool. I'd used the same chair for Margaux's treatments, but I tried to erase that thought from my mind.

Beau's den had a lived-in look and I guessed that cleaning people had do-not-enter, do-not-touch orders. Floor-to-ceiling bookshelves lined three walls: some of the books had been pulled forward, some of them placed horizontally across the tops of other volumes. The array of books made it clear to me that Beau didn't get all the research information for his columns from the Internet. Papers and notebooks lay stacked on a mahogany desk beside a computer. The thing that held my attention was a small box of gold rings.

Following my gaze, Beau smiled.

"Artifacts from the *Atocha*?" I asked as I began to set up my portable foot bath and arranged lotions and towels.

"Yes. The rings were personal possessions of the passengers aboard that ill-fated galleon." He picked up one of the rings and offered it to me. "See if you have a finger it will fit."

The ring was far too small for most of my fingers, but it fit perfectly on my right pinky. I examined the gold circlet with its green stone carefully, turning it this way and that. An emerald? A priceless antique? Who had this ring belonged to? Who had worn it centuries ago? I suddenly felt speechless as I eased the emerald from my finger and laid it in his hand. Our eyes met in an unusual directness.

"Oh, my." That was all I could think of to say. When I broke our gaze and again looked down at the ring box, Beau dropped a heavy gold chain around my neck—a chain with gleaming links that dangled to my waist. Its weight made me want to stand straighter. "Oh, my."

"Breathtaking, isn't it?" Beau asked. "This gold affects me

the same way, Keely. Makes me want to say, 'Oh, my.' After centuries of tumbling around in sea and sand, silver corrodes, turning ugly and black, but gold holds its gleam forever."

"These rings and the chain—they belonged to . . . to people who lost their lives centuries ago, right?"

"Right. These artifacts weren't listed on the ship's manifest a scholar found in Madrid. The manifest listed mainly gold bars, silver bars, doubloons, pieces of eight. Oh, and maybe some anchors and astrolabes."

"The manifest failed to mention the jewelry?"

"If it was a notable piece, perhaps one belonging to some crowned head, it might have been listed. The rings in this box were contraband probably smuggled aboard in the passengers' pockets. They might've worn the rings and lockets, of course, but if the ship authorities saw them, the owner would have been taxed."

"So even in those days, people hated paying taxes, tried to avoid them."

"Remember however, back in those days gold chains served as money. When the owner wanted to buy something, he paid for it by snipping off a link of his chain—or perhaps several links."

"The doubloons?"

"Of course they were spendable, too. Ever seen one up close?"

"Only in Mel Fisher's museum."

Beau removed the doubloon he wore around his neck and placed it in my hand. "The Spaniards were a two-faced bunch, Keely. Pious. See the cross of Christ on this side of the coin?"

After I nodded, he flipped the coin over. "They were also mercenary. There's the king's mark on the back—the mark that shows that the king's tax had been paid. Those aspects of

Spanish personality were to be the subject of this week's column in the *Citizen*, but I've no heart for writing today. I may beg off and repeat a column from last year."

Beau replaced the gold chain and doubloon around his neck. "To me the real and lasting treasure of the *Atocha* lies in the found jewelry such as the rings. Those pieces tell the human story of the galleon."

"A human story and a very sad story, too."

"I can't look at a ring or a chain without thinking of the people aboard that ship—people with hopes, dreams, desires. People from across the centuries may have differed a lot in their thoughts, but little in their feelings. The sensations of hurt or happiness, jealousy or joy, remain the same even when separated by hundreds of years."

I could tell how much Beau enjoyed touching and thinking about the treasures from the *Atocha*, telling me their stories. I hated to pull him back into the present moment, but I knew he had other appointments this afternoon, and I remembered Punt who'd soon be waiting for me. Again, Beau eased the situation by moving the box of rings aside and pushing some buttons on the adjustable lounger.

I spread a towel in front of a low chair suitable for him to use during the footbath and he sat down with a sigh. Once the lime-scented water swished around his feet I sensed his mood lift slightly.

"Best thing I've felt today." He smiled and I let him enjoy the water an extra minute or so before I dried his feet and motioned to the lounge chair.

"Anything special you want me to work on today, Beau?"

"My eyes and my lungs burn. My joints hurt. Feel like I haven't slept for a month."

I began therapeutic pressure on the small toe next to his large toe, and immediately we both felt the crystalline deposits begin to break up.

"Wow!" he exclaimed, but he didn't withdraw his toe from my grasp.

"Too much pain?"

"Of course not. I'm no lily. Use whatever pressure's necessary. It's the end result I'm interested in."

I took him at his word as I applied more pressure. "The discomfort you feel is in direct proportion to the quantity and size of the crystal buildup."

"Some of them seem a lot sharper than others." Beau closed his eyes, but I knew he wouldn't fall asleep. Now and then a frown etched his forehead and I felt his foot grow tense. When that happened, I worked on his arch and he relaxed again.

Over an hour had passed before I'd done all I could to help his eyes, lungs, and joints, and to relieve his stress. When I finished I offered a hand to help him up and out of the chair.

"Thanks, Keely. I may need more than one treatment before this week ends."

"Give me a call and I'll see if I can work you in—at your convenience. Always glad to help."

Beau let me out of the house by a side door and I appreciated his thoughtfulness. Two-fifteen. Punt would be waiting. When I arrived at my office, he sat enjoying a cup of espresso and visiting with Gram. I unlocked my door and he joined me, helping carry my work equipment inside. Once things were back in place, I prepared to lock up and leave.

"Car's on Angela Street." Punt grinned. "That is, it's on Angela if it hasn't been towed away at its owner's expense."

Gram frowned as I told her goodbye and we headed for Angela.

"No more work today?" she called after me.

"Had a cancellation, Gram. Be back ready to work in the

morning. Or maybe in the afternoon if . . . Punt, do you know when Margaux's memorial service will be?"

"Cremation's later today and the service will be at two o'clock tomorrow afternoon in the garden at their Grinnell Street home."

We walked the few blocks to Angela Street and eased into the Karmann Ghia.

"I'd like to go home and change from this jumpsuit. We'll have time, won't we?"

"Sure. It'll take only a little over an hour or so to drive up to Key Colony Beach in light week-day traffic. You know the turnoff—right before you cross the bridge leaving Marathon."

He headed toward Georgia Street, and when he stopped in front of my house, I ran inside to change while he waited in the car. I seldom went out on a dinner date, so I had few choices in outfits. The blue pantsuit? Or the green silk shift? I chose the green silk, telling myself that it didn't matter that it brought out the green in my eyes, but at the same time I wondered if Punt would notice.

After a quick shower, I slipped on the shift, enjoying the way the soft fabric slithered over my skin. The humidity of the shower had put extra curl in my hair and I gave it a quick brushing before I applied fresh lipstick and slipped on my green sandals. In moments I joined Punt in the car.

Punt gave a low whistle of approval when he saw me. "Very cool, Keely. You'll turn lots of heads."

My face flushed. It'd been a long time since I'd heard a man's whistle and compliment and I had to admit that I liked it. In a couple of blocks we were on Highway 1 headed northeast toward the middle Keys. I liked the feel of the wind in my hair, the sun warming my cheeks. Even the salt scent of the sea had an exhilarating tang I could almost taste.

"I haven't been up this way for a long time," Punt said. "Dad's always attending a fishing tournament or a boat show, or visiting some old timer who may have an interesting tale to tell. He drives up here now and then."

We passed Stock Island, Sugarloaf, Cudjoe. Quite a few cars headed toward Miami, but nothing like the bumper-to-bumper traffic headed into Key West. Punt turned off at a tiki bar, *The Boondocks,* and we sipped a Coke before we drove on. We left Ramrod Key and were heading into the Torch Keys when I saw the same gray car I'd noticed behind us before we stopped for a Coke. Again it hung three or four cars behind us. Sun glinting on its windshield deflected my view of the driver, but my throat tightened. I try not to be a wimp, but Jude taught me caution—among other things.

"Punt." I touched his arm and whispered his name as if someone else might be listening.

Punt reached over, taking my hand. "What?"

"There's a car following us. Four cars behind. Gray."

Punt peered into the rearview mirror. "Be real, Keely. I see at least fifteen cars following us and several of them are gray. A driver takes a risk if he passes on this highway. Lots of drivers play it safe and follow the car ahead of them 'til they get where they're going."

"That gray car's deliberately following us. It tagged behind us before we stopped at Ramrod and now it's behind us once more. It must have pulled off the highway somewhere and waited until we started out again."

"You think it might be Jude?"

"I can't tell, and I don't know what kind of car he's driving these days."

"Okay, we'll check it out. When it comes to Jude, you're smart to be seriously cautious." Punt hung a quick right when we reached the boat ramp turnoff to Little Palm Island.

Then, braking quickly, we sat watching, partially hidden by palm and mangrove trees. We both saw Jude's bald head at the same time as the gray car sped on past us.

"Now what?" Fear froze my throat and I could hardly speak. "Maybe we should turn back."

"You going to let that bastard scare us out? You're through letting him control your life, Keely. Remember? He's forbidden by law to come anywhere near you. We'll follow *him* for a while—give him a dose of his own medicine."

Gravel flew and tires screeched as Punt found a break in the traffic and roared back onto the highway. He left four cars behind us as he passed them on the right. Horns honked either in protest or in warning. I hoped no cops were watching. Two passes on the left put us directly behind Jude.

Punt honked his horn and rode Jude's bumper until he turned off at *Sea Center Marina* on Big Pine Key.

"I think we're rid of him now, Keely. He knows we could report him, claiming harassment, and he knows the law's on your side. Forget about him for now."

Easier said than done. My hands were icy cold in spite of the sunshine bearing down on us in the open convertible. I nodded and tried to relax against the leather seat cushion.

Neither of us spoke as we passed Sunshine Key, the state park on Bahia Honda, and then Seven-Mile Bridge. Traffic moved more slowly through Marathon, and at last we turned onto the long causeway leading to Key Colony Beach. On our left a posh shop offered upscale clothing, another displayed upscale fishing tackle. Everything on Key Colony Beach fit into the upscale description.

In a few moments we turned onto the island, driving until we reached *Fisherman's Cove Beach House.*

"Here's the place where they held the tournament on Saturday," Punt said, stopping in the parking lot. "Come on inside with me and we'll see if we can find Dad's friend."

The beach house offered a bar and restaurant overlooking the sea. Now, a little past four o'clock, customers were already dropping in for happy hour. Silver and gold lanterns hung from the palm-thatched roof and a boy in a white jumpsuit busied himself lighting torches mounted in huge clay pots at the edge of the deck railing. Three cocktail waitresses wearing black mesh hose and scarlet tutus placed gold-colored napkins on the tables, taking care not to damage the bird-of-paradise centerpieces.

"May I seat you?" A hostess wearing an ankle-length silver lamé gown smiled as she stepped forward to greet us.

"We'd like to talk with Mr. Sam Smothers," Punt said. "Is he available?"

"You're looking at him right now." A barrel-chested man wearing khaki shorts and shirt approached us from behind and we turned at the sound of his voice. Punt reached to shake the ham-like hand he offered.

"I'm here on an errand for my father, Beau Ashford," Punt said. "He spent Saturday and Sunday here working at the fishing tournament. He thinks he may accidentally have left his favorite yachting cap here. Would you have a way of checking on that for us?"

"Excuse me for a moment," Sam Smothers said. "I'll see what I can do."

He disappeared into what appeared to be an office and remained there for quite some time before he returned. I knew from his slight frown that he had bad news.

"Sir," Mr. Smothers said, "we have no record of your father having been here on Saturday. His name's not on our tournament work list, and there're no yachting caps in the lost and found box. Perhaps he worked a derby farther north—Plantation Key, maybe."

He looked at a space just above Punt's head and I knew he recognized the Ashford name, the murder investigation headlines.

"Is there anything else I can do for you?" he asked.

"No, but thank you for checking on this for us." Punt nodded to Sam Smothers, took my arm, and headed toward our car. His face a mask of worry, Punt said nothing until we were settled in the car again.

"Dad lied to us." He spat the words like pills that left a bitter aftertaste on his tongue. "Dad lied. Why?"

Chapter 14

We sat in the car for several minutes, silent, concerned. When a Ford sedan pulled in at the other end of the parking lot, I paid no attention to it until the driver got out. He didn't seem to notice us, and after my first glimpse, I kept my back turned toward him.

"Punt, don't be obvious, but case the tall guy entering the bar."

"Don't think I know him," Punt said. "You recognize him?"

"It's Detective Curry. Plain clothes. Unmarked car. I guess he hasn't been around to talk to you yet, right?"

"Right. He hasn't. But obviously he's talked to Dad and Jass, and I'm guessing he's here for the same reason we are. He'll get the same information we did. So go figure."

Punt started the car and I heard gravel spew as he turned and headed back toward the causeway, the highway.

"What now?" I asked. "Should we go home and warn Beau?"

Punt shook his head. "Let's think this over before we do anything." He drove slowly through Marathon, passing *The Quay* where people were gathering to have drinks and watch the sunset from the outdoor patio, passing *Herbie's* where people sat in a screened-in porch at pine tables probably enjoying seafood or foot-long hotdogs. When we reached the stop light, he turned left and headed for Sombrero Beach.

Swimmers and sunbathers were leaving the shore and we easily found a parking place near an entry gate. Gulls soared overhead, screeching like laughing children at play.

"Let's take a walk." Punt slipped from beneath the wheel and came around to open my door and guide me toward the white sand beach. "Kick off your sandals." He shed his Birkenstocks like unwanted skin, dangling them from the fingers of his left hand. "Maybe we can think better with a little sand between our toes."

I welcomed the feel of sand gritting against my feet as we strolled through the sea-scented air toward the water. Now and then we skirted temporarily abandoned beach towels and tubes of aloe lotion.

"Why do you think Beau lied about the fishing tournament, Punt? Surely he knew he couldn't get away with it."

"I've no idea. No idea at all, but since he wasn't at the fishing tournament, we have to find out where he was. That's the big question. We may not like the answer."

"You don't think . . . you don't think he had anything to do with Margaux's death, do you? I just can't believe a thing like that. I spent a lot of time at your house during my growing-up years. Beau's honest as they come." Punt didn't reply and we walked on toward hard wet-packed sand and then into the water, letting the sea swirl first around our ankles then rise almost to our knees.

"Had he and Margaux been having problems? Something wrong in their marriage?"

"How would I know that? Dad and I haven't been close for several years. He hated my drug problem. He hated my run-ins with the law. It's only been recently that we've been able to talk to each other with any sort of compatibility."

"He never gave up on you."

"Yeah, he bailed me out of so many jams we both lost count. When Mom died, I thought someone had cut the family anchor line. We all drifted. Then Margaux arrived on the scene and the rest's history. Jass handled Dad's new marriage a whole lot better than I did."

"Were you openly hostile?"

"No. I tried to keep my mouth shut about Margaux. Didn't want people saying wimpy Punt missed his mama, resented his stepmom. I've no idea what went on in Dad's mind or in his marriage. I can't imagine he shot Margaux, but that's looking like a possibility we're going to have to investigate."

"I'm jumping to no conclusions." I picked up a broken scallop shell and lobbed it into the waves. "Beau may have a perfectly good reason for being a no-show at the tournament. So he lied. Why? Maybe giving a phony alibi is one cut worse than having no alibi at all, but maybe when he lied, he had no idea how soon he'd be in deep need of proving his whereabouts on Saturday night."

"Who've you talked to so far?" Punt asked. "Who had no alibi?"

"You and Jass are in the clear—witnesses and all that. Shandy said she went walking alone, but she has no proof. Consuela said she spent Saturday night dancing with two different partners. We'll have a hard time checking that out. I haven't had a chance to talk to Otto or Nikko, but if they keep their appointments, I'll question them soon."

"There's still Jude. He could be the one. Or a street person. I still say a street person could have entered the house and . . ."

"But why? Nothing turned up missing. The police found no forced entry. Why would a street person have possessed my gun? Margaux answered the door and let someone inside the house, someone she knew; surely she wouldn't have admitted a stranger off the street."

"She might have let Jude in, since he worked for *Hubble & Hubble*. He could have pretended to have some legal paper for her to sign."

"You'd like to see Jude charged, wouldn't you, Punt?"

"It sure wouldn't break my heart."

"Well, that's unfair. People aren't guilty because you'd like it to happen that way. We're going to have to talk to Beau. Either that, or figure out for ourselves why he failed to show at the tournament."

Punt sighed. "There's nothing we can do right now. I think we need to get through the memorial service tomorrow before we say anything to Dad. Right now let's see if we can enjoy the rest of the evening. I promised you dinner and as soon as we've watched the sunset, we'll find a place to dine."

"Good idea. You're right. There's nothing else we can do until tomorrow."

The sun was a bright coin, slipping into a bank of clouds that turned scarlet, then pink, then to twilight gray. I smiled.

"More people should realize the sun sets at places other than Key West's *Mallory Dock*."

"Right," Punt said, "but here at Sombrero you miss seeing the Key Lime Tart Lady, the Frenchman with his trained cats, the high-wire walker."

"I heard that the Key Lime Tart Lady moved to Ohio, but don't forget the bagpiper. Few people can forget his haunting melodies. The tourists fill his open instrument case with dollars to keep him playing."

Punt laughed. "To each his own. I offered him a twenty one night if he'd pack up his pipes and go home."

"Punt! How could you!"

"It was a joke—sort of. Then a guy beside me offered him another twenty and I thought the two twenties tempted him to pocket them and go. But he kept playing. Maybe there aren't any pockets in those kilts."

We returned to the car, rinsing our sandy feet in the open air shower at the beach entrance. Punt steadied me as I slipped my damp feet into dry leather, pulling me a bit closer to him than necessary, I thought.

We drove slowly back to the Torch keys, turning right for a short distance and stopping at *The Sandbar*. The cool trade wind ruffled my hair as we climbed a dozen stairs to the restaurant perched on pilings and overlooking the bay. Darkness had fallen, and a full moon lit the water, glinting against the dock where other diners had moored their boats. The smell of fried shrimp made my mouth water.

Luck smiled on us and we found a table by one of the huge open windows that afforded us a clear view of the scene below. The running lights on a sailboat looked like slow-moving stars. Moonlight etched a couple pausing to enjoy a kiss on the dock, but closer at hand a waitress arrived, presenting us with a wine list and asking for our drink order.

I tensed, waiting to see how Punt would handle that.

"Would you care for a drink?" he asked.

"I'd like club soda with a twist of lime, please."

"Make mine the same," Punt told the waitress.

"Do you miss the wine?" I asked after the waitress left.

"Sometimes, but never a lot. It's surprising what a person can get used to—when it's necessary. Don't let my being on the wagon stop you from enjoying a glass of wine. They used to have excellent Chardonnay here."

"Thanks, but maybe another time, Punt."

A few minutes later I enjoyed the fizz of sparkling water and lime on my tongue as we studied the dinner menus the waitress placed before us.

"Punt, look. They serve alligator steak. Have you ever tried that? I thought alligators were endangered."

"I think that's past." Punt grinned at me. "So let's order alligator and see what happens."

"What do you think'll happen? Is there something about

alligator steak I should know?"

Before Punt could answer, the waitress returned, pencil and pad in hand. "What would you like this evening?"

"We'll try the alligator steak," Punt said.

She looked up, smiling. "I'm sorry, but we're out of alligator tonight."

"Give us a bit more time, please." Punt waited until she walked away, then he grinned. "Restaurants are frequently out of alligator unless area security officers have recently had to dispose of some 'gator that dined on a pet-owner's dog."

"You're making that up, right? Tell me it's something you read in a book."

Punt avoided my question and changed the subject. "Do you still like seafood as much as you used to?"

I felt flattered he'd remembered. It'd been a long time since we'd enjoyed a meal together. "Yes, I still love seafood."

"Then how about ordering the seafood platter for two?" He pointed to the listing on the menu. "Shrimp, oysters, crab, lobster."

"Sounds good to me."

"See this isn't so bad after all." Punt grinned at me.

"What do you mean, not so bad after all?"

"I've been asking you out now and then for years and you've always said no. Tonight, I feel like I'm gaining ground."

"We've had our problems, haven't we? We got along great in high school—for a while."

"Then I played jerk and went for any drug I could get my hands on. That turned you off, and rightfully so, and the next thing I knew you married Jude Cardell. Mrs. Jude Cardell. What on earth did you see in that guy? Do I dare ask you that question?"

I wished he hadn't asked. Why spoil an evening by talking about Jude? My face flushed and I took a drink of fizz water to cool down. No point in letting Punt know he could upset me with his questions or that his mentioning Jude could flood me with the frightening memories I tried hard to hold in check.

"Ask whatever you like. Hindsight's better than foresight. All I can say now is Jude and all his phony sophistication dazzled me. He's several years older than I, you know, and at the time I thought him a debonair man about town. The community respected him. I didn't see his dark side until after we married. Before that, he wined me and dined me and brought me gifts for every occasion and many times for no occasion at all." I forced myself to stop talking when I heard my words rattling on and on.

"Jass told me Jude's ability to enchant ended once you married."

"Right. It did. Jude insisted we move to Miami where I had no friends or relatives. Then he became jealous to the extreme. He tried to control everything I did. And I let him. I think now that's why he did it—because he knew he could, because it made him feel big and important. If I even looked at another man, he accused me of having an affair behind his back."

"That's when the abuse started?"

"Yes. I suppose Jass told you about it. She tried to get me to leave Jude after my first broken jaw, but my stubbornness and my fear held me in place. Finally I had the courage to walk out and, although I've sometimes still been afraid, I've certainly never been sorry. I do regret the fear Jude left with me, a fear of being around men, a fear of even thinking about another relationship."

"I hope you notice that I've done nothing to scare you to death today."

"I've noticed, and I appreciate that, Punt. I'm going to have to bury my fears as we face the days ahead, the murder investigation."

We stopped all serious talk when the seafood platter arrived, and we had playful arguments over who ate the biggest shrimp, the best piece of lobster. We laughed as we debated over whether the scallops were really scallops or just cookie-cutter pieces of breaded gray shark. But what did it matter when everything tasted so delicious? We took our time enjoying the meal and watching the moonlight play on the bay.

After we ate we climbed back down the stairs and walked around the building to a shallow lighted pool where we watched baby barracuda, sharks, and some rays swimming among coral rocks and a bit of floating seaweed. Sea water splashed into the pool through a length of copper tubing, keeping the enclosure fresh and clean. Two children dropped pieces of bread on the water's surface, and we could almost see those meat eaters turning up their noses at such poor fare. When one of the groundskeepers tossed some chum into the pool, the water swirled as the creatures vied for it.

After watching the fish for awhile, we strolled onto the dock. The boards swayed beneath my feet and I clung to the rope railing strung between sturdy uprights.

"Let's go see who's docked here tonight." I liked reading the names painted on the boat sterns. Punt took my hand to steady me. "Look. *The High Sea* from Big Pine Key. *The Sea Witch* from Little Torch Key. *Janice* from Sugarloaf Key."

I leaned over to try to read another name, but Punt pulled me up and into his arms. The evening had grown cooler, and his body warmed me. In the next moment his lips pressed against mine in a sweet, lingering kiss that I returned—because I wanted to. I enjoyed the lime scent of his after-shave for several moments before I gently eased from his embrace, determined to keep our relationship platonic.

"Punt, be real." My voice sounded throaty and shaky. "We're probably putting on a moonlight show for all the diners with window seats."

"Do you really care?" Punt released me, but kept one arm around my waist as we headed back toward the car.

I didn't answer. I considered his question and I wasn't at all sure of the best reply. The truth? Or something I made up in order to sound glib? Punt didn't repeat the question. Maybe he was as afraid of the answer as I.

We rode back to Key West in a passive silence that belied our concern over Beau's lack of an alibi, over what might happen to all of us the next day. A few cars passed us, but for the most part the drivers held to the speed limit. Shandy says there are a dozen speed limit changes between Key West and Big Pine Key—forty-five to fifty to fifty-five. I didn't count them. I trusted Shandy when it came to counting things.

At first, North Roosevelt was relatively quiet for that time of night, then sirens wailed, demanding right-of way. Punt managed to pull the convertible to the curbing to let two fire trucks whiz by.

"Wonder what's up?" I asked.

"Want to go see?"

Without waiting for my reply, Punt followed the sound of the sirens, and we gasped when both trucks turned onto Georgia Street. At first we couldn't tell where they were going to stop, then all at once we saw they were slowing at my house.

We saw small flames licking from the two windows that opened onto the front porch. Then Punt drove on past the fire trucks and we saw more flames snaking out the side windows and charring the siding. Even brighter flames shot into the air near the back entrance, flaring higher than the roof.

"Stand back folks! Give the firemen room!"

"More hose. Connect that hose!"

Firefighters shouted orders, pulled a hose from the truck, hooked it to the fire hydrant.

"My things! I've got to save my things!" I released my seatbelt and shouted as I opened the car door and fought to get out, straining against Punt's grip on my arm and hating the way he pulled me back.

"It's too late, Keely," Punt yelled in my ear, but I continued to struggle.

"Let me go! Let me go!"

"Don't risk your life." Punt's fingers were like a vise clamping me to the car. "The house's going up like tinder. There's not a chance in hell of saving anything."

Physically, I stopped struggling, but my thoughts raced with the flames. "What do you suppose caused it?" I hoped Punt would say something like "faulty wiring" or "stove burner left on." He said nothing. Nor did I. But my mind's eye saw Jude Cardell carrying a match and a can of gasoline.

Chapter 15

A police car arrived, sirens wailing, warning lights flashing. It stopped in the middle of the street and a cop sprinted to our car.

"Move on! Move on! You're blocking the right-of-way. Let the police cars through. No parking here! Move on."

Punt pulled the car ahead slowly and we craned our necks, trying to see the extent of the fire. Were flames leaping higher, or was the blaze dying down? We couldn't tell.

"Move on," the cop ordered again. "Move on or I'll ticket you."

"Drive around the block, Punt. Please. I've got to get back to the house. I'm responsible for it. The Moores expect me to look after it." I felt tears wetting my cheeks and my breath snagged in my throat.

"There's nothing either of us can do to help. The firefighters know their business. The best thing we can do is to keep out of their way."

Punt had to circle two blocks before he found a parking place. He took time to raise the top on the convertible, lock the doors, and although I could barely stand the delay, I waited for him. Nobody leaves an unlocked convertible on the street at night. A smog of smoke filled the air and my throat ached as I choked on it as well as on my tears.

"Fire! Fire!" Somebody behind us shouted, and footsteps pounded the sidewalk passing us by. "House afire! House afire!"

We joined the throng running down the street and heading

for the blaze. When we reached Georgia Street, policemen holding restraining ropes and Billy clubs struggled to hold the crowd at bay.

"Stand back! Stand back!" An officer shouted through a bullhorn.

Neighbors stood on their porches gawking. A pudgy man in a green plaid nightshirt stood barefoot on his front sidewalk, shouting orders to the firemen.

"Around back! Around back!" he shouted. "I heard an explosion."

"Henry, shut up," a woman yelled. Her baby-doll nightgown reached mid-thigh, revealing thin sparrow legs and bare feet thrust into a man's loafers.

I heard gushing water splashing the front porch siding, smelled the pungent odor of smoke, oily, black. Punt tried to hold me back, but I pushed my way forward until I felt the heat from the blaze, tasted gritty ash on my tongue. Something inside the house exploded, and in the flare of the explosion, light glinted on a bald head. I grabbed Punt's hand, but in the next moment the bald head disappeared and I said nothing. Lots of men had bald heads.

"Lady, if you don't get back, we'll have to restrain you in the patrol car." The policeman pushed on my shoulders, forcing me back a few steps.

"But it's my house," I shouted. "I live here." I shrank from his touch, darted behind him, and jogged toward the rear of the house just as the flaming roof over the back porch crashed. Support posts fell like jackstraws and sparks flew in all directions. Only when a bit of burning debris landed in my hair, did I realize I could do nothing to stop the fire. Punt knocked the debris to the ground and stamped on it. The smell of my singed hair sickened me.

"Are you okay?" Punt brushed his fingers through my hair

to make sure there were no more live sparks.

"I'm fine. I'm fine."

Punt slid his arm around my waist and pulled me close, and I sagged against him, exhausted.

"Let's get out of here, Keely. There's nothing either of us can do. Maybe in the morning we can come back, sort through the rubble. You might be able to salvage a few things. Is there a back path we can leave by? No point in antagonizing those cops again if we don't have to."

"We can follow this chain-link fence to the alley behind the house. The fence surrounds the yard and the pool and there's a back gate. Maybe the firemen could bring their hoses through it and reach the flames at the rear of the house."

"You got the gate key with you?"

"No. I keep it inside on the key rack beside the kitchen door."

"It doesn't matter. The house's a goner. Let's follow the fence and then the alley. We need to get back to the car."

Punt took my hand and I followed his lead, feeling an exhausting numbness I couldn't describe. When he squeezed my hand, my ring cut into my finger.

"You're hurting me!"

He dropped my hand. "Sorry, but look." He pointed to the ground and I gasped.

A black sweatshirt lay in the dirt beside the locked gate. I picked it up.

"That yours?" Punt asked.

"No, but I'm taking it with me."

"Maybe you should leave it here and let the police or the fire chief find it. There's always some kind of an investigation into the cause of a fire. The sweatshirt might be a clue."

"You think someone deliberately started the fire?"

"That's always a possibility."

"If I leave the shirt here, the owner may realize he left it and return for it. Or if the police or fire chief find it, they may pay no attention to it, believing it belongs to me." I slung the shirt over my arm, thinking of that instant flash of light gleaming against a bald head. "I've read that people who deliberately start fires sometimes hang around the scene—even offer to help the firefighters."

We walked past the gate and headed down a narrow alley toward the car.

"So you think someone deliberately started the fire?" Punt asked at last.

"As you said, that's a possibility. Why would an empty house catch fire?"

"There could be many reasons. Faulty wiring comes to mind first. Or maybe an appliance left on accidentally."

"I know I didn't leave anything on. I seldom iron. This's wash-and-wear country. I didn't leave a stove burner on because we planned to go out for dinner, remember? I didn't think to turn on a night light because we left for Key Colony Beach in bright sunshine."

By the time we reached the car, the crowd had thinned. Punt skirted around a few stragglers who stood on the sidewalk discussing the blaze. When Punt drove down the street, turning toward Duval and my office, he squeezed my hand.

"I could stay the night if you're afraid," he offered.

"Thanks a lot, but no thanks, Punt. This has been some kind of a day! We still don't know what Beau was doing the night of the murder, and now I suppose I'll be questioned about this fire."

"No doubt about that."

"What will I tell Mr. and Mrs. Moore? I hope they don't

think me negligent. I feel so sorry for their loss. They had high hopes for that house."

"Are you going to call them tonight?"

"No. There's nothing they can do right now. No use waking them up in the middle of the night with bad news."

"I suppose you're right. You have enough clothes and things on Duval to see you until tomorrow?"

"Yes. I'll be fine. The Moores are due to arrive next week and I'd already started clearing some of my things from the house."

"Think you'll be able to keep your appointment with Nikko in the morning?"

"I hope so. And Otto's, too. Once I've talked to those two, that's about it for checking alibis."

"Except for Jude. I can't see any way that either of us can talk to Jude."

"The police probably won't think he had any motive."

"Unless I point it out to them," Punt said. "Enough for now."

Punt parked in front of my office, pulled me toward him, and kissed me. I returned the kiss, surprised that it seemed like such a natural thing to do.

Punt hadn't been gone two minutes before Gram tapped on my door. I supposed she'd seen Punt's embrace, but I didn't care. I felt too drained of all strength to care about anything, nor did I want to talk about my day or the fire. I only wanted to be alone with my thoughts so I could sort them out and maybe make some sort of sense of them. Or maybe I just wanted to go to bed and erase all my problems with sleep. I heard Moose's claws clicking on the floor overhead, heard Nikko's TV playing softly as I tossed the black sweatshirt onto the bed in my living quarters.

"What's up, Keely?" Gram knocked again then pushed

her way inside almost before I could open the door. Without her scarlet caftan, her hoop earrings, her headband, she looked like—a grandmother. I smiled, doubting that she wanted to project that image to the public. "Radio say house on Georgia Street afire."

At that point, Nikko appeared behind Gram in the doorway with Moose at his heel.

"You all right, Keely?" he asked. "We're guessing that the house was your rental. The announcer didn't give the exact address, but the description—everything fit."

I opened the door wider so Nikko and Moose could come in.

"Right. My house. Or rather Mr. and Mrs. Moore's house. Punt and I just came from there. Nothing the firemen could do to save the place, but they did save neighboring homes. I'll be living back here sooner than I planned."

"What start fire?" Gram asked.

"Too soon to tell. The police were busy trying to keep everyone back and out of the way. Maybe tomorrow they'll have some information." I reached down to pat Moose, feeling his heavy hair, his thick leather collar. He licked my hand with his sandpaper tongue.

"You call me if police come with questions." Gram shook a forefinger at me.

"I will. You'll be first to know—as usual. Nikko, didn't you and Moose investigate suspicious fires before you retired?"

"Many times," Nikko said. "You think this was a suspicious fire?"

"Hah!" Gram said. "Any fire in Key West a suspicious fire. Street people break in. Druggies light up. Shoot up. Any fire suspicious."

"What do you think, Keely?" Nikko asked. "Something

special about this fire that makes you wonder about it?"

I wanted to tell Nikko about the sweatshirt, but not in front of Gram. No point in worrying her. Time enough to talk to Nikko tomorrow.

"No. Nothing special about this fire. I hate it that it happened at a house I feel responsible for."

"You be tired now," Gram said. "You get rest. Things look better in morning."

"Right," Nikko said. "Moose and I may drop by Georgia Street tomorrow to see what we can see. Or should I say sniff what we can sniff."

Gram and I smiled at each other, I hugged her goodnight, and everyone left me alone. Everything about me smelled of smoke and soot. I hung my green silk up to be hand-washed later, then I showered and dropped into bed, but sleep wouldn't come. Scenes from the crazy day kept replaying through my mind. Too much had happened too fast. Why had Beau lied to everyone? I didn't want him to be the one accused of Margaux's murder. Nor did I want to find myself in that position. Big problems. And now this fire.

It seemed I had hardly hit the bed when my clock radio announced the new day. Tuesday. I yawned and stretched and wished I could sit this day out. Two patients to see and then the memorial service. My feet had barely touched the floor when the telephone rang.

"Foot reflexology. Keely Moreno speaking."

"Keely! This's Ruth Moore. We just heard the news from the police down there. Are you all right?"

"I'm fine, Mrs. Moore. I'm so sorry about your house . . . all your plans for it. I haven't had time to go over this morning to view the damage again, but . . ."

"We're concerned and shocked," she said, interrupting me, "but we've had time to calm down a bit. Insurance will cover the monetary loss, and we're so relieved that you weren't injured."

"No, I'm fine. I'd gone out for the evening and I was away when the fire started. Thanks for your concern. Do you plan to come down?"

"Not today," she said. "We'll see about plane reservations."

"Sometimes planes are booked full at this time of the year."

"We'll call our insurance carrier to take care of the details as soon as the offices open. Then we'll hire workers to do the cleanup." Now Mr. Moore's voice flowed over their extension.

"We'll try to come down soon, find a rental while we take care of rebuilding—or perhaps selling. This's a real shock. It's hard to know what to do or which way to go."

"I can understand that. If there's any way I can help you, please let me know. I've lived here all my life and I can put you in touch with salvage and clean-up people."

"Thank you, Keely," Mrs. Moore said. "I'm upset, of course, but I'm so, so relieved that you're okay. I'll let you go for now. We'll probably be in touch later after we've had more time to think and to adjust our plans."

"Thanks for calling, Mr. and Mrs. Moore. Again, let me tell you how sorry I feel about your loss." I began to hate those words. Why were they springing to my lips so frequently?

I'd hardly replaced the receiver when the phone rang again.

"Detective Curry here, Miss Moreno. I'd like to speak to you about the fire on Georgia Street last night."

My heart pounded. I'd expected this, but not so soon. I slid my warm feet into cool sandals, and when I didn't respond, he continued.

"May I stop by to talk to you?"

I took a deep breath as I glanced at my watch. I didn't want to talk to this man at this time—or any other time. Nor did I want to seem reluctant to answer his questions. "I have a patient scheduled at nine. Could you arrive before or after that?"

"I could come right now if it's convenient."

"That will be fine, sir."

"Thank you. I'll be right there."

I barely had time to dress and make us some coffee before he knocked on my door. When I let him in, I saw a curtain move at Gram's shop. No need to let her know anything; she had an inner antenna tuned for news.

"Good morning, Detective. Please come in." I motioned him to the chair beside my desk where he had sat before, surprised that my voice sounded steady and unafraid. "Would you care for a cup of coffee?"

"No thank you, Miss Moreno, but do have some yourself if you care to."

I shook my head and sat down behind my desk. I usually felt that the behind-the-desk position helped me control any situation. Again, that feeling vanished when Detective Curry spoke.

"Of course you know there's always an investigation of any fire. It's routine." His laser-beam eyes bored into mine.

"Yes, I understand that." I decided to keep my responses brief.

"You rent the Georgia Street house?"

"Yes." He knew that. Why was he asking again? "The Moores called me moments ago. They'd heard the news."

"Where were you last night when the fire started?"

I'd expected that question, yet hearing it verbalized shocked me. I countered with a question of my own, stalling for thinking time. "What time did the fire start? It looked full-blown by the time I arrived."

"The fire chief's estimate is around ten o'clock. Where were you at that time?"

Fat chance I had of diverting his attention! "I was somewhere on Highway 1 between Little Torch Key and Key West."

"Alone?"

"No. With a friend."

"The friend's name, please?"

"Punt Ashford."

"You'd been away the whole evening?"

"The whole afternoon and evening, Detective."

"The fire investigator thinks the fire started in the attic. Have you ever been in the attic of that house?"

"No. Mr. Moore said getting to the small crawl space in the attic required climbing a ladder propped against the kitchen wall. He saw no need for me to go up there."

"So you never did?"

"No. Did you find an indication of arson?"

Detective Curry straightened in his chair and his eyes bored into me until I felt like an ant under a microscope. "Do you have reason to suspect arson, Miss Moreno?"

I wished I could withdraw my question. Thank goodness he couldn't read the thoughts that swirled in my mind concerning the black sweatshirt.

"I know little about arson." Mentally, I congratulated myself on having avoided his question without lying. "Since the house was in rather deplorable shape, I thought some homeless person might have entered, perhaps deliberately started the blaze. That happens in Key West now and then— especially if the night's been chilly."

"The temperature last night reached the seventies."

Detective Curry stared at me until I wanted to squirm, but I managed to keep meeting his gaze until he looked away. "Miss Moreno, I find it rather remarkable that you have been so closely aligned with two recent disasters."

It wasn't a question, so I made no response.

Chapter 16

Detective Curry left, and Nikko arrived for his appointment almost before I'd had time to regain my composure and hide Curry's insinuations deep inside myself. As usual, Moose accompanied him, walking sedately at his heel. They made a formidable pair, Nikko with his heavy black eyebrows and piercing eyes, Moose with his lean muscular body and pointed ears on the alert. The police force lost two good workers when those two retired. Nikko was too macho to admit to any physical failings. At first he said he came in for treatments to help me get my business started, but he still stopped by for monthly tune-ups. At least that's what he called his sessions.

While Nikko sat enjoying the scented footbath, we talked about the fire.

"Rotten luck, Keely. I know you enjoyed getting away from the hustle-bustle of Duval Street part of the year. Maybe you should find a house of your own. I try to look at setbacks as opportunities."

"Right now I feel safer right here on Duval. It's noisy and full of all kinds of people, but it's also full of police who keep a sharp eye on things."

"You've been afraid?"

"Let's just say I've felt apprehensive. Go figure. We know for sure there's a killer at large, and now I think there may be an arsonist running loose, too. Maybe they're the same person."

"Arson?" Nikko dried his feet on the towel I provided, then moved to my work chair. "I knew last night you were holding back things you wanted to say. So you suspect arson?"

146

I waited until I'd adjusted the chair for ease in working on his feet before I answered. "Arson, yes, and for several reasons. First, I can think of no reason why an occupied house would suddenly catch on fire. It's not as if the place had been standing vacant like an open invitation to intruders. Second, Punt and I found a black sweatshirt lying on the ground outside the backyard fence—a sweatshirt that didn't belong to me. And third . . ." I hesitated before saying more.

"And third?" Nikko flinched a bit as I applied pressure to his little toe.

"I think I saw Jude's bald head in the crowd of onlookers. I think he stood nearby watching the fire, the crowd, the hullabaloo."

Nikko suddenly raised up in the chair and I had to ease him back down before I could continue my work. For a few moments he said nothing, then questions gushed forth. "Did Punt see Jude? Did you point out the sweatshirt to the police? Do you think Jude saw you?"

"Hey! Slow down. One question at a time." I put pressure on his left heel in the area corresponding to the sciatic nerve and he winced as crystalline deposits broke away. "Your back pain been any better this week?"

"What back pain? You're changing the subject."

"When I feel crystalline deposits in the heel area, I think in terms of back pain."

"Maybe a little back pain. Not much."

"Good, but maybe we should increase your treatments to every other week for a while. Would you like to try that?"

"Monthly. Bi-monthly. Whatever you say. You're avoiding my questions. Did Punt see Jude?"

"You think I imagined seeing Jude?"

"I didn't mean to imply that at all, Keely, but I know a fear of Jude always resides in the back of your mind. No one can blame you for that. Did Punt see Jude, too?"

"I don't think so. At least I didn't point him out to Punt, but maybe Punt saw him, too, and said nothing, disliking to upset me. It works both ways, you know."

"What about the sweatshirt? You give it to the police?"

"No. I brought it home with me."

Again, Nikko raised up, scowling this time. "You may have tampered with a crime scene—again. What possessed you to take the sweatshirt? If you suspect arson, you must know the sweatshirt could belong to the arsonist."

"Right. That's exactly what I thought, and that's why I kept it. I thought the arsonist, if there is one, might realize he dropped it and return for it before the police discovered it. They were very busy and I doubt they would have listened to anything I had to say. All they wanted me to do was to keep moving, to keep out of their path. The way I see it, I have preserved evidence."

"That's reasonable, I suppose, but you could have turned the sweatshirt over to the police."

I knew Nikko was right. I could have given the sweatshirt to Detective Curry a few minutes ago, too, but I didn't.

"The cops scare me, Nikko. They might say the sweatshirt belongs to me without trying to find its true owner. I'm already high on their suspect list concerning Margaux's murder, but I have an airtight alibi for last night. At the time of the fire I was with Punt. Lots of people saw us on Key Colony Beach. Lots more saw us eating dinner at *The Sand Bar*. Yet in spite of witnesses, I'm afraid the police might manage to use that sweatshirt to my disadvantage."

"Do you have an alibi for the night Margaux died?"

"No. Do you?" I had hated the thought of asking Nikko for an alibi, but now he had opened the subject.

"Afraid not. I'd been working earlier in the evening. When

the dining room closed at ten, I left the clean-up to the bus boys and came on home. No witnesses to that except Moose. So what? I don't expect the police to question me about Margaux's death. I had no motive."

At the sound of his name, Moose lifted his head to look at us, then relaxed again and closed his eyes.

I hated to question Nikko about the rumor that he and Margaux were more than good friends. Maybe they had been lovers. Maybe they hadn't. It was none of my business, yet I had to warn Nikko of the gossip.

"Nikko, you may need an alibi." He started to sit up, but I eased him back down.

"Why would I need an alibi? Be real, Keely."

"Please hear me out. The local tongue-waggers are saying you and Margaux were lovers. Some are hinting you may have killed her as a way of dropping her for some other woman. Others are guessing she may have dropped you."

"What are you saying? It's all b.s. You know that, don't you?"

"I don't believe any of it. I'm telling you because I don't want the rumors to hit you as a surprise. You need to be prepared if the police question you."

Now Nikko jerked his foot from my grasp and sat up straight, straddling the middle of the contour chair.

"I'm making no judgment, Nikko. Your relationship with Margaux never concerned me."

"I'll tell you about our relationship, and then I'll go straight to headquarters and tell the police, too. I have proof. The police will find more proof if they go through Margaux's papers and notebooks."

I eased Nikko down onto the chair and began working on his foot again, and he began talking without my prompting.

"Margaux was Greek. You know that. Everybody in Key

West knows that. She and I shared that common bond, but lovers? No. Margaux wanted me to publish my Greek recipes and she offered to edit the book manuscript. She says there's a demand for authentic recipes from other countries. So people may have seen us together frequently as we worked. Sometimes the work involved library research. Sometimes it involved my treating Margaux to an after hours dinner at *The Wharf*."

Tension left my body and relief flowed in. "I believe you, Nikko. I think the police'll believe you, too, once you produce some rough drafts of the cookbook."

"I'm not really worried about police questioning, but I am worried about you. You've got to trust someone. What do you intend to do with that sweatshirt?"

"At the time I took it, I had no idea. Maybe in the back of my mind, I knew all along. I want you to take it, Nikko. You and Moose have worked to catch arsonists and druggies. Just because you've retired doesn't mean Moose has forgotten his scenting skills. Will you take the sweatshirt and see what you and Moose can learn from it?"

"If I'm caught with that sweatshirt and the police find out where it came from, we both could be accused of tampering with evidence."

"So don't get caught."

"Keely, Moose has been trained for just one thing—to track human scent. Even if sniffing the sweatshirt enabled Moose to find its owner, it would prove nothing to the police. Such evidence can't be admitted in a court of law."

"The evidence would prove something to me."

"You think the sweatshirt might belong to Jude?"

"That's a possibility, but if dog-tracking evidence can't be used in court, how come the police can arrest druggies when a dog pinpoints them with hemp or coke?"

"Some dogs are trained to track specific drugs. If a dog identifies a culprit and the police find the evidence on him, that evidence is admissible in court." Nikko left the treatment chair and began slipping on his sandals.

I went to my apartment and returned with the sweatshirt. "Please take this. Please see if you can find its owner. Do it for me. I need to know who came sneaking around my house. So what if your findings won't stand up in court? If Jude owned that sweatshirt, if he came near my house . . . I've got to know, Nikko."

"That restraining order still in effect?"

"Yes. If he skulked around my house last night, he broke the law."

"I'll see what I can do, Keely." Nikko took the shirt and left my office, and as he went out the door, Punt arrived.

"You've got a free hour between patients, right?"

"Right." I lifted the coffee pot and started to pour him a cup, but he shook his head.

"Let's make a quick trip to Georgia Street and look at the fire scene in the daylight."

"That's something I never want to see again."

"I think you should see it again. The police may have questions for you, and viewing the burn site may help you with answers."

"Okay. If you insist."

"Did you get a chance to quiz Nikko about his alibi for Saturday night?"

I smiled. "He made it easy for me. He asked me my alibi, and when I asked for his and mentioned the gossip circulating about him, he said he and Margaux were seen together because they had been working on a Greek cookbook. He has a rough draft of the manuscript as proof of a platonic relationship. He went home alone on the night of the murder."

"Good work on that one, Keely. Maybe you should go into the private detective business."

"Thanks a lot, but I'll leave that up to you and Nikko."

We only had to walk three blocks to Punt's car and traffic was light on this Tuesday morning. When we reached my Georgia Street address, a couple of people stood on the sidewalk, staring at the blackened scene. They nodded in greeting and we returned their nods, saying nothing.

My stomach tightened like a clenched fist when I saw the total destruction of the house I'd called a home. Only a twisted mind could deliberately have caused such ruin. My eyes burned as I blinked back angry tears.

Blackened beams lay under the charred roof. We walked to the back of the house where the carcass of a stove and a refrigerator poked up through the other debris. The odor of smoke hung in the air and my throat began to sting. We walked on to the back of the lot and I looked around but I saw nothing unusual.

"I thought whoever dropped the sweatshirt might have dropped something else, too, but I don't see anything."

"So let's leave." Punt took my hand and we returned to the front of the house. I tried not to imagine the Moores' charred furniture and/or my destroyed clothing. Those things could be replaced. I tried not to imagine what might have happened had I been inside the house and asleep at the time the fire started. Would I have heard it? Heard the crackling flames in time to escape?

"Is anyone allowed to poke through the ashes?" I managed to keep my voice strong.

"Doesn't look as if anyone would care. They must not suspect arson or someone would have surrounded the area with yellow fire scene tape. Something you especially wanted to look for?"

Again, I mentally accused the police of taking the easy way out in order to avoid a full-blown investigation, but I didn't say that to Punt. Nor did I tell him about giving the sweatshirt to Nikko.

"If you lost some special piece of jewelry, I suppose we could sift through some of the ashes."

"No. I think nothing would have survived that fire. Let's go now, Punt. I've seen enough of this and it's etched in my memory. I really need to get back to my office."

"Okay. Guess there wasn't much here to view after all."

As we stopped at Punt's convertible, I pointed at our shoes. "Got anything we can use to wipe away this soot? Don't want to mess up the inside of your car."

Punt unlocked the trunk and pulled out an old towel. "Here, we can use this."

He stooped to wipe off my sandals and then worked on his own. "Stuff doesn't want to come off, but I think I got the worst of it."

We wiped the soles of our sandals on the grass again, then climbed into the car. In spite of our care, a few black smudges darkened the carpeting.

"Rats," I said.

"Don't sweat it. I've some good carpet cleaner at home."

We reached my office as Otto Koffan shuffled down the sidewalk and stopped, waiting at my door. The door stood slightly ajar and the sign on it said OPEN, but Otto stood waiting. A tall stoop-shouldered man, Otto looked as if he'd lost his last friend. I can't remember if he always looked that way or if it became more pronounced after Margaux dumped him. I doubted that my treatments were helping him, but he said they always made him feel more relaxed. I didn't argue.

Punt braked the car, blocking traffic, and I got out as motorists behind us honked and called obscene advice complete with hand gestures. Ignoring the comments and the gestures, I flung my office door wide and invited Otto inside.

"How are you today, Otto?"

"Was a lot better when I was younger."

I think he intended his standard comment as a joke, so I smiled. Otto's been suffering from a clinical depression ever since Margaux and Beau married, and I never expected him to respond, "Just fine." And he never did. His comments matched his clothing—drab brown shirt, drab brown walking shorts. I readied his foot bath and started the water swirling around his feet. The lemon-scented water lifted my spirits even if it didn't lift his. I wondered if a bit of Prozac or Zoloft in the water might help.

"How's your work-in-progress coming along?" I let the water swirl for a few minutes before snapping off the switch. "That's a safe question in Key West where there's a would-be writer or artist lurking behind every palm tree. You're still writing, aren't you?"

"Every day. Every day of the world, but I'm progressing slowly. Very slowly." Removing his feet from the water, he dried them on the towel I provided, then took his place in the treatment chair.

"What are you writing, Otto? Novel? Nonfiction?" I doubted he had a work-in-progress. I think he enjoyed hanging out with the writers that met on Saturday mornings at *Kelly's*. "Or maybe you're into poetry?"

"You've guessed it. Poetry. Please don't tell anyone. Not yet. I'm not quite ready to come out of the closet as a poet. Maybe never will be."

"Okay, Otto. It's our secret. After my mother's death, I wrote a bit of poetry, too, and I've never showed it to anyone. It was too dark and down—too private. Maybe that's the way you feel about yours, too."

"That's exactly the way I feel about it. Private. The police never found who shot your mother?"

"Yes. They did. The guy's doing time up north—a lifetime of time. Before they caught him, they questioned dozens of people, but everyone had an alibi of sorts."

"I suppose the police'll be around, asking for my alibi for last Saturday night," Otto said.

Otto, too, was making it easy for me to learn some answers. "I'm surprised they haven't already questioned you."

"Oh, they have, but I know they'll return, asking for more answers."

I studied Otto carefully. "You mean they've asked you for an official statement?"

"No. How about you? The one who finds the body . . . I thought . . ."

"I've no alibi. I was home on Georgia Street alone. Do you remember where you were?"

"Barely. At home, I think, but I was so zonked on drugs, I don't remember for sure. Anyway, I woke up at home in my own bed on Sunday morning."

"That the story you're going to stick to if the police query you again?"

"Don't know for sure. It might be better to tell them I was home alone. Don't want them searching the house for drugs. I keep a little coke hidden from Shandy. She'd have a fit if she knew. Says she doesn't want any truck with the police. Guess I can keep my stash hidden from the police, too. Any advice?"

"No advice. None." Otto scared me. Who knew what a druggie might do, a druggie who had good reason to be deeply angry at his former wife? I thought it interesting that Otto felt Shandy expressed more interest in whether the police might find drugs in the house than she did in his health. Maybe she used drugs, too. I cut his treatment a bit short and he didn't seem to notice. He didn't comment or complain. Maybe he still felt hung over. A chill made the back of my neck tingle. I wondered if I'd just given a foot treatment to a killer.

After Otto left, I put the CLOSED sign in my window, drew the drapery. I stepped over to Gram's shop for an espresso to calm my nerves although Nikko always said that caffeine only made a person jumpy.

"Gram, are you going to close shop for the service?"

"Who say I go to service? I no say that."

"You were invited. Beau said so."

"Then I turn down invite. Margaux no good woman."

I saw no point in arguing with Gram once she had made her mind up to a thing. I returned to my shop without drinking an espresso. Although a noon whistle blew from a cruise ship, I didn't feel hungry. In two hours I'd be at Margaux's memorial service and I had no idea of how I should dress. I owned nothing black. Black clothes fit poorly into my lifestyle or into the paradise of Key West. I stood in front of my closet shoving hangers this way and that. My usual work garb wouldn't do. No, a khaki jumpsuit wouldn't be appropriate. Nor would the slinky green silk I wore last night with Punt. I could smell it. It still reeked of smoke.

And in addition to the memorial service here in Key West, I had to remember the burial at sea. Beau had insisted that I be aboard the boat that would carry Margaux's ashes to their final resting place. I'd never attended a burial at sea before. My mother's body lay in the Key West cemetery. Would one boat hold everyone who attended the burial? I wished I'd been excluded from that bit of drama.

Finally, I reached to the back of my closet and pulled out a plain navy blue skirt, straight and with a generous back slit I hoped would allow me to board a boat gracefully and without mishap. I found a white blouse, a white belt somewhat yellowed with age, and a pearl choker. I arranged the outfit on my bed and studied it. Yes, I supposed it would do, but it certainly wasn't an outfit I looked forward to wearing. I felt as if I were going to a costume party disguised as a nice girl.

Chapter 17

I'd stepped from the shower when the phone rang and Punt's voice flowed over the line.

"May I pick you up in twenty minutes?" he asked.

"I'd really appreciate a ride." I smiled at the thought of pedaling across town in a long skirt.

"Nikko's riding with us, too. The mortuary's lending the family a car and placing some reserved parking signs in front of the house. Since we need to carpool to save parking space, I can pull the loaner into the carport and leave on-street slots for others."

"I suppose Gram told you she isn't attending."

Punt laughed. "Yes, she mentioned that. I understand her feelings."

"How many people will be there?"

"A couple dozen—immediate family, close friends, and Dad's life-long business associates. Only a few will go out on the boat. Harley Hubble's invited the heirs to meet at the *Hubble & Hubble* office following the burial. He'll discuss the highlights of the will for those who're concerned."

"Oh, my. It's going to be a long afternoon."

"Agreed. See you in a few minutes. Wish it were under more pleasant circumstances, but maybe there's an up-side to all this tragedy."

"An up-side?" I had a hard time imagining an up-side to Margaux's death.

"These varied circumstances have pulled us back together, Keely. I like that and I hope you do too."

"Oh, excuse me, Punt. There's someone at my door."

"See ya."

Punt broke the connection and I felt guilty about lying, about cutting him off. Nobody waited at my door. I'd been at a loss for words. Circumstances certainly had pulled us back together, but I wasn't all that sure that I liked it. I had to admit that I'd enjoyed yesterday's afternoon and evening together, but that had been business—avoiding Jude on the highway, checking into Beau's alibi, accepting the reality of the fire. Business.

To be honest, I had to admit that Punt's kisses had aroused a kind of warmth within me I'd almost forgotten. Pleasant sensations. Urgent sensations. But my soul still suffered unhealed bruises from my marriage. I wasn't any place close to being ready for a new relationship. Maybe I'd never be ready. That thought loomed as a strong possibility.

I pulled on my "nice girl" outfit and waited, feeling as unreal as a paper doll wearing an outfit cut from a Sears catalog. Nikko came down from his apartment with Moose at his side on a leash.

"Nikko! You're not taking Moose to a memorial service! I mean . . ." I leaned to pat Moose's coarse hair and give him a scratch behind the ear. "I don't think it's the thing to do."

"How many memorial services you been to lately?" Nikko kept Moose at his heel.

"None, of course, but . . ."

"Not to worry. Moose's my partner. Where I go, Moose goes. We're a package deal."

Punt double-parked the loaner in the street, leaned over, and opened the passenger door for me while Nikko and Moose climbed into the back seat. As usual, car horns blared as we delayed the drivers behind us. Some, risking head-on collisions, managed to pass us, but others depended on their horns to express their sentiments.

"Thought we were going to Grinnell Street." Nikko leaned toward the front seat as Punt turned the car in the opposite direction.

"Dad decided to hold the service in the garden at *Ashford Mansion*. He had originally planned on Grinnell Street, but there isn't enough room."

Punt made no further explanation and it surprised me that Beau would hold a memorial service for his second wife at the home he and his first wife had shared for a quarter of a century. It was none of my business. The garden at *Ashford Mansion* offered more room, so I supposed that explained Beau's choice.

Punt drove into the carport when we reached the house and helped me from the car while Nikko and Moose exited from the rear. An attendant from the mortuary greeted us and showed us to our seats. Had he raised an eyebrow when he saw Moose? I wasn't sure. But he said nothing about the dog.

White lawn chairs had been arranged in a wide semicircle beneath the palms. To one side sat a round table draped with a white linen cloth that brushed the grass. Someone had set two white tapers in burnished brass holders on either side of Margaux's gold-framed portrait. A dozen or so of the well-known books she had edited lay in front of the photograph. Everything looked stiff and proper as a gentle trade wind sighing through the palm fronds wafted the scent of candle wax toward me.

On the other side of the circle of chairs stood an electric piano—a white one. White drop cords partially hidden in the grass snaked across the lawn to the house. I wondered where they'd found white drop cords. The only ones I'd ever seen were brown or orange. I pulled my thoughts from such mundane details when a pianist eased onto the bench and began softly playing hymns. *Amazing Grace. The Old Rugged Cross. In the Garden.* I hummed along when I heard *In the Garden.* It'd been one of my mother's favorite hymns.

We were the first guests to be seated and that pleased me. I'd rather watch others arrive than to have them watch me arrive, especially since I felt ill-at-ease wearing clothes I so seldom chose. Nikko took a chair next to me and Moose lay quietly beside him. Jass joined us, as usual wearing green— long flowing skirt and hibiscus-print shirt.

When Consuela approached us, I hardly recognized her. The Cuban bombshell did own ordinary clothes. Gone were her Cher imitations, her jingly bracelets. She wore a gray silk pantsuit with matching sandals and no jewelry at all except for small button-type earrings in silver gray.

Other guests began arriving so quickly I lost track of them until they settled in their seats. Otto and Shandy. Detective Curry. Detective Winslow? I didn't see her anywhere. Curry's presence surprised me. Maybe he'd invited himself. I gave an involuntary gasp and reached for Nikko's hand when Jude strolled in and sat at the other end of the semicircle.

"What's he doing here?" I whispered.

"Probably representing *Hubble & Hubble.*" Nikko squeezed my hand. "Not to worry. Ignore him. Make no eye contact."

Other people arrived claiming the rest of the chairs. Some of them I knew. Others I didn't. Then a minister, Reverend Sotto, robed in white, took his place before us, reading scriptures from a white, gilt-edged Bible, then giving such an upbeat eulogy that I almost envied Margaux's being dead. I tried to close my ears to this whole performance. That's what it amounted to—a performance.

During a prayer, I saw Nikko hold his hand close to Moose's nose then give the dog a silent command. Moose rose and began pacing near the circled chairs. Guests who had closed their eyes in reverence didn't notice Moose, but during the prayer, Otto leaped to his feet.

"Get that dog out of here!" he shouted. He held his chair between himself and Moose like a circus lion tamer. Beau hurried to Otto's side, took his arm and quieted him, helped him back into his chair as Moose walked on, paying no attention to Otto's outburst.

The minister continued his lengthy prayer as if nothing unusual had taken place. I wondered, if in seminary, theology students studied Short Prayer 101 their first semester, Mid-length Prayer 201 their second semester, and Long Prayer 301 before graduating into the real world of clergymen. If so, why did they so frequently choose to do the long scene?

Before the prayer ended, Moose passed Otto's chair, and then three chairs farther along, he paused and sat silently at Jude's side. I held my breath until I saw Nikko's unobtrusive hand signal that released Moose from his stance. The dog strolled back to Nikko and lay at his side, looking up until Nikko slipped him a doggie treat.

After the prayer, the minister left his place before the small congregation, Beau thanked the guests for their expressions of sympathy, and the mortuary attendant dismissed everyone. And that ended the service.

"What was the scene with Moose all about?" I whispered to Nikko. I thought I knew the answer, but I wanted to hear it from Nikko.

"I let Moose sleep with that black sweatshirt last night," Nikko said. Then he showed me a piece of black cloth he had secreted in his hand. "Moose didn't have to track far to find the source of the scent."

"So I did see Jude at the fire scene."

"You were right, but remember, I warned you that such

evidence can't be admitted in court. He could have been there for several reasons. Maybe he was just trying to keep track of you, to be aware of your whereabouts."

"What about the restraining order?"

Nikko nodded. "He was taking a chance by ignoring it."

That didn't matter to me now, but it did matter that I knew Jude had probably started the fire. He'd done it to frighten me, of course. More important, he'd done it to try to make me look guilty, or at least to point up the fact that I was closely connected with two major disasters. *I'll see you dead.* Jude's long-ago threat still hid in my mind, haunting my thoughts.

Beau had asked the people invited to the sea burial to remain behind—five of us. Beau, Punt, Jass, the minister, and me. Beau drove us bayside to *Seaview Marina* where he moored his boat. *Margaux's Dream.* The name gleamed in gold and black on the yacht's white stern.

A dockmaster had readied the craft and I felt the narrow walkway branching off from the cement dock sway on its wooden pilings as we walked along. We waited on the walkway until Beau took his place behind the wheel and invited us aboard. The minister boarded first and then Jass. Punt helped me over the gunwale, and a slight ripping sound told me the slit in my skirt had increased in length.

We sat on the cushioned seats around the gunwale while Beau maneuvered the yacht from its berth, easing it at no-wake speed from the marina and then into the harbor. Would I get seasick? Suddenly I worried. I'd never been seasick in backcountry shallows, but a ride in the open sea might be a different story.

"How far are we going?" I whispered to Punt.

"It's twelve miles or so out to the reef."

He slipped me a Dramamine, but I knew it probably

wouldn't help at this point. Seasick pills have to be swallowed an hour or so prior to the time of need. I had no water to wash it down so I held the pill under my tongue, and after awhile it dissolved, emitting bitterness throughout my mouth.

Under ordinary circumstances, it would have been a great day for enjoying the sea. I guessed the winds at eight to ten, and few whitecaps frothed the gentle waves. Overhead the air filled with pelican-speak as five huge birds followed us until they saw we had no raw fish tidbits to offer.

As we approached a sailboat carrying red sails, another with yellow sails, and three more with white sails, Beau adjusted our course to give them right-of-way. I realize sailboats have problems with tacking, with catching the wind, but sometimes they think having the right-of-way makes them kings of the seas. I saw Beau's jaw muscles tighten as he gritted his teeth.

We motored along without speaking until Beau found a spot over the reef that suited him and stopped the boat. Since dropping anchor on the reef in this marine sanctuary defies federal and state laws and damages the coral, Beau tethered his yacht to a buoy environmentalists have floated there for that purpose. When the yacht was secure, we stood at the gunwale. I saw a variety of formations—brain coral, sea fans, staghorn, and elkhorn coral. Colorful neon gobies and coral shrimp swam in and out of the coral formations, now and then running from a yellow shark or a barracuda.

The minister stood at the bow, holding a round white box with a golden handle on top. Beau joined him at the bow as the minister read scripture. "For everything there is a season, a time to be born, a time to die." We listened to many verses with heads bowed until he finished reading. At that time he placed the white box in Beau's hands and motioned toward the water.

Leaning low over the bow, Beau lowered the box into the sea and we all stood watching in silence. As the box sank into the waves, compartments on its side opened and rose petals floated to the water's surface. Jass stepped forward and dropped an array of hibiscus blossoms beside the rose petals. After a few brief moments of contemplation, the minister ended the service with a short prayer.

And it was over.

Beau returned to the wheel and pointed the boat toward Key West. When we reached the marina, the stench of dead bait fish sullied the air. Cormorants high overhead drifted on updrafts, but the ever-present pelicans hovered close to our stern, hoping for a handout while Beau maneuvered the boat into its slip. Harley Hubble and Detective Curry sat waiting for us on a bench near the chandlery. They rose as Beau turned the boat's care over to a dockmaster and we strolled along the walkway toward them. Both men wore business suits and ties, garb that set them apart from most of the locals and tourists who hang out at the marina.

"What's this all about?" I whispered to Punt, but before he could answer, Attorney Hubble spoke up, reminding me of Punt's words earlier in the afternoon.

"Detective Curry and I invite all of you to join the rest of Margaux Ashford's beneficiaries at the *Hubble & Hubble* office to receive information concerning her will. The will won't be read in its entirety due to its complexity and its length, but you'll hear the specific details that pertain to each of you."

I wanted to escape.

"It's been a long day." Beau stepped forward, shaking his head and placing his hand on Hubble's arm. "May we put this meeting off until another time—or is it a command performance?"

"The other beneficiaries are waiting at my office." Hubble eased away from Beau's touch. "They've been waiting for some time. I strongly suggest you accompany us to join the others."

"Fine," Beau said. "I'll drive Reverend Soto home, then Jass and I'll come to your office immediately. Punt, please bring Keely and Nikko and join us."

And that's what we did. Punt drove to Simonton Street where the Hubble offices occupied a small home converted by the Hubble family for business use—a practice common in Key West where property values had skyrocketed in the past few years. Both the house and its roof glowed sky blue in the late afternoon sunshine, but once we passed through the doorway we stepped onto somber gray carpeting that matched the walls, an upholstered couch, and a multitude of steel file cabinets.

Nikko and Otto and Shandy Koffan sat beside Beau and Jass, who had managed to arrive ahead of us. Harley Hubble motioned Detective Curry, Punt, and me to the remaining chairs. Moose lay at Nikko's side. At the sight of the dog, Otto reached for Shandy's hand and she eased her chair toward him in a protective way. I wondered why Otto feared Moose so much. Did he think Moose might detect drugs on his person? Maybe Otto didn't know that Nikko and Moose had retired from locating missing people, not missing drugs.

"A few of you may be familiar with some of the bequests listed in Margaux Ashford's will, but this reading of the will's highlights should serve to underline your previous knowledge." Harley Hubble cleared his throat and read in a sonorous voice. I watched Detective Curry as he studied each of us. I wondered what he expected to see. Did he think something in our expressions, our reactions, would pinpoint one of us as Margaux's killer?

166

The reading lasted only a few minutes and it relieved me to note that Harley Hubble hadn't required Jude's secretarial services. Punt and I drove Nikko home, Nikko who had been bequeathed only a book contract and a few thousand dollars, then Punt and I joined Jass at *Ashford Mansion* to discuss other aspects of the will, although my mind already buzzed on overload. It relieved me to learn that Beau had returned to the Hubble office to sign some additional papers.

"You heard it," Jass said, offering us seats on her couch and then joining us in an easy chair. "Margaux's will leaves Punt and me each one million dollars. In the eyes of the police that amount would give us strong motive for murder. The will also leaves Dad the bulk of her estate, which gives him an even strong motive, but . . ."

"But now we know just how much Margaux's ex comes into the inheritance picture, too," Punt said, interrupting. "And the plot thickens." Jass brought us tumblers of iced tea. "Otto Koffan wanted more from Margaux than his elbow-patched sport coat and custody of their CD collection of jazz greats."

I almost choked on my tea. "I can't believe she left her ex a chunk of her estate. No way would I have left Jude anything but bad wishes, even if I'd had an estate—which I hadn't."

"You heard what Harley H. had to say," Jass said. "Margaux was under court order to divvy with Otto. I'm guessing the divorce judge didn't like the way Margaux dumped Otto."

"Probably jealous of Margaux's lifestyle here in the Keys," Punt said.

"During the thirty years of their marriage, Otto had worked as Margaux's secretary and business manager," Jass said. "Dad had already told us that and also that after

Margaux's marriage to him, he took over her business matters."

"I'm guessing that the judge ruled that because of Otto's being left in meager circumstances, Margaux had to take care of him financially," Punt said.

"You mean Margaux had to pay alimony?" I asked. "I didn't hear that lawyer say anything about alimony, and if that's true, I don't see why Otto's inheritance would make him a suspect. Wouldn't he have wanted Margaux to live forever—to keep those alimony payments dropping into his mailbox along with his Social Security checks?"

"Dad told me that pride kept Otto from accepting alimony," Jass said, "so the judge placed a stipulation on the divorce. You heard what Hubble said. If Margaux married, she had to provide Otto a home to live in while she remained alive, a home of equal value to her own. And she had to agree that upon her death, Otto would inherit ten million bucks."

"Ten million big ones," Punt said, laughing. "I'm putting Otto at the top of my suspect list."

"That lawyer talked so fast I can't remember half of what he read," I said, "I'm surprised that after Otto's inheritance, there still remained money for Beau."

"For Beau," Jass said. "And for you, too. Half a million for you. Don't forget that."

"That I remember very clearly, but I don't understand why Margaux would leave me anything."

"Because your reflexology treatments relieved her back pain," Jass said. "That's what Hubble said. How could you have missed that?"

I sat speechless.

"Couldn't happen to a nicer person, Keely."

I was still sitting there when Jass stood and excused herself to run an errand in her greenhouse.

"May I take you to dinner?" Punt asked.

"Not tonight, Punt." I pulled my hand away. "We need to talk about . . . we need to discuss . . ."

"Discuss what?" Punt asked. "I'm ready to discuss a dinner menu."

"We need to think carefully about working together now that we know the exact stipulations of Margaux's will. A killer's at large and there's a possibility that we may be able to identify that person before the police start in-depth questioning of suspects."

"So far the police have lurked in the background—observing, checking on the gun." Punt reached for my hand again. "I think the in-depth questioning may start tomorrow, now that the memorial service and the reading of the will are behind us."

"I'd like to avoid that questioning, if possible." I withdrew my hand from his a second time. "I agree that we need to work together, but I want to keep our togetherness on a platonic basis. Please understand that."

He reached for my hand a third time and I didn't have the heart to withdraw it again.

"You liked that kiss last night as much as I did, Keely. Admit it. Be real."

"I am being real. Yes, I enjoyed our kiss, but I'm not ready for a new relationship with any man right now. I may never be ready. I don't want to hurt you—to hurt either of us, but our lifestyles are too far apart, our values too different." I was out of breath from talking so fast.

"Maybe you're right. Maybe not. We'll play it platonic—for a while at least. Bearing that in mind, may I take you to dinner tonight?"

"It's been a long day, Punt . . . maybe . . ."

"Maybe we could eat on the patio at *Two Friends* and nose

around a little more concerning Consuela's alibi. There's no time to waste."

"You're right, of course, but this day has been almost beyond bearing."

"You'll feel better—we'll both feel better after a good meal. May I call for you around seven?"

Chapter 18

As usual Punt arrived promptly and we walked to *Two Friends* through a soft moonlit night like the ones pictured on the Chamber of Commerce brochures. Punt held my hand but I drew it away. Platonic. I tried to etch that word in my mind. Walking felt good and I welcomed the sense of freedom and independence it gave me as I watched motorists vie for parking slots. The cruise ships had sailed from Mallory and many of the sunset watching–crowd had left the dock and taken refuge in restaurants and bars. Even Punt's attempt at bribing a waiter for a table on the *Two Friends* patio failed. We perched on high stools at the bar beside an old man who looked like Father Time—if Father Time happened to be wearing jeans, a tank top, and a green straw hat decorated with fishing lures.

We both ordered shrimp steamed in beer and garden salads with special house dressing on the side. Luckily, Bennie worked the bar tonight, and Punt quickly turned the conversation to Consuela.

"I told you all I know about her," Bennie said. "She's a noise-maker dressed like a sexy slut and I've convinced the boss I've earned a drink on the house whenever she leaves. Saturday night she wore a banana and a mango pinned in her hair."

"You talking about that Carmen Miranda type in here last Saturday night?" Father Time asked.

I turned to him quickly. "Who's Carmen Miranda?"

He looked at me and grinned. "Oh to be young! You kids probably can't remember Carmen Miranda. Singer. Actress. Wore slinky dresses and hats that looked like fruit baskets.

Folks laughed, but they liked her."

"You saw someone in here Saturday night that looked like that?" Punt asked.

"Right," Father Time said. "Why, her picture's right there on the wall behind the bandstand. Guess she's some famous babe. She's hanging there right beside President Clinton, George no-W. Bush, Marilyn Monroe."

Punt and I both slipped off our bar stools to take a closer look at the pictures taped and thumbtacked to the wall. Father Time spoke true. A small glossy of Consuela and her dance partner vied for space with a larger glossy of Frank Sinatra. I hurried back to the bar.

"Bennie, who's the guy in the picture with Consuela?"

"Don't keep track of Consuela's men friends," Bennie said. "Too many of them. I'd lose count."

"May we borrow that picture?" I asked. "We'll bring it back. Promise."

Bennie shrugged and shook his head. "Not my picture to lend."

Again Punt produced a twenty and this time Bennie grinned, nodded, and reached for the bill. I stepped onto the bandstand, removed the picture, and took it to our seats where we studied it carefully.

"I don't know her partner, Punt, do you?"

"Never saw him before, but the shot's small and blurred. Let's take it to a copy shop at the mall. They can blow it up, enlarge it. Maybe I'll recognize the guy."

We ate the rest of our meal in a hurry, picked up Punt's car at my office, and drove to the Mall on North Roosevelt. The copy shop smelled of new paper, ink, and fluids I couldn't identify, and the clerk looked as if he had never hurried in his life.

A toothpick dangled from the corner of his mouth and he

combed his greasy hair with tobacco-stained fingers as he slouched forward to greet us. "How ya guys doin' tonight?"

"Fine," Punt said. "We'd like to get an enlargement of this photo. Can you manage that while we wait?"

"Sure thing, pal. What kind of paper youse want?"

"The best kind for getting a clear shot of the guy in the pic," Punt said.

The clerk fumbled through several drawers, then he went to the file cabinets and fumbled through envelopes of paper. At last he made a decision and placed our original in the copy machine and his chosen reprint paper in its tray. Lights flashed as the machine pulsed to life, and in a few moments we held both the original and the enlargement.

"That help you any?" the clerk asked, then without waiting for our reply, he added, "That'll be two-fifty. Cash."

Punt paid and we took the enlarged the photo to the car to study it again in private.

"The likeness of Consuela's clear enough," I said, "and the guy's a bit easier to identify. You ever seen him around?"

"He looks vaguely familiar, but I can't quite place him."

"So let's take both pictures back to *Two Friends*. Maybe Bennie can identify him in this blow-up."

Bennie stood wiping the bar with a grimy rag when we arrived. The band had started setting up stands and lights. A short guy, ponytailed and barefoot, blew a glissando on his sax while a stringbean of a drummer rat-a-tatted on his snare, eager to begin the first set. Someone had claimed our seats at the bar, but Bennie approached us, reaching for the original photo.

"Recognize this guy?" Punt flashed the enlargement.

Bennie squinted at the picture for a few seconds. "Don't know him by name, but I think he's a shrimper. You might ask around at the shrimp docks. Someone there might recognize him, know him by name."

"Let's go." Punt grabbed my hand. "It's late, but someone may still be at the docks."

"Tonight? It's a smelly place. We've had a long day. Let's wait . . ."

"No point in waiting, but if you don't feel up to going now, I'll drive you home and check out the docks by myself."

"You're not going without me."

We drove to *Land's End Village* where throngs of tourists crowded the streets, the tiny tourist-trap shops, the bars. At a parking lot where a crude sign on the gate said FULL, Punt called to the gatekeeper. "Hey, Slim. You owe me one."

Slim ambled toward us, drinking something from a bottle wrapped in a brown paper sack. "Full up, buddy."

"Find us a place. We're in a hurry. Only be here a few minutes."

Slim shrugged and made no move to open the gate. "Full up, I tell you, but I know a spot that's empty behind *The Raw Bar*. My pal just left it. Little slot, but you can wedge this car in it. Anybody give you lip, tell 'em to come talk to me."

We inched the car toward *The Raw Bar*, sometimes brushing against tourists walking in the street. The area behind the bar was black as the inside of a cat, but we found the empty slot and Punt eased the car into it. He raised the top although the weather was clear and warm, then he locked up, double-checking each door. As we walked toward the street, he kept glancing over his shoulder as if he'd like to slip the Karmann Ghia into his pocket and take it with us.

"Now what?" I dropped the photo into my shoulder bag. "Looks like most of the boats are out tonight. Probably won't come in until morning. So what else is new? You know that night-fishing drill."

Punt led the way to the dock. "There may be someone

hanging around. A watchman, probably. These shrimpers all know each other."

Moonlight silvered the dock, making it look more attractive at night than it did in the daylight when the sun glinted on rust-encrusted hulls and silhouetted spindly riggings against the sky like bony fingers. The shrimp docks were my least favorite spot in Key West, yet they were one cut above the *Turtle Kraals*. A museum now stood at the *Kraals*, marking the place where butchers used to kill and clean green turtles for the entertainment of a bloodthirsty crowd. The whole area reeked of dead shrimp and decay.

We walked onto the dock and saw some furtive movement at the far end. Cautiously we approached a person half-hidden by a weather-beaten shrimp shack.

"Can we talk to you for a minute, buddy?" Punt called.

"About what?" a deep voice asked.

"We got a picture we'd like to show you. Need some identification. Hope you can help us out."

I pulled the photo from my shoulder bag, knowing nobody could identify anything in this gloomy spot. A barefoot man wearing a hooded sweatshirt approached us, eyeing us as warily as we eyed him. Punt took the photo from me and held it toward him.

"We may need to step to a spot with more light," Punt said.

The stranger pulled out a flashlight from his sweatshirt and shone it onto the photo. Before we could say anything else, the man spoke.

"Consuela. That's who she be." He chuckled. "Know her well."

"We know Consuela," Punt said. "It's the man we need to identify. Recognize him?"

"No. Looks familiar. Can't put a name to him, though."

The man snapped off his flashlight, handed the photo back to Punt, and slunk into the shadows.

"So much for that one." I slipped the picture back into my bag and we left the dock. I squelched the urge to keep looking over my shoulder. "Now what? That guy seems to be the only one around."

"Let's step into this souvenir shop and talk to someone in there." Punt led the way and I followed, approaching the nearest clerk and presenting the photo.

"We're trying to locate the man in this picture," I said. "Would you happen to know him or have seen him around here?"

The woman studied the photo until a customer vied for her attention.

"Miss. Miss. Wait on me, please. I have a taxi outside with the meter running."

"Excuse me, please." The clerk wrapped a pink conch shell, rang up the sale on her cash register. I wondered if the customer knew that conchs were a protected species in the Keys and that her souvenir probably came from the Bahamas. Maybe she didn't care. Nor did I, but I came to full attention when the clerk gave us her attention again as she studied the photo.

"The woman is Consuela somebody-or-other. Don't know her last name."

"The man?" Punt pointed as if she might be unable to distinguish Consuela from a man. "He's the one whose name we need."

At last the clerk shook her head. "Sorry, but I can't help you. Have you asked at *The Raw Bar?* Someone there might recognize the guy."

We thanked her and left the shop. I eyed *The Raw Bar,* guessing that if I entered it, I'd be the only woman present.

"Do we have to go in there tonight?"

"Would you rather wait in the car? I can go in alone. Probably only take a minute or two."

I led the way toward the entrance. Once inside, Punt kept close to me as an eerie silence hushed the crowd. I felt unnerved by the scrutiny of dozens of eyes. A man sitting to my left continued slurping raw oysters. He salted each one, added a bit of pepper, then tipping his head back and chewing only slightly, he let the slimy morsel slip down his throat. My stomach churned and I looked away. A poster at the side of the cash register announced Hank Culpepper as the winner of that day's oyster-eating contest, having consumed two dozen at one sitting at two o'clock that afternoon. I didn't even want to think about what the prize might have been.

Taking the photo from me, Punt strode to the man at the cash register. Had he worn a headband and a patch over his eye, he could have passed for Blackbeard. Punt thrust the picture toward him.

"We're trying to identify the man in this picture. Can you help us out?"

Blackbeard looked at the photo briefly and shook his head. "Want me to pass it around?" He nodded to his customers. "Most of these guys are locals. Someone may know your friend."

Punt nodded consent and Blackbeard handed the picture to the guys at a nearby table. Finally one of them smiled up at us.

"That's Gus Helmer. Know him well." He licked his lips and kissed his forefinger as he ran it over the likeness of Consuela.

"Know where we could find him?" Punt asked. "Tonight?"

"Might try at *Shorty's Dry Dock*. Think Gus planned to take his boat in for repair. He may not be around there tonight, though." He handed the photo back and we headed for the door. "If he is around, he might be aboard his boat—*The Pink Gold*," the man called after us.

"Thanks, fella." Punt ordered the man a plate of oysters, paid, and we left the bar.

"Never say I don't take you anywhere." Punt reached for my hand as we stepped outside, and this time I didn't pull away. "The dry dock may be even more glamorous than *The Raw Bar*. I think it's down this way and to our left. I've taken my boats there for repair a few times."

We stepped carefully over beer bottles and fast food containers as we made our way to the dry dock where boats in various stages of repair or disrepair either hung from davits or rested on sturdy foam pads. A dim bulb above a doorway glinted on black letters: SHORTY'S DRY DOCK. We threaded our way through the maze of sailboats, runabouts, and shrimpers, checking names on the sterns. Usually that's one of my favorite pastimes. Tonight wasn't one of those times.

"There it is." Punt pointed and stepped closer to a shrimper that looked as if rust might be the only thing holding it together. "*The Pink Gold.*"

"Do we knock to announce our presence or just shout to anyone who might be near?"

"Let's try this." Punt pulled on a salt-encrusted cord and a brass bell clanged into the silence. No response. Punt jerked the cord again, but nobody answered the summons.

I squelched a sigh in relief. "Guess we'll have to come back tomorrow, right?"

"Suppose so. If Gus isn't home, he's not home, but first thing in the morning we'll . . ."

We were turning to leave when a guttural voice called out. "What you up to? Speak out or I'll have the cops on you like white on rice."

Chapter 19

Punt and I both turned to face the short bulldog of a man who had appeared from nowhere, holding his right hand hidden in the pocket of a fisherman's vest.

"We were just leaving," Punt said. "Looking for Shorty. Hoping he could identify the guy in a picture for us."

"Let's see the picture. Don't believe you for a minute. Somebody's always poking around the dry docks looking to snitch a few spare parts. Well, that won't happen tonight as long as I'm on duty."

I handed over the picture, and Bulldog beamed a flashlight into our eyes before he aimed it at the picture. I blinked and squinted and blinked again.

"Consuela," Bulldog said. "Ha. Everyone knows Consuela. She in some sort of trouble? She hate the dead broad—Margaux Ashford. Heard her say so myself. I'd not testify to that in court, though. Consuela's my friend. She treats me well."

"Consuela's our friend," Punt said. "We needed the identity of her companion here, and we know the man's Gus Helmer and that *The Pink Gold*'s his boat. We need to talk to him and we thought he might be aboard."

"Helmer's not here, so be away with you and don't come nosing around these parts again."

"We were just leaving," Punt said again in an ultra-polite voice. "Pardon us for disturbing you. Rest assured, it won't happen again."

Bulldog's flashlight went out and Punt grabbed my wrist as we headed back for our car. I couldn't wait to get out of there, but Punt held me back. We moved slowly enough to let the Bulldog know we weren't running from him, yet fast enough to get us out of there without more delay. I had visions of home. A hot shower. A soft bed.

The Karmann'll be there, I told myself. Punt locked it. Nobody'd dare take it, would they? Of course not. It'll be there.

Right. Nobody'd stolen the car, but when we tried the doors, we found them unlocked, and the lid to the glove compartment hung out like a hound's panting tongue. Someone had entered the car. I shuddered. "Anything missing?" I asked.

Punt snapped on the overhead light. "Registration. Flashlight. Owner's manual. Junk. Guess everything's here." He closed the glove compartment then circled the car, kicking tires. No slashes. I checked the small area behind the front seat. Nobody waiting there to attack us. So why were my hands shaking and my heart pounding?

"At least they didn't hot wire it and take off." Punt helped me into the passenger seat then slid behind the wheel and sat leaning a bit to one side as he inserted the ignition key. A low voice at the driver's window startled both of us. I gasped and almost choked on saliva that slid down the wrong way.

"Give me the keys." A male voice dripped with menace, and his beery breath filled the car.

"Who are you?" Punt demanded. "This's my car."

"This's my fist." The man raised his clenched hand. "Give. I want your keys."

"Do it," I whispered. "Just do it."

Punt jangled the keys for a moment before dropping them into the stranger's outstretched hand. "What do you want from us? You could have taken the car. Why didn't you take it and go?"

"Don't want your car. Piece of junk. I want you. Both of you. Get out and follow me. Move it along."

"May I lock my car again? I don't want it stolen."

"I didn't steal it. I'm no thief."

"Someone else might be. May I lock it?"

"Lock it." The man laughed. "It's a rattletrap. Don't know who'd want it."

If the guy was asking for a rebuttal, he didn't get it. Punt took his time locking the car, checking the top, checking the trunk. Then he turned toward our captor.

"Now lead the way," the man said. "Head toward the dry dock."

"Who are you?" Punt asked.

"Call me Gus. Gus Helmer."

"The guy in the photo," I said.

"Right. I'm your guy and we need to talk. Keep walking straight ahead."

"We've already been to the dry dock," Punt said. "A guy there asked us to leave. We didn't touch a thing. Rang the bell at *The Pink Gold*. Nobody answered and we made no attempt to board."

"I know."

"How do you know?"

"Watchman paged me. Your car's hard to miss, you know. I saw you park it. Everyone saw you. Lots of folks saw that picture, too. Not that it mattered to any of them."

"What's going on here?" Punt demanded. "Take me with you if you want to, but how about letting my friend drive on home?"

"Ha! Double ha! No way. Keep walking. Straight ahead."

Fear dragged at my feet and my tongue. I couldn't talk and I could barely walk, but constant urging from our captor kept me moving forward. I tried not to imagine what he might have in store for us. When I slipped on a beer bottle and fell, Punt pulled me back to my feet.

"Clumsy," Gus said. "No drunks toss their beer bottles in your part of town?"

Neither of us replied, and we walked on until we reached the boat.

"Come aboard." Gus propped a ladder against the hull and motioned Punt up first. "Okay, sister." He bowed from the waist then pointed to the ladder.

Holding tightly to the splintery ladder, I managed the climb and Punt gave me a hand, helping me over the gunwale and onto the deck. Gus followed us aboard and led us into a small wheelhouse that reeked of stale cigar smoke and over-ripe shrimp. He took the seat behind the wheel and lit a bat-tery light. We sat silently for a few moments in the eerie glow before Gus spoke again.

"I want that blowup picture," he said, "and then I want the original."

I gave him the enlargement without argument.

He tore it to shreds and held his hand out toward me again. "Where's the other one?"

"We returned it to *Two Friends,*" Punt said. "It belongs to them. They've got a picture gallery of sorts on the wall. Pics of famous people who've patronized the place. Maybe you've noticed it behind the piano on the bandstand."

"Don't go there to see no pictures," Gus said. "Go there to drink and dance with the babes. Gotta have that other pic-ture. Where'd it come from?"

I shrugged and looked away. It's hard to act calm and cool when your teeth are rattling from fear and your mouth feels dry as a sand dune.

"Don't dummy up on me, broad. Where'd that picture come from?"

182

"I've no idea," I said. "Bennie showed it to us and let us borrow it."

Punt spoke up. "Bennie said a roving photographer snapped it, tried to sell it to *Two Friends*. He makes a living of sorts that way, snapping candid shots, trying to get people to buy a picture of themselves visiting Key West. Bennie can probably give you the name of the photographer—probably some guy who hangs around Mallory."

"Why you so interested in my picture?"

"Why're you so interested in our interest?" Punt countered.

Gus stood and doubled his fist. "Bastard! You trying to start trouble for me?"

"Easy, Gus. Easy." Punt managed to smile. "We're not trying to start trouble for you. We're trying to save Consuela from trouble. If she's your friend, here's your chance to help her out."

"Didn't know she was in trouble."

"She may be, or she may not be. At this point it's sort of up to you—in a way. Keely and I are hoping Consuela has an explanation for where she spent her time last Saturday night. That's the night a killer murdered Margaux Ashford."

"That's the rich-bitch broad Consuela's always saying she hates, right? She mouths off to everyone who'll listen about how the Ashford broad badmouthed her writing." Gus slapped his forehead as the reason behind our visit came clear in his mind. "You telling me Consuela may be up for a murder rap?"

"We're not saying that at all," I said. "If she can prove where she was between ten o'clock and midnight on that Saturday night, there's no way she can be charged. So far Consuela's failed to come up with an airtight alibi."

"I enjoy being with Consuela and I can give her an airtight

alibi if you'll make me one large promise."

"What kind of a promise?" Punt asked.

"It's like this." Gus shrugged. "I got a steady lady friend up on Largo. Susie Lohman. Last Saturday night Susie had to go to Miami to visit her sick mama in the hospital." Gus shrugged again, a more elaborate shrug this time. "Well, what's a guy to do with a Saturday night and no woman?"

"So you picked up Consuela at *Two Friends*." Punt made it a statement.

I wondered if Gus's shoulders ever ached from over-shrugging.

"Consuela there and we dance. We dance a long time."

"Consuela told me she had two partners," I said.

"She lie to you. She likes to make herself seem in big demand, but she had only one partner on Saturday night. Me. Gus Helmer. I keep Consuela well occupied all night on Saturday. You two gotta git that other picture off the wall at *Two Friends*. You gotta promise not to tell my Susie Consuela spent the night with me. Susie and I are getting hitched in April. If Susie ever sees that picture of me with Consuela, it'll all be over between us."

I thought of many things I could say, but I said none of them. I just hoped Susie had enjoyed a good time last Saturday visiting her sick mother in Miami.

"We'll make a deal with you," Punt said. "If you'll promise to vouch for Consuela's whereabouts last Saturday night, if that should become necessary, we'll get that picture and place it in your hands."

"It's a deal." Gus shook Punt's hand and escorted us from his boat. Ladders are easier to climb going up than going down, but I didn't fall. Gus returned Punt's car keys, and we made our way through the dark back to the car and left *Land's End Village* and Gus behind us. Now Consuela had an alibi.

Chapter 20

On Wednesday morning, Punt knocked on my door an hour or so before my first patient was due, and I invited him in as I hid my surprise.

"Good morning! You're out and about early." I kept my voice crisp and businesslike as I tried to guess what he could want at this time of day.

Punt pushed his sunglasses to the top of his head where they were almost lost in his thick hair as he looked directly into my eyes. "I wanted to talk to you before you opened your office. How about taking the day off?"

I motioned him to a chair although I wanted him to leave. "I can't afford to cancel appointments. I'll lose clients. People depend on me and I have a stack of bills to pay before the end of the month."

"That one of the lifestyle differences you mentioned—you work, I play?"

"It's something to consider. At least I think so."

Punt looked out the window and changed the subject without commenting. "Detective Curry called Dad in for questioning this morning. I think they know he missed Saturday's fishing tournament. Maybe they'll concentrate their investigation on him for a while or maybe they won't, but I'm guessing they'll soon get around to you. If your name hits the newspapers as a murder suspect, what do you think that'll do to your business?"

"Nothing good."

"Right. So bail out for a day or two. Grab some vacation time." Punt stood and began pacing.

"I don't have a boss to ask for vacation days."

"I need your help, Keely, and you need my help. If we can pinpoint Dad's whereabouts on Saturday night, it could turn the police investigation in a different direction."

"What direction? I mean, I don't think Beau's guilty, but . . . I don't want the investigation pointed my way, that's for sure."

"I'd like to see Jude put under some police scrutiny. I think he planned for you to find Margaux's body. I think he torched your house to put you under more police pressure plus some added pressure from fire investigators. Jude's a control freak, Keely, and he lost control of you. He's a guy who can't stand losing. In his inimitable way, I think he's trying to even the score by making you pay big time and in a way nobody will discover."

"I can't imagine him risking his own life to ruin mine." *I'll see you dead.* Again, Jude's threat rang in my mind. Punt continued to pace and both his movements and his words unnerved me.

"Keely, you may be the only thing Jude ever lost. He's sly and he's conniving, but you know that. He'd really gloat if the police hung a murder rap on you, put you away in some slammer for life."

Punt voiced all the fears I had locked deep inside myself. "We don't even know if Jude has an alibi for Saturday night. He may have one and he may have a dozen people to corroborate it. Punt, why should the police think about checking on Jude? He hasn't done anything to make him suspect in their eyes."

"Maybe we can tell them a few things, but not yet. For starters, let's find out where Dad hung out on Saturday. Close your office for the day. Let's get started."

"All right. Since I only have two clients this morning, I'll reschedule. I hope they'll be understanding and accept makeup times."

I made the two calls while Punt continued pacing. Once I had rearranged my schedule, I placed the CLOSED sign in my window and drew the drapery. I disliked admitting that I looked forward to spending the morning with Punt, but before we could make more plans, the phone rang.

"Keely Moreno speaking."

"It's Jass, Keely. I hope you have a few free minutes before your first patient arrives. I need your help. It won't take long."

"What's up? Got problems?" It wasn't like Jass to call on a brown-thumb like me for help. Maybe she felt desperate. Or maybe she was trying to keep so busy she didn't have time to think about the police investigation.

"I'm getting ready to experiment with propagating some plants and I need two more hands to assist with the soil mixture. Shandy's here helping me cut the stems and we need to get them into the potting soil quickly. It won't take long, but we need to work fast in order to keep the cut stems from drying out."

"I'll be right there, Jass. Glad you called."

I broke our connection and looked at Punt who scowled then shrugged.

"Okay, do it and get it over with. I suppose you should feel flattered. She won't let me or Dad step inside her precious greenhouse. Let me drive you over. That'll save a little time and as soon as you finish in the greenhouse, we can go on with our plans."

"My plans involved working right here in my office."

"My plans involved changing your plans." Punt grinned at me.

"Jass said this job wouldn't take long." I slung my bag over my shoulder and followed Punt to his car. He had one thing right. I did feel flattered at Jass's request. She allowed few people inside her greenhouse other than Shandy, but now that her plant had won the prize in Miami, secrecy was less important. Nobody could take that blue ribbon away from her.

When we arrived at the greenhouse, Jass met us at the door and I saw Shandy near the potting tables. She gave me a wave and a shy nod then turned her back and busied herself with a knife, cutting stems from mature plants.

"You're a doll to do this for me," Jass said. "Come on in."

"If I helped, would the work go faster?" Punt asked. "I'm a good twig-cutter. I can mix soil, too. You really haven't discovered the true extent of my many and super-useful talents."

Jass laughed. "No thanks. I appreciate your offer, but you're all thumbs when it comes to working with plants. Didn't know you and Keely had plans this morning. Sorry to interrupt."

It was an invitation for us to tell all, but neither of us volunteered. Punt shrugged and winked at me. "Nothing important, Jass. Nothing that can't wait a *few minutes.*"

"Good." Jass ignored his emphasis on the last two words. "It really won't take long. You can join us and watch if you want to. No charge for that today."

"Thanks, but no thanks." Punt headed upstairs to his apartment, then paused to call over his shoulder. "Be right here, Keely. See you in a *few minutes.*"

I felt the hair around my ears begin to frizz the minute I stepped into the humid air of the greenhouse. Not a lot of fun working in here, I thought, but Jass and Shandy loved it. Their faces shone with perspiration and they'd pulled their hair back with headbands. Both of them wore short shorts and tank tops, and they stood barefoot. I should have thought to change into something cooler. Much cooler. Too late now. I inhaled the earthy scent of soil and growing plants as Jass led the way to the sink near the potting tables. Shandy continued working with the knife and stems, slowly turning a plant this way and that as she searched for the best stem to cut.

"Wash up, okay?" Jass asked.

It seemed crazy to wash my hands before getting them caked with dirt, but Jass was particular about not introducing foreign elements into the potting soil. I knew that and I didn't argue. The soap emitted an antiseptic odor and I felt germ-free as Jass showed me how to mix the potting soil.

"I use a mixture of half peat and half perlite." Jass handed me a measuring cup and pointed to two bags of soil. "Use one cup of each and mix them with this wooden spoon in this sterilized bowl. When that bowl's full, fill the next bowl."

"Will do." I counted three empty bowls. This really shouldn't take too long.

"When you have the soil mixed, you can fill the pots I've set on the tables in row three."

I tried not to sigh as I saw so many empty pots I couldn't count them at a glance.

"While you do that, Shandy'll be cutting the stems from my strongest plants to the proper length for propagating. I'll be shredding the bottom of each stem a bit, dip it in my special formula rooting powder, and insert it into the prepared pots."

"Wow, Jass. Will you ever sell all those plants? How long does it take them to root? And to grow? And . . ."

Jass grinned. "You're asking for my trade secrets."

"Don't worry about that. I'm no danger to you."

"I know. Only kidding. I do try to start a lot more plants than I need, because some of them won't take root no matter how much I baby them."

I started mixing the potting soil, stirring it with the wooden spoon, dipping it into the prepared pots. I knew Jass had probably sanitized the pots and I smiled at the idea of sterile dirt.

"By the time you have some of the pots filled, I'll begin inserting the stems. When Shandy has enough stems cut, she'll begin preparing the water and then we'll both water the plants."

"Preparing the water? The water at my house flows from the tap already prepared."

"Sometimes would-be hibiscus plants are more particular than humans."

Shandy had stopped cutting stems and now she held up a bag labeled MSG. "I mix two tablespoons of this to a quart of water, then I give each stem a drink."

"I use MSG to cook with," I said. "Didn't know it was a magic formula for hibiscus plants."

"This's only one experiment," Jass said. "I do lots of experimenting with different soil mixtures, different water mixtures. This's the one I happen to be using today."

"You mean it may work or it may not work?"

"Right. I'm fairly sure that many of these stems will root and thrive. The things we're doing today are the things I did to create the blossom color that won Sunday in Miami. It took me three years to create that winning blossom."

"Will you enter that show again next year?" I asked.

"Yes, but not with plants from any of these cuttings. In a year or two these types of plants will be old hat. I'll have to show something new next year and I can only hope that I'm ready."

"You have some new ideas?"

"Sure. I always have new ideas. The trick is to have new

ideas that work. That's the iffy part. I have experimental cuttings going most of the time."

"With secret formulas, I suppose."

"Right. Top secret. That's why I keep the greenhouse locked. Each season I try a few new soil and water mixtures and I keep written records of each experiment." She glanced at a steel filing cabinet standing next to an old desk. "I tell nobody about my experiments. If two people know a secret, that's one person too many."

"I didn't realize all this took so much organizing."

"I love every minute of the work. I devote my life to it."

Jass had a faraway expression when she said that and I wondered if we both were thinking of Scott Murdock who lost his life in Afghanistan. I doubted that loving hibiscus plants made up for not having Scott to love. I thought of the wedding dress she had made and never used, the wedding invitations never sent, and I changed the subject and my thoughts quickly.

"I see you're setting some plants on heating pads, Jass. Is the why of that a secret?"

"No. Some plants require bottom warmth in order to thrive. So I humor them with the heating pads."

We worked in silence a long time before all the pots were filled with soil and once that was done, Jass thanked me for helping out and walked with me to the sink while I washed up.

"Shandy and I can finish now that the pots are ready. I'll let Punt know you're through." She keyed in Punt's number on her cell phone.

"It's been interesting, Jass. I enjoyed the work. Call me again if you need help."

Punt must have answered his phone on the first ring. He stood at the door waiting for me almost before I had time to finish washing Jass's magic formula from my fingers.

Chapter 21

Punt hurried me into his car and we left the greenhouse.

"Do you need to go home before we start out?" Punt asked. "I'm not suggesting. You look fine to me, but that greenhouse can make a person feel mighty hot and sticky."

"I guess I'm okay, Punt. Since I usually take Wednesday afternoons off, I only had to make two quick calls to free up my day and I've done that and placed the CLOSED sign in my window. So what's the plan? I'd like to get back in time to go fishing—mid to late afternoon, maybe."

"How can you think about fishing at a time like this?"

"Hours spent on the water help me relax. I think it's sorta like the way hours in the greenhouse ease Jass's mind. I wish her win in Miami had come at a better moment—a time when she could keep it uppermost in her thinking."

"A win is a win. Don't think she isn't enjoying it."

"I suppose you're right. So what are your plans for the morning?"

"Jass and I know Dad's car wasn't at home Saturday night, and we know he wasn't at Key Colony Beach. I'm guessing he might have gone to the marina. Let's check that out as a starting point. If he parked his car there, someone must have seen it."

Punt headed toward *Seaview Marina,* and after we claimed a visitor's parking slot, I turned up the collar on my jumpsuit against the cool trade wind. Dozens of boats bobbed in their moorings. *The Vitamin Sea,* my backcountry skiff, floated at the end of the first row. A cormorant perched on the stern, wings outstretched as if drying underarm deodorant. Then a gull circled over its head screaming seagull invective. I mentally thanked the gull as the cormorant took off, winging toward the Tortugas, but a pelican soon claimed its place. Even from this distance I could see white droppings decorating my boat seat. I sighed. Weekly cleanups were a given.

I followed Punt from the salt-scented air into the marina office where the faint odor of diesel fuel mingled with that of hemp line and motor oil. Hotdogs turning in a countertop broiler made my mouth water, but I resisted the temptation to buy one. Nearby, the cash register clanged, and voices echoed in the cavernous structure as I looked up at an array of boats, their bows poking from overhead storage units.

"Morning, Keely, Punt. How may I help you?" The counter clerk stuck a yellow pencil behind his right ear and grabbed a ringing telephone, punching buttons that directed the call to another office.

Punt waited until he had the man's attention. "Were you working here last Saturday, Ben?"

"Right. Got a problem?"

"Did you notice if Dad took his boat out that day?"

Ben jabbed his pencil behind his left ear and frowned thoughtfully. "As a matter of fact, I did see him here mid-morning. Waited on him when he bought a Coke. Then he asked me to fix up a sack lunch for two."

"So did he take his boat out, or did he leave with someone else?"

"You really checking up on him, right?" Ben backed off a step, cocked his head, and looked at Punt from beneath lowered lids. "Maybe I shouldn't blab about him—what with Margaux's death and all. Last thing I need is a summons to testify in court. Need no part of that scene."

Punt shoved a twenty across the counter and waited.

Ben pocketed the twenty. "He and Slone Pierce went out in Pierce's dive boat."

"What direction?"

"Never noticed."

I wondered if another twenty might help Ben's memory, but Punt didn't try for that. Was Ben really afraid of having to appear in court, or was he playing hard to get?

"Seen Slone around today?" Punt asked.

Ben shook his head and nodded to the slips. "His boat's still here."

"Thanks, Ben. See ya around."

Punt nudged me toward the door and we headed back to his car where he pulled out a Bell South book, then keyed Pierce's number on his cell phone. I could only hear Punt's side of the conversation, but after he slipped the phone back into his pocket, he nodded.

"Pierce took Dad out Saturday morning, but he'll only talk about it at his house, one on one. Cell phones never guarantee privacy, so we're heading for Slone's place, okay?"

I nodded. "This guy must be onto something he doesn't want the whole world to know."

We left the marina and drove to Flagler Avenue where we found plenty of parking places at the Pierce address in the newer part of Key West. A coral rock privacy fence enclosed a tiny yard and provided a backdrop for an abundance of blooming poinsettia plants. Slone had seen us coming and he stepped onto the front porch of his frame house, wearing red short shorts and the short-sleeved top to a black wet suit. He reminded me of a trained seal: heavyset, sleek, slow moving. The three of us knew each other slightly, and we exchanged greetings as Slone offered us seats on a rattan couch while he claimed the porch swing that squeaked on rusty chains. Nothing unusual about that. Even plastic tends to rust in the Keys.

"We're trying to check on Dad's activities last Saturday," Punt said. "We hope you'll be able to share some information."

"Helping the police out?" Slone's expression never changed, but I sensed a guarded look darken his eyes as his gaze went slightly to the left of Punt's head.

"We may help them if we can." Punt smiled in a way that invited Slone's confidence. "We thought Dad was supposed to keep records at a black-fin shark tournament at Key Colony Beach last Saturday, but the tournament officials didn't have his name on their roster. Have any idea about why? Had he engaged you for the day?"

"It's a long story," Slone said. "I'm guessing maybe Beau'd rather keep that story private."

"He swear you to secrecy?" Punt asked.

"No. But . . ."

"I'll wait in the car if you want to talk to Punt alone," I offered as I started to stand.

"No." Punt took my hand before I could step from the porch. "Slone, I think the police may call on you soon with these same questions. It might help Keely and me a lot if we had the information first."

"Don't want no mix-up with the police," Slone said. "Don't want to get Beau in any sort of trouble. Don't want to tarnish my own reputation. I run a clean operation, a reputable business."

"We're trying to keep Beau out of trouble, Slone. What was he doing on Saturday that you're being so secretive about? What's it got to do with your business reputation?"

Punt pulled another twenty from his pocket, but Slone shook his head and looked into the distance.

"Want no part of your bribe. If you want to know more

about Saturday, ask Beau. I got no more information to offer you." Slone stood, clearly giving us a signal to leave. His words chilled me, but Punt smiled and remained seated.

"I'm just guessing, Slone, but did Beau have an accident? A serious accident involving both of you?"

Slone gave a deep sigh. "Why else would we go to the hyperbaric unit?"

"Didn't know you went there until this minute. Lucky guess on my part. Come on, Slone. Give me a break."

Slone walked to the porch steps, giving us only a follow-me-then-leave-my-property look. "Check with the hyperbaric unit. That's all I'm going to say to you now or in the future. The accident wasn't my fault. Never my fault at all. If Beau says different, then he's lying."

I followed Punt to the car. "What's a hyperbaric unit?"

"A decompression chamber for bent divers."

"Guys who've gone down too deep?"

"Maybe. Maybe not. It's a decompression tank used to help divers who've tried to surface too quickly. Sometimes divers do that—either accidentally or purposely while they're showing off."

"Beau's no show-off. We both know that."

"Let's drive to Marathon—to the hospital. Dad may have a legitimate alibi after all. If he does, I want the police to know about it quickly."

We were about to pull away from the curbing when Beau drove up beside us, squealed his tires, called to us through the open car windows. "Follow me," he ordered. He took off before we could ask questions or refuse to follow.

We trailed him to the park across from Higg's Beach, left our cars in the small visitors' parking strip, and joined him at a picnic table. A group of kids shouted and laughed as they played tag around a swing set. Near a tennis court, an old man walked his dog, carrying a plastic bag for cleanup duty.

"What's going on, Dad? Are you okay?"

"I am now, but I guess Slone's already told you I wasn't so okay on Saturday afternoon."

"Slone told us very little. You and Slone had a diving accident?"

Beau nodded. "I called Margaux to tell her I'd be away all night on Saturday and maybe most of Sunday. She knew the truth. She could do nothing at the hyperbaric unit to help me, so I urged her to stay away. She tried to protect me by making up the story about my working the fishing tournament—thought the white lie would help me save face and that it'd make no difference to anyone."

"How does Slone come into the picture?" Punt asked.

"I'd promised Slone to help him with his dive boat on Saturday and that's where I went. We left the marina and headed for Hawk Channel in his boat about mid-morning."

"I guess Margaux's lie explains why the tournament people said they didn't have your name on their work list," Punt said.

"Hear me out, please." Beau shook his head as he looked at the ground. Guilt? I couldn't tell, but I felt sorry for him, for his discomfort.

"Margaux always hated to see me to go diving even though she knew diving was one of my lifelong passions and that I was an expert at it. Every year a few Keys scuba divers die in the sea, usually as a result of carelessness, or sometimes as a result of sudden illness. Margaux frequently let that knowledge cloud her thinking, and she had begged me to stay ashore last Saturday."

"You went anyway," Punt said.

"Yes, I went against Margaux's wishes, but when I got into trouble and called her, she wasn't the kind to say I told you so. She knew I'd be deeply embarrassed, so she tried to cover for me. She always had my best interest at heart."

"Her little white lie turned out to be very important." Punt sighed. "I don't understand all of this. Tell us about the accident."

"Are you okay?" I broke in. "You looked really exhausted when you came home late Sunday afternoon. Of course, you were grief-stricken, but now I see more to the situation than that."

"Exactly what happened, Dad?"

Beau flushed. "The whole thing embarrasses me. I hate having prompted Margaux's lie. I hate being involved in a dumb accident. The whole situation's something I'd rather forget."

"Let's hear the story," Punt said. "The true story. I don't see how it can be all that bad."

Beau's flush deepened as he began talking in subdued tones. "Most divers like to brag about finding treasure. They like to talk big about the dangerous sharks and huge barracuda they encounter. They love to exaggerate about how deep they can dive. But they hate to mention the time they have to spend in a hyperbaric chamber following a dive accident."

"That sort of accident that happened to you?" I asked. "Too deep a dive? Surfacing too quickly?"

"How bad was it?" Punt demanded.

"I hate admitting my ego's as big as that of most divers. Slone and I were in Hawk Channel where I planned to help him rig a new depth sounder, but as I peered over the gunwale, a giant-size loggerhead caught my eye. They're an endangered species, you know. I wanted to get a good look at this one to see if it appeared to be healthy or if it had *fibropapillomatosis,* those strange growths that result from the disease that's killing so many sea turtles."

"You risked your life for a turtle!" Punt exclaimed.

"I never realized that's what I was doing. When I dived overboard, the turtle sounded. My air gauge showed plenty of air, so I thought it'd be safe to follow it down a ways. That's when it happened. One minute I had plenty of oxygen and the next minute—none at all. I yanked on my air hose to signal Slone. No response. I had no choice but to surface quickly. Luckily, I had a lung full of air before I got cut off."

"So you surfaced too fast," I said.

"Yes, far too fast. Slone helped me into the boat, surprised to see me and surprised to see that a hose attached to my air tank had worked loose. Bad connection."

"Whose fault?" Punt asked.

"Maybe both of us stand at fault. The tank belonged to me, so I accept responsibility for not maintaining it in perfect condition. The boat belonged to Slone, so as captain, his responsibility lay in checking the condition of his passenger's dive equipment. We both fouled up."

"Thus the accident," I said. "How did all that affect you? Heart attack? Lung problems? I'm sorry, Beau. I shouldn't be prying. Maybe you dislike talking about the details."

Beau shook his head and continued his story. "I felt a profound fatigue—so tired I could barely move. I gasped for breath and dropped onto the bottom of the boat. Had extreme pain in my joints—all of them. It felt like someone was sticking pins and needles into my arms and legs."

"Slone rushed you to the hospital?" Punt asked. "How'd he do that? Call for a helicopter? Marine Patrol boat? Surely he didn't waste time driving you to Fisherman's in Marathon."

"None of the above. That hospital has the only civilian-operated hyperbaric unit in the Keys, right, but Slone drove me to Fleming Key. An Army Special Forces team has two hyperbaric chambers there. Underwater operations."

"Chambers available for public use?" Punt asked.

"Not usually, but they're available to anyone in case of an extreme emergency. Slone took me there. A diver can get in a real mess if he delays treatment. I lucked out. Slone carried a nasal mask and some pure oxygen aboard his boat and he administered that on the way. Probably saved my life. He phoned in our emergency, and they were expecting us when we arrived."

"What happened there?" I asked. "Obviously, they saved you."

"They put me in a chamber where the air is pressurized to create a specific underwater atmospheric pressure. Then, attendants depressurize the air gradually to simulate a safe rate of ascending to the surface. In my case, it took eight hours on Saturday—into late afternoon and night—then I rested under their watchful eyes, isolated until late Sunday morning when I had to go back into the unit for additional hours of decompression."

"Are you all okay now?" I asked.

"I think so, but I'll return for periodic checkups for a while."

Punt snorted. "When Jass and I were little, you and Mom always emphasized the importance of telling the truth. Margaux should have heard that advice."

"Hindsight," Beau said. "I knew what she planned to do, what she planned to tell people. At the time all I could think of was hiding my embarrassment from the public. I didn't want everyone in the state to know their favorite big-time treasure diver had been foolish enough to get the bends."

"I'm sorry for all you've been through, Dad, but at least you have an alibi for Saturday night. We were concerned about that, especially when Margaux's story turned out to be a big lie."

"I regret the whole situation and that's the pure truth. Maybe sometime in the future I'll be brave enough to admit all and write up that rotten dive experience in one of my columns. It could save some young diver from a similar experience."

As we all stood, ready to leave the park, Beau linked his arm through Punt's. "Son, those hours in the chamber gave me a lot of thinking time—thinking about what's important in this life and what's not. A lot of our differences come under the heading of 'what's not.' "

"Truce, Dad. Truce."

It had been years since I'd heard Beau call Punt "son," and when they smiled at each other, I knew they'd made a big step toward reconciliation.

"Have the police questioned you yet?" Punt asked.

"Yes. They picked me up at the house and then we drove to Police Headquarters. I'm sure they'll check out my story just as you have. They may be visiting Fleming Key right now, and again, they ordered me not to leave Key West without their permission."

"They told me that, too," I said. "It scares me to know there's a killer still at large."

"Whoever shot Margaux won't get away with it," Beau said. "I trust the police, but I may hire a special detective, to do some private investigating. 'Private' is the key word. A special investigator might have access to facts that the police don't have, and he might be able to keep some of our private life out of the newspapers. We've already made headlines in the Miami *Herald*."

"Where you going to find a private investigator?" Punt asked.

I waited for Punt to mention the P.I. agency he and Nikko planned to open, but he said nothing about it.

"Don't know yet," Beau said. "May have to go to Miami for that. Why don't you two take a break from your private snooping? I'm concerned for you. There's a killer at large, and if you put pressure on him, you could be the next victims. Let the police handle it. They'll probably be calling on you again soon, Keely."

Chapter 22

After Beau left us, I began to realize that he might be right about letting the police handle the case. We'd done a lot of running here and there trying to protect Beau when he hadn't really needed that kind of help at all. We'd failed to discover his true alibi. We'd failed to save him from embarrassment over the dive accident.

"Let's go somewhere for lunch, Keely." Punt took my arm and guided me back to his car.

"Not today, thanks. Please drive me to my office. I really need to be alone for a while—need to give myself time to think."

"Think about a killer on the loose? I hate knowing you'll be alone on the water—alone and afraid. You'll be in less danger if you have someone with you." Punt squeezed my hand as he helped me into the car. "I'd like to be that person. If you have to go out in your boat, let me go along."

"I appreciate your concern. Really, I do, but I need time alone to plan my words carefully, to be sure of what I'm going to say when the police call me in again for questioning. I'm sure they'll call me. I also need to think back, to remember exactly what I've already told them. They'll check on that, won't they?"

"Yes. I'm sure they will, but if you've told them the truth, it shouldn't be hard to remember what you've said."

"Detective Curry took notes when he talked with me on Sunday morning, and he took notes again on Sunday night when he told me the gun in Margaux's hand belonged to me. He asked endless questions about it. I have to remember exactly what I told him. If I change my story, even accidentally, I'll be under even more careful scrutiny."

"I'm trying to help you. Why're you giving me the brush-off? You said something about our lifestyles being too different. I'm not sure that's true and I'm not sure exactly what you mean. We have lots of things in common—lots more now than we had years ago."

"I'm not giving you a brush-off. I'm trying to give myself some think time—some time alone. That has nothing to do with our lifestyles, either past or present."

"You still afraid I may revert to druggie life?"

"No. You've been there, done that. I believe you're on a better course."

Punt grinned at me as he managed to find a parking place in front of my office. "You still see me as a beach bum? You afraid I'll never be able to support myself—or want to?"

I smiled. "Give me a break, Punt. I'll see you tomorrow."

"What about tonight? Dinner? You have to eat somewhere and it might as well be with me."

"Call me around seven and we'll talk about it then, okay?"

Punt sighed. "Okay."

I entered my office and closed the door quickly. I wanted no one to see me and maybe think I might be open for business. Gram followed me inside and Nikko and Moose followed her. I sighed. So much for entering on the Q.T.

"So who's minding your shop?" I asked Gram as I inhaled mingled fragrances of peppermint and lemon that permeated my office.

"Honor system. Left coffee pot on counter. Left coin box beside it."

"That might work with the locals," I leaned to pet Moose. "I'm not so sure about the tourists."

"Where you been?" Gram asked.

I told her about part of our morning, but not about Beau's experience in the decompression chamber. She and Nikko could read about that in the newspaper. Or would Beau be able to pull some strings and keep it hush-hush?

"You closed for the day?" Nikko asked.

"Yes. Wednesday afternoon's always been my time off. I'm going to take *The Vitamin Sea* to the backcountry and try for bonefish or permit."

"Want me to go along?" Nikko asked. "Don't like to see you out on the water alone."

"I'll be safe enough in my boat, and I know deep channels that lead to secret coves on the flats that even you haven't fished. Besides, if someone's trying to pin a murder rap on me, they'll want me in good health. Nobody's going to give me a bad time."

"Nikko tell me about funeral," Gram said. "I hear Moose sit by Jude. What you make of that?"

"That Jude had something to do with the fire, Gram. We can't prove it in court, but we know. It helps us keep our guard up."

"What good to know—to know and do nada?"

"We know for sure who our enemy is," I said. "Right, Nikko?"

"Right. We know your enemy hasn't changed. It's always been Jude. Take care, Keely."

"Maybe you and Moose should take care. I think Moose scared Otto half to death yesterday. Otto may not take that lightly."

"Maybe he had drugs on him." Nikko shrugged. "Moose's trained to track humans, not drugs."

"Otto didn't know that. Don't try to shrug off your own danger. Otto's afraid of you and Moose, and people hate the ones they fear. Otto probably thinks you're onto his secret.

Detective Curry saw his reaction to Moose, and he'll probably have a few questions to ask Otto about that scene."

"Glad I no go to memorial," Gram said. "Don't want police questions about secrets."

Nikko laughed. "Forget it, Celia. Your only secret is your age. Even the police couldn't pry that from you."

"I no tell. Not even to police."

I kept a straight face. Gram's secretive about her age. She and I are probably the only ones who know she's seventy-two. Sometimes thugs prey on the elderly if they think they're too weak to defend themselves, and Gram doesn't intend for that to happen to her. She tries to put up a strong front. And she succeeds.

"Out of here. Both of you." I smiled when I shooed them toward the door, but I meant it. "I need some down time, and I need it now."

Reluctantly, they left, and I made myself a peanut butter and banana sandwich and a salad. Gram's favorite recipe, I thought smiling. After eating, I changed into jeans, T-shirt, and boat shoes. Sweatshirt. Boat keys. Was that everything I needed? I slipped my cell phone into my sweatshirt pocket, tied the sweatshirt around my waist, and left my office.

I pedaled slowly to the marina, enjoying the sun, the trade wind, and even the throngs of tourists. As I passed Mallory Square, I saw Punt and Nikko in Punt's car, but they were in such deep conversation they didn't notice me. Good. I didn't want to talk to them right now, but I couldn't help thinking they were discussing business matters. Maybe there was hope for them in a detective agency.

At the marina, I chained my bike to a piling outside the office before I took my rod and reel from my storage locker inside the office, trying not to sniff the ever-present stench of diesel fuel. Walking along the dock, I headed for the bait bar where I bought a carton of frozen squid and half a dozen live shrimp.

As I turned onto the narrow walkway that led to *The Vitamin Sea*, I passed Nikko's skiff, Punt's cabin cruiser. I hated to look, didn't want anyone to notice my interest, but I peered behind me and to the far left. Jude's black and silver speed boat bobbed in its slip. I looked ahead again quickly. I wasn't afraid, but when I went out in the backcountry, I always liked to know that Jude's boat bobbed in its slip. My sea-gray skiff blended with the water, and once I left the harbor behind me and headed west, I could easily disappear into hidden coves and mangrove thickets.

Drat those pelicans. I stepped over the gunwale into my boat, grabbed a bucket, and lowered it into the sea. Before I began scrubbing, I opened the package of squid and set it in a sunny spot on the bow to thaw and then filled my bait tank with sea water and splashed the shrimp into it.

White droppings covered the area around the motors and I spent several minutes applying the scrub brush before the fiberglass gleamed again. As I gave the stern a final rinse, I saw Shandy approaching on another walkway, her lips moving as she counted the boats between the dock and her skiff. She didn't wave, but I started my motor and eased from my slip in case she might suggest we go out together. Such worries about invasion of privacy were probably groundless. Shandy seldom sought company. Maybe she hated to reveal her secret fishing holes as much as I hated revealing mine. Fishermen are like that.

Taking care to leave no wake, I steered slowly toward a deep-water channel, and a few minutes later my bow cut a V-shaped wedge into the sea as I throttled the boat on plane, and headed west. Sea spray dampened my arms, and I tasted a salty mist on my lips. Hello Paradise.

I waited until Key West harbor lay in the distance before I changed course, speeding into backcountry waters that I knew well. A few minutes later I slowed down, heading into a small bight surrounded on three sides by the sandy shores of an islet I had nicknamed Osprey Key—a mere flyspeck on area charts. This spot rated tops as one of my favorite fishing holes and I suppose other fishermen knew of it, too, but I'd never seen anyone else here.

I cast anchor, watching line snake over the gunwale until the orange mushroom settled in the gray-green turtle grass. Securing the line to the stern cleat, I sat for a few moments enjoying the sunny day, the billowing clouds, the undulating sea. With the sun almost directly overhead, I could see into the water. A stingray glided beneath the boat. To the left a five-foot barracuda nosed slowly toward me, but when I moved, it saw me and darted toward the horizon.

Sitting statue still, I listened and watched the surface for bonefish. Sometimes a school of bones raised clouds of mud as they nosed the bottom for food. Bonefish on a feeding frenzy could be noisy. I scanned the surface for tails fanning the air, but saw none, heard none. At last I reached into the bait well, caught a shrimp, and threaded it onto my hook. Yuck! I started to wipe my hands on my jeans, then I remembered to use the old towel hanging near the wheel. No point in wiping shrimp aroma on my jeans. Sometimes I wished for the good old days when Gram took me fishing, baited my hooks, gill-threaded my catch onto a stringer. Forget that, Keely. You're a big girl now.

I stepped lightly onto the bow with rod in hand. It helped to be able to look down into the water. Still. Still. Quiet. Quiet. Once a fish spotted unusual movement overhead it'd take off like an arrow. Adjusting my stance to the motion of the boat, I watched a white sandy spot on the sea bottom surrounded by turtle grass that lay about twenty feet ahead of me. A small nurse shark swam lazily across the area, but I didn't cast. In no mood to fight a shark today.

Then I saw it—a permit. My mind and body tensed. The fish's silvery body flashed in the water and I made my cast. Missed target. Rotten aim. The shrimp still wiggled on my hook while I waited again. Where I saw one permit, I frequently saw others. My legs ached from standing still for so long, then another fish headed toward me. Good cast this time.

Line shrieked from the reel as the fish took the bait. Permit? Bonefish? Shark? I wasn't sure, but I played out line until the fish stopped running, then I forced the rod tip up and reeled in line until the fish took off again. We played that game for about fifteen minutes before I brought my catch to boatside. A 'cuda. Barracudas put up a good fight, but I'd hoped for bonefish—or permit.

Now I had to deal with the critter. I'm not a meat-on-the-table fisherman and 'cuda aren't good eating fish. I'm a strong believer in catch-and-release. No point in killing a fish you neither want nor need. I reached for the pliers on my console before I knelt at the gunwale and eased the fish up until I could reach its head. The hook was only slightly embedded in the 'cuda's lower lip, and a quick twist with the pliers released it. For a moment it lay dazed near the surface. I leaned farther over the gunwale and grabbed its tail, pulling it back and forth to send water flowing through its gills. After a few moments it regained strength and pulled from my grip, heading for the horizon. I always wondered if a fish once caught would be dumb enough to bite on another lure—to let itself get caught again. Scientists may know the answer; they tag and release lots of fish.

I reached for the half-frozen squid, cut off a piece, and

prepared to bait up again when I heard another boat approaching. Strange. I'd never encountered others in this bight. I straightened up and stood on the bow so the interloper could see me easily and have the courtesy to leave. One person per fishing hole makes a crowd. This interloper didn't leave and he showed no sign of intending to leave. Jumping from the bow, I eased back toward the console and grabbed the wheel for support.

What was this idiot doing? The sun now slanting in from the west blinded me, but I saw his boat on a direct course toward me. As the distance between our crafts shortened, I made out the black and silver of Jude's speedboat. Did he intend to wreck us both? My boat lay at his mercy. Maybe I could pull anchor, start the motor, escape. But no. Impossible. My skiff pitched so badly I struggled to keep my footing. No way could I grab the anchor line. Paralyzed with terror I braced myself for impact.

Jude sped directly toward me, but at the last moment he jerked his wheel and turned. Our boats missed colliding by a few inches—less than a foot. I gasped for breath as I struggled to keep upright, then I breathed easier when I saw the stern of his speedboat as he headed away from me.

Reaching for my radio, I planned to call the Marine Patrol for help. Jude Cardell wasn't going to get by with this. I fumbled with the radio dials, but before I could turn it on and get it working, I saw Jude's boat heading for me again. A cloud passed over the sun and this time I saw his shaded face clearly. He made a large semicircle in front of my boat, then he cut toward me again, turning at the last possible instant and heading away. I continued to grip my wheel for support, expecting him to return for another go at me. But no. Not this time.

At last I forced myself to relax, to radio for help. No such luck. The radio refused to come to life. I grabbed the cell phone from my sweatshirt pocket and keyed in the Marine Patrol's emergency number. The phone rang six times. No answer. I tried the Coast Guard number and a faint voice responded.

"Need help," I shouted into the phone.

"Where are you?" a voice asked.

I gave my location.

"Sorry, can't hear you. Repeat location again, please."

I gave my location again, but that time I received no response. I broke that connection and tried again. No response. Maybe they were too far away. I tried the Marine Patrol number once more. Again, no response. I started to key in Nikko's number, but the battery went dead. Damn phone! I shoved it back into my pocket, wishing for the spare phone I kept in my desk drawer.

Did I dare return to Key West? Maybe Jude lay hiding in one of these out-of-the-way coves, waiting for me to make a run for help. Maybe he'd strike again in deep water. I didn't want to take the risk of leaving. It's hard to know that someone hates you as much as Jude hates me.

It'd be sundown before too long. I disliked boating after dark, but I had running lights and a compass. I knew my way around these waters. I'd have a good chance of sneaking past Jude without him seeing me if I waited. I'd lost the mood for more fishing, and I sat behind the wheel waiting. Waiting. That's where I was when I saw Jude approaching again. This time his slow approach scared me more than his great speed.

"Scared to go home?" he taunted.

I didn't reply.

"Maybe you want some company. Maybe I should come aboard and show you a little fun."

Now I found my voice. "Don't come near me," I shouted,

but my voice sounded ragged and afraid. Somehow I managed to turn on the boat motor. Maybe I could gun it, swerve to one side of him and then shoot straight ahead. Yet I knew that wouldn't work. Jude's speedboat had much more power than my skiff.

His bow nudged mine and he let his motor idle as he moved forward and started to step onto the bow. From there it would be only a short jump from his boat to mine. I threw my boat into reverse and increased the distance between us. Jude pulled forward and tried to board again. Again I reversed, avoiding his approach. It was a cat and mouse game until my last reverse maneuver.

The stern of my boat hit a sandbar. I'd been too scared to look behind me, and I hadn't realized that danger. Now Jude'd have no problem boarding my boat. *I'll see you dead.* His threat screamed through my mind, and in desperation I jerked my boat knife from its sheath. Anger and fear all but choked me as Jude stood on his bow laughing.

"Have fun tonight, you bitch. I'm leaving you here. There's no way you're going to pull from that sand during low tide." He stood there laughing at me. "Oh, one more thing, bitch. Toss me your cell phone."

"Damn you, no!"

"Then I'll come aboard and get it."

Chapter 23

How do you prepare yourself to die on the spur of the moment? Pray? I could only think of now-I-lay-me-down-to-sleep and that didn't seem to fit this situation. My whole life didn't flash before my eyes as I've heard happens to others at times like these. No. I lived totally in the horrifying present, my body like a coiled spring ready to fly into action, yet tense with fear. Only strong determination kept me from begging Jude for mercy. I clamped my jaws shut until my teeth ached, determined that my days of begging Jude for anything were behind me, gone forever.

Jude killed his motor, and using a yellow emergency paddle, he silently poled his boat a few feet forward until its bow nudged the bow of *The Vitamin Sea*. No use retreating aft. My only hope aft would be to jump from the stern onto the sandbar and then splash to land. On shore, mangrove roots arched above the sand like dark snakes, ready to trip me. I'd be no match for Jude in a foot race on the island.

Clutching my fillet knife so hard my nails bit into my palm, I eased forward. Maybe I could defend myself. Maybe I could throw Jude off guard momentarily by shoving him into the water. Or, more likely, maybe he'd kill me with my own knife. That possibility loomed large in my thinking. Yet would he kill me if he were the one trying to lay a murder rap on my doorstep? He'd want me alive and suffering from righteous anger in a prison cell, wouldn't he?

With a thud that reverberated through the soles of my shoes, Jude leaped easily to the bow of my boat. Then he jumped to the boat bottom, stiffened his knees, and paused only long enough to regain his balance. Grabbing my radio from the console, he smashed it against the floor, kicked it to the stern, then retrieved it and threw it overboard. When he spoke, his breathing clogged his throat and his voice came in angry spurts. I dodged around the console and leaped onto the bow.

"Where's your cell?" He stood behind the wheel and began searching, tossing pliers, compass, pens aside. While he searched, I leaped from the bow of my boat onto his, flailing my arms and bending my knees to keep my balance. Now I stood on the operable boat, and Jude's search for my cell phone intensified. The cell would do him no good with a dead battery, but he didn't know that and I wasn't about to tell.

Unfortunately, in my terror I'd left the phone in my sweat-shirt pocket. He'd know all too soon that it wouldn't work, but I'd tucked the sweatshirt under the passenger seat storage bin and Jude stooped, searching in the deep box under the driver's seat.

Escape! I had to make a fast start out of here! Jude's boat key dangled from the ignition, but my fear-numbed fingers could barely activate it. There! The key turned, and as I tried to start the motor, Jude heard the grinding.

"Stop that, you bitch! I'll make you sorry!"

I tried the starter again and again. No luck. The motor refused to catch. Jude could leap aboard his speedboat in a matter of moments ready to make good his threat once he found my phone. Panic rose in my chest like a hot air bal-loon expanding until it threatened to choke me. In despera-tion I looked toward the stern. When I saw Jude's anchor and the coil of line beside it, I saw my only slim chance of evening the score. Quickly, I tied the anchor line to a stern cleat.

"Damn you! Where's that cell?" Jude's face flushed and

his eyes stabbed me as he shouted. "Tell me or you're a dead bitch."

I knew I'd be crazy to try to bargain with him, but I saw bargaining as a small avenue of hope. I eased back to the bow of his boat, hoping to draw his attention away from the anchor.

"If I give you the cell, will you go away and leave me alone?"

"You've got it, you slut. Give me that phone and I'll leave you to rot out here on this devil-forsaken sandbar with the mosquitoes. It'll serve you right to spend a night here alone. Do you good."

"The cell's in my sweatshirt pocket."

Jude looked at me as if to make sure I wasn't wearing the sweatshirt. "Okay, bitch, where's the shirt?"

"Under the passenger seat. Take it and go."

"You dumb butt!"

His voice became muffled as he bent to open the storage bin, and in moments he held the phone, raising it high in a gesture of triumph before he spit on it and threw it overboard. Would he go? Or had I been a fool to expect him to keep his word? Again, I held my knife at the ready as I leaped back into my own boat.

Jude eyed me, then he eyed the knife, and with a swift and vicious chop to my wrist, he knocked it from my hand. It fell into the boat, clattering against the passenger seat before it hit the bottom, landing easily within his reach. But he didn't go for it. For a second we both stared at it lying there. Then our eyes met.

"You're daring me to kill you, aren't you, Keely? You rat's ass? You hate me so much I think you'd actually die to know that I'd live to face the murder rap. Well, it'll never come down that way. Not tonight. I'm not nearly through toying with you yet. We'll play games together again another time, Keely, another time and another place. You can depend on it, you turd."

Before Jude left my skiff, he gave me a flat hand slap to the face that sent me reeling to the bottom of the boat. My ribs hit the gunwale and hot arrows of pain shot throughout my body. Broken ribs? Broken jaw? I lay there vulnerable and unable to move. Jude ground at his starter switch, swearing and making several attempts to engage the motor before it spluttered, caught, and roared.

Unwanted memories flooded in through my pain. On my eighth birthday, I'd been out fishing with my mother. Before sunset she'd hauled in the anchor, untied it, and was preparing to head for home when she paused to consult a chart of the area. Childlike, I got tired of waiting and I entertained myself by tying the anchor line to the stern cleat as it had been when the anchor lay overboard.

When my mother finished studying the chart, she started the motor, put the boat on plane, and made a fast turn toward Key West. I can still see a wave catching that anchor line, jerking it over the gunwale, pulling the anchor after it. I screamed as the anchor slammed into the water then bounced back, hitting my mother's hand. Blood spurted everywhere, but even at age eight I knew where to find the first-aid kit. In spite of choking sobs, I opened the kit and followed my mother's directions for holding bandages and cutting tape to help her bind her broken fingers.

Once we reached the hospital emergency room, the doctors examined my mother's hand and gave us the terrible news. Her two middle fingers had to be amputated immediately. I'd never felt such guilt. I blamed myself for that horror. My mother tried to console me, telling me that accidents happen, that it wasn't my fault. She said the ricocheting anchor could have landed anywhere, anywhere at all, and of course she was right. The anchor accidentally happened to hit her hand. Gram agreed with everything Mom said. Nobody ever scolded me for what I'd done.

I've lived almost twenty years with the guilt of that accident buried deep in my heart. Nobody ever mentioned it to me again. Not my mother. Not Gram. Never again had I tied an anchor line to a stern cleat while a boat was to be in motion—never again until today. Today I acted in self defense. I hoped Jude would make a fast turn. I hoped the anchor would hit the water and ricochet. But it was wishful thinking on my part to dream the anchor would do Jude any real damage. Nobody could pinpoint what target a ricocheting anchor might hit. It could hit the hull, or the wheel, or the console. Or it could drop harmlessly back into the sea. In my heart, I hoped the anchor would target Jude.

The stench of gasoline floated toward me and I wondered if he'd try to ram my skiff just hard enough to jab a hole in the hull that would sink it or at least put it totally out of commission for the rest of this day. Even in the unlikely event that help might arrive, I hoped he'd leave *The Vitamin Sea* intact. Jude must have thought he'd damage his own boat in trying to sink mine because he shifted into reverse and jerked on the wheel until his bow pointed toward Key West.

Tears streamed down my face, but I forced myself upright and eased onto the passenger seat. To my relief, Jude revved his motor and put his boat on plane. He headed some distance toward Key West before he did what I'd guessed and feared he'd do. He circled, making a broad turn, then with throttle wide open, he sliced the sea as he sped back toward me.

As his motor roared in the late afternoon stillness, egrets roosting in the mangroves took flight like puffs of cotton floating toward the sky. I watched in fascinated horror, unable to move. The sand bank near shore dropped off into deeper water, but did Jude think he could smash my skiff at that speed without damaging his own craft and killing us both?

I sank back onto the bottom, covering my head with both arms in an effort to protect myself from the impending shock. Then at the last moment, I heard Jude pull his old trick, turning his boat seconds before it reached mine and then speeding away into the distance. I couldn't bear to watch. I lay on the boat bottom in exhaustion and pain. Jude could come back again and again if he decided to. I lay beyond caring.

Staring upward, I watched the sky turn from blue to fiery red, to gray-black. I counted the stars appearing one by one until so many pricked the sky I could no longer keep track. Soon, true night shrouded me, black, quiet, frightening, and eerie night sounds reminded me of what a fool I had been to come here alone. Water lapped my boat hull and the shoreline, making an obscene sucking sound. A heron's cry wavered into the darkness. While leaves and fallen branches whispered threats, some unknown creature slunk nearby. Raccoon? Maybe. Wild dog? I hoped not.

I lay safe from critters as long as I stayed aboard the boat. When the onshore wind ceased, mosquitoes began zinging around my ears and a do-something-or-perish reality forced me to sit up, to ignore the pain that stabbed from my chest through to my back. How many ribs does a person have? I guessed all of mine were either broken or bruised.

Crawling along the boat bottom I found my sweatshirt, eased my arms into the sleeves, then pulled the soft cotton slowly and painfully over my head. Now moonlight silvered the sea and the incoming tide lifted the bow until it made slapping noises against the water, but the stern still lay deeply embedded in the sand. I started the motor, revved it, and tried to dislodge the boat and move it forward. No such luck. The stench of gasoline left me sickened as I wasted fuel and my own energy. At last I cut the motor and relaxed against the wheel, trying to relieve my pain.

The mosquitoes still came after me and their itchy bites stung my face, the backs of my hands, my ankles. West Nile Virus? I shuddered. Wishing I'd worn socks, I yanked my jeans down to the tops of my boat shoes and pulled the sweat-shirt hood around my head until only my nose stuck out. The mosquitoes used my nose for their target and hordes of them swarmed around me like flying teeth.

In great pain, I raised the lid on the bow's storage bin and pulled out a canvas tarp and a life vest, dragging them to the starboard side of the console. Then I remembered my emergency flares. It meant another trip to the bow, but my pain had eased a little. Maybe the ribs weren't broken after all. Inch by inch I crawled to the bow and opened the storage bin. My fingers fumbled against life jackets and boat cushions before I touched the emergency kit and found three flares inside the box along with a waterproof canister of matches.

Closing the bin, I sat on the bow to catch my breath before I struck a match and lit the fuse on the first flare, holding it like a Roman candle and pointing it toward Key West. It sizzled for a few seconds and died. Damn! Trying to avoid inhaling the sulphur fumes, I pinched the fuse between my thumb and forefinger to be sure it was out before I lit another match and touched it to the fuse on the second flare. This time the fuse caught and sizzled and the flare exploded, leaving heavy smoke plus a red streak in its wake before it fanned out into a yellow-orange brightness.

I waited a few minutes, slapping at mosquitoes every

second, then I released the third flare before I dropped down once more and managed to wrap myself in the tarp and rest my head on the life jacket. It promised to be a long night—a long frightening night, but at least the mosquitoes couldn't eat me alive now.

A fishy odor clung to the tarp and it, along with my painful ribs, made it impossible to sleep. I wondered if anyone would find me. I'd been crazy not to let Punt or Nikko come along with me. Maybe they'd miss me and come searching. Or maybe they'd call the Marine Patrol or the Coast Guard. Those officials might look for me, but most of their boats were too big to navigate in these shallow waters. My only hope in calling them earlier had been that they might lower a dinghy and rescue me in that. After dark, rescue by dinghy was highly unlikely.

Chapter 24

I lay wrapped in the tarp for over an hour before I heard the sound of a boat motor, first in the distance, then coming closer and closer. Jude? Stomach contents threatened to rise into my throat. I tasted bile. Was Jude returning to torment me again? I didn't dare look. If I didn't rise up and show myself, maybe he'd think I'd left the boat. Unlikely. Jude would know this sandbar offered nowhere to hide. I strained my ears listening, expecting any moment to hear him revving his motor and speeding toward me. Instead I heard the splash of an anchor and in the next instant I heard Punt shouting my name.

"Keely! Keely, are you there? Are you okay?" Even before he started splashing toward my boat, I ignored my pain, threw the tarp aside, and sat up so he could see me.

"Punt! Oh, Punt! Am I ever glad you're here." My voice failed and in the next moment he boarded my boat and pulled me into his arms. I clung to him, forgetting my painful ribs. When his lips found mine, I welcomed their warmth, but after only seconds, hordes of mosquitoes intruded on our embrace and reluctantly I pushed him away. "How did you find me?"

"Tell you later. Right now you need to get into my boat and let me tow your boat in."

"That'll take forever, Punt. Let's take my ignition key and leave *The Vitamin Sea* here. I can hire Ace Towing to bring it in tomorrow."

"Guess that'd get us home quicker. Your boat'll be safe. Nobody's likely to be poking around back here after dark."

Nobody but Jude, I thought, but at this point I wanted to believe that even Jude wouldn't return again tonight.

Punt helped me overboard and the cold water chilled me as it flooded my deck shoes and soaked my jeans. To look at the shallows in the backcountry, one might think boarding a boat from the water would be easy. Not. The sea bottom where we stood was like quicksand. The more we struggled for leverage to hoist our bodies up, over the gunwale, and into Punt's boat, the deeper the muck sucked us down.

Water that had been ankle deep when we entered it soon measured waist deep, and then chest deep—at least on me. At last Punt released my hand, and with great effort he managed to hoist himself onto the motor prop, the motor itself, and from there onto the stern. Turning, he offered me his hand, and I splashed and struggled until I stood aboard with him, dripping muck and water all over his carpeted boat bottom. We collapsed onto the boat seat until we caught our breath and rested for a few moments.

"I thought we might not make it," I admitted at last.

"The sea has serious ways of showing us humans who's boss." Punt sat on the stern still catching his breath. "Want to tell me what happened out here?"

I sat on the bottom protected from a slight breeze as I began talking. "Jude trailed me here. I'd no idea anyone was near—hadn't heard a sound. He must have followed at a very safe distance."

"Probably not the first time he's followed you. I'm guessing that he spent lots of time spying on you before letting you know he'd discovered your special cove. Did he hurt you?" Punt leaned toward me and the boat tilted then righted again. "If he touched you . . ."

"No, he didn't hurt me, not physically. He smashed my radio and threw it overboard. He wanted my cell phone so I couldn't call for help."

"Did he find it?"

I hesitated, leaving out the part about boarding Jude's boat and being unable to start it and escape. "I finally told him where I'd hidden the cell, told him to take it—with the agreement that he'd go away, leave me alone. I didn't tell him about the dead battery."

"Bargain with the devil. Since Jude's nowhere in sight now, I suppose he did leave."

"Right." Then I told Punt about Jude's showing up a second time, threatening to smash my boat. "I'm guessing he wants me alive to face the police. I really think he murdered Margaux."

"I agree." Punt pulled the anchor and turned the boat, pointing it toward Key West harbor. "It's going to be hard to prove that. Jude's slick as spit. You said you saw him near Margaux's house on Sunday morning. I believe you, but we can't prove that. Nor can we prove he dropped his sweatshirt at the Georgia Street fire. We have no proof he's breaking the restraining order by stalking you here and tormenting you. It'd be your word against his. But enough of Jude for now. We need to get home."

I breathed a sigh of relief when the motor came to life. Engine roar made talking impossible and we rode without speaking until we could see the lights of Key West in the distance. When we reached the marina and he slowed to "no wake" speed, I moved to sit on the bow.

"How did you find me, Punt? I didn't think anyone knew about that cove. After tonight I'll always believe in miracles."

"I hated seeing you go fishing alone this afternoon. I worried about you from the start. When I stopped at the marina a little before dusk and saw your boat slip empty, I smelled trouble."

"Glad you checked on me." What if he hadn't checked? I refused to imagine spending the night wrapped in that smelly tarp with mosquitoes at the ready, waiting to eat me alive if I poked my head out.

"I knew you were too smart to stay out after dark. I tried to radio you. No go. I tried to call you on your cell. Thought you must have had it turned off. So I waited a while, thinking you might come in soon. When you didn't, I saw no use going out and searching aimlessly. You could have been anywhere. A long time passed before I saw a flare and then another."

"Lucky for me that you saw them. I've never had much confidence in flares—until tonight."

"I pointed the *Sea Deuced* in the general direction of the flares . . . and finally, I found you."

"I can never thank you enough."

"Oh, I can think of a few ways." Punt grinned.

I eased from the bow to the passenger seat, leaning a bit to the right to keep the boat in trim. The pain around my ribs reminded me of the ordeal I'd rather have forgotten. Under most other circumstances this trip might have been a romantic boat ride on a moonlit sea. Instead, I felt cold and wet, grubby and dirty, and itchy. I knew I must smell like dead fish.

Punt secured the boat in its slip, helped me over the gunwale, then took my arm as we headed toward his car. I thought it must be almost morning, but my watch said only a little after eight o'clock.

"Let's go to my place first," Punt said. "You know your grandmother'll be watching for you. You don't want her to see you looking like . . ."

"Okay. You're right, I don't, and I don't want to be responsible for staining the interior of your car."

"I suppose we could walk home." Punt grinned as he looked down at his slimy shoes and then at mine. "I keep some old beach towels in the trunk. We can spread them over the seats and the floor. I'm fond of that upholstery and carpet."

I helped Punt arrange the towels, saving a couple of them to wrap around our shoulders, to ward off the chill.

Punt drove to his private entrance at *Ashford Mansion* and we climbed the stairs to his apartment, our wet feet in wet shoes squish-squishing at every step. We both kicked off our shoes at the door, and the white tile floor inside the apartment felt warm to my cold feet.

Punt's apartment consisted of one large white-walled room with white wicker furniture dividing the space into living-dining room, bedroom, and kitchen. Dive flags, boat flags, and flags I didn't recognize decorated the walls, giving the apartment a nautical look without the usual clichés of rope-framed seascapes, life preservers, and fishing nets. An open door led past the bedroom into the bathroom.

"So how about a shower?" Punt invited. "You can use this one and I'll use the one in Jass's laundry room."

"I won't argue showers with you. I can hardly wait to get cleaned up."

"Want some help? I'm good at backs and also at the other two thousand body places available for a scrub-down." Punt grinned and his smile barely missed being a leer.

"I'll manage on my own, thanks, if you'll only lend me towel, soap, and some dry clothes."

"Okay, but you're missing a good thing. I never share my shower with just anyone."

Punt supplied towels and soap and I stepped into the shower stall. After adjusting the temperature to hot, I let the needle-like spray sluice over my body. Heaven. No other word would do. I lathered and rinsed twice. By the time I finished the second time I'd also lathered and rinsed my hair. The in-shower time washed away many of my aches and pains. My ribs felt sore, but I doubted they were broken.

Punt had left a slinky robe and some strappy sandals on a low stool beside the sink. Who had those belonged to? Jass? Much too small for Jass. I really didn't want to know who Punt might have entertained. Gratefully, I slipped into the robe, feeling it glide over my body before I took his hair dryer from a wall rack and dried my hair.

When I stepped from the bathroom, Punt was sitting in clean fresh clothes at the coffee table where he had arranged a tray of peanut butter and jelly sandwiches and a dish of macadamia nuts. A bottle of Chardonnay and a bottle of Coke sat near two frosted glasses, and he poured our drinks.

Chapter 25

Punt placed the frosted wine glass in my hand, clinked his glass against it, and offered a toast. "To us, Keely. A happy celebration of good times past and many more good times to come."

We drank to that and I liked both the taste of the Chardonnay and the smooth feel of the cool liquid in my mouth.

"You're smiling." Punt offered me a sandwich. "I hope that means you're pleased with me as well as with the toast."

I smiled at him. "There's something touching about a sophisticated man-about-town offering a sentimental toast, enjoying peanut butter and jelly sandwiches, and washing them down with a cola."

"When we were kids, Mom made the sandwiches for us and we washed them down with lemonade. Remember those days?"

"I remember a lot of good times at this house with you and Jass, your parents. Sometimes I wish we could turn the clock back and start over again."

"Maybe we can draw on those memories and move on. People in-the-know say the good old days were often more old than good." Punt left his chair, joined me on the couch, and eased close. "I've been in love with you since high school days. You know that, don't you, Keely?"

I eased away from him, suddenly uncomfortable. "I remember that for a while you were very much in love with cocaine and you had the money to support your habit. I couldn't get through to you."

"I'm clean now. Been clean for three years, and I intend to

227

stay clean forever. Cocaine and booze have no part of my life now."

"I want to believe that, Punt. Everyone wants to believe that."

Punt took my hand and inched closer to me. "I tried to put you out of my mind the second time I came out of rehab. I tried to accept the fact that you were married, that you had chosen Jude Cardell. Believe me I really hated that low blow. Jude Cardell!"

"Let's not talk about Jude. Not tonight. I've had enough of him for today—for today and forever."

Again Punt inched closer and dropped his arm around my shoulder. I took a sip of wine, lifting my glass in a way that kept us a bit apart.

"Keely, could we start over? Could we begin a new relationship, take up where we left off ten years ago? Now that I'm older, I feel much wiser."

The warm touch of Punt's arm around my shoulder made me want to ease closer to him, to relax against his lean body. The temptation to say yes to his invitation played on the tip of my tongue, but I forced myself to pull away. In my mind's eye I saw him lounging on the beach, hanging out at *Sloppy's*, scooping the loop in the Karmann Ghia with a variety of girls at his side. I wondered whose robe I wore right at the moment.

"I think we've drifted too far apart, Punt. I'll always be your friend, but during the past ten years I've grown up. I've a horrible marriage behind me, one I need to forget completely. I can do that only by concentrating on my career. For a while I doubted I had the strength to make it go. I've worked hard to create a niche for myself."

Ignoring my words, Punt pulled me close and stopped my words with his lips. The wine, his nearness, the touch of his mouth against mine dissolved my resistance. Warmth spread throughout my body, and I welcomed his kiss and the next one—and the next. When at last I eased away from him, I felt a great reluctance.

"Please take me home now, Punt."

"You want to stay, don't you? Please tell me you want to stay, to spend the night here with me."

I hedged. "A person can't always have what she wants."

"But you can. You can have what you want as long as what you want is me."

"If it were only that easy." I laughed and forced myself to stand and to pretend as if I really wanted to go home.

Punt saw through my amateur acting and he covered my hand with both of his. "Got a really comfortable bed over there." He nodded toward the bedroom area where a circular bed with a white plush spread invited occupants.

I avoided looking overhead at the mirrored ceiling, tried not to wonder who else might have shared his bed. "No thanks, Punt. After tonight's ordeal, I'm totally exhausted."

Punt stood and grinned down at me. "Well, I can't guarantee you much sleep if you stay here."

"So please take me home."

"Okay. Your call—this time."

Punt brought me my clothes which he had put through the washer while I showered and the dryer while we talked. I stepped back into the bathroom to slip from the robe and into my own jeans and shirt. It was after eleven o'clock by the time we reached my apartment and Punt stopped at the back door where Gram was less likely to hear us, especially if she'd put her ear plugs in for the night. He got out and saw me to the door, waited until I unlocked it, opened it before he gave me a lingering goodnight kiss.

"See you tomorrow, Keely. Keep me in your dreams."

"See ya." I made no promises about my dreams.

I thought I'd fall into a profound sleep as soon as my head hit the pillow, but no. I squirmed and tossed on the bed as crazy garbled scenes played through my mind like reruns on late-night TV. One minute I stood back on *The Vitamin Sea* with Jude swearing and threatening me, slapping me, hurting me, and the next moment I sat in Punt's apartment lost in his deep kiss and wondering why it tasted of Chardonnay-flavored peanut butter and jelly.

At first, the rapping on my door reminded me of thunder and hurricane warnings. Then Gram's voice brought the early morning into sharper focus. Wednesday. No today was Thursday. That's right. Thursday.

"Keely! Keely! Open door. I bring news."

Flinging back the covers, I finger combed my hair, thrust my arms into a robe, and padded barefoot to the door.

"Come in, Gram." I stepped back. "What time is it?" I glanced at my watch. "Gram! It's only seven o'clock."

"Dress quickly, child. Mr. Moore come here last night. I tell him you out. Although you no tell me where you be. None of his business where you be."

I ignored the guilt trip Gram tried to lay on me. "Mr. Moore? Oh, my. What did he want?" I could think of a lot of things he might want, but I hoped Gram could be specific.

"He no tell me what he want."

Sometimes Gram likes to be begged for information. I begged, hoping it would delay her from asking where I'd been last night. Usually I kept little from Gram, but right now I wasn't ready to tell her anything about Punt—or my encounter with Jude. I wanted to know what Mr. Moore had said. Did he blame me for burning down his house?

"Did he seem angry and upset?" I asked.

"You decide for yourself."

Sometimes I think Gram deliberately tries to irritate me as another part of her guilt trip syndrome. "How can I decide anything about his mood or his feelings when I didn't see him?"

"He return soon. He tell me that. He say he return early morning. Get dressed. Pronto."

"Sit down, Gram. We'll talk while I'm dressing." I picked up the jeans and shirt I'd worn yesterday, then shoved them aside as they brought back too many memories of Jude—and Punt. Besides, I wore khaki jumpsuits for work and a Thursday meant a workday. I found fresh underwear, a clean jumpsuit, and slipped them on, and as I sat giving my tangled hair another comb, the phone rang.

"Maybe Mr. Moore call you," Gram said.

"Miss Moreno?" a familiar voice asked. "Gladys Blackburn here."

"Yes, Miss Blackburn. How may I help you?"

"I'm calling to cancel my morning appointment. Have to make an . . . an unexpected trip to Miami. I hate to foul up your schedule like this. I would have called you sooner, but . . ."

"Don't worry about it, Miss Blackburn. Emergencies come up now and then. Would you like to reschedule?"

For a moment the line hummed, then Miss Blackburn cleared her throat and the line hummed again before she spoke. "I'd rather not reschedule right at this time. May I call you for a make-up appointment later?"

"That'll be fine. Thanks for letting me know your change of plans."

I hung up, knowing I'd probably face a lot of cancellations. People dislike being associated with suspects in a murder case.

I rammed my feet into sandals as another knock sounded.

"Mr. Moore. There he be, Keely. I stay here. Want to know what he say about house fire."

I didn't argue, but when I opened the door, Punt smiled down at me, dangling my chain and ring on his forefinger. "Found this in my car. Didn't want you to worry about it and I knew you'd be concerned once you missed it."

"Oh, thank you, thank you. I hadn't missed it yet, but I would have. And soon. Come on in."

Punt stepped inside. "Morning, Celia." He nodded to Gram. "You closed today, or can I get some espresso?"

"No be closed. Plenty of espresso. Come with me."

As Gram started to leave, we all drew in quick breaths when we saw Detective Curry standing on the sidewalk ready to knock on the door. He stepped inside without invitation and Gram, Punt, and I backed up and stood staring at him. Something inside me shriveled and died each time I encountered this man. After all my problems with Jude, I doubted I could ever feel at ease with police authorities. Did this detective plan to haul me in for questioning—again? If so, what for this time?

"Won't you come in?" I asked at last, although he already stood inside.

"Have you heard the news?" His laser-beam gaze cut directly toward me.

"Gram's told me that Mr. Moore's in town and plans to see me this morning. Is that the news you mean?"

"No. It . . . is . . . not."

Let's not play guessing games. I wanted to shout those words at him, but I choked them back. No point in irritating the police unnecessarily.

For a moment the four of us stood waiting in a suffocating silence I could hardly bear. Then Detective Curry spoke again.

"Jude Cardell died last night."

Chapter 26

That's all he said, and his words hung in the room like time bombs sizzling and ready to explode. Shock sent my mind, my body into standby mode, and faraway sounds crept in, momentarily blotting out Curry's words and his message. A rooster crowed. My refrigerator hummed. The rooster crowed again. Seconds passed before I could make myself speak.

"What happened to him?" I asked.

"When did you see him last?"

Curry's gaze bored directly into me as he hurled his question, and my heart plunged to my toes. I knew I had to reply. He'd already told me his questions were informal and that I could always refuse to answer. Hah! We both knew I could refuse to reply only if I wanted to heap suspicion upon myself.

My throat felt cotton dry and I wondered if I could speak. I hated his answering my question with another question. Did he plan to blame Jude's death on me? Is that why he had come here so early in the morning? Questions raced through my mind. Did Curry plan to point out for a third time my seeming predilection for tragedy? I delayed answering him as long as I could. When I spoke, I chose my words carefully, trying to reveal as little concerning yesterday afternoon's encounter with Jude as I could without appearing evasive.

"I saw Jude for a few minutes yesterday afternoon when I went out fishing west of the harbor."

"Had you planned the meeting?"

"No. We met by accident." I doubted that. I felt sure Jude had stalked me into my well-hidden cove, but I refused to tell Curry that. He would call my feelings speculation.

"An unplanned meeting, right?"

"Right."

Then Punt spoke up. "What happened to Jude? How did he die?"

"Boating accident," Curry snapped his reply, and his gaze probed into each of our faces in turn. Even Gram squirmed. Again, nobody spoke. At last Curry's gaze rested on me.

I could imagine Jude killing himself by revving his motor to top speed and accidentally ramming some submerged boat or underwater coral formation. I could also imagine him ramming another boat on purpose, using a super-clever maneuver that would avoid great bodily injury to himself or his boat. I said nothing, and Punt broke the silence.

"What sort of an accident, Detective Curry? Jude defied all safety rules. All the locals know he raced his boat on the water like a crazy man, but what happened this time?"

"Marine Patrol found him this morning. Slumped in his boat. Empty gas tank. He lay dead from a single head wound."

"A bullet wound?" Punt asked.

"No. A wound from a blunt object. It appeared he'd left his anchor line tied to a stern cleat while running at high speed."

I forced myself to keep a blank face when I realized I'd accidentally caused Jude's death. Accidentally? I'd wished to harm him, hadn't I? But wishing couldn't make that sort of an accident happen. I admitted that to myself, glad that all I could read on Gram's face was surprise and shock.

"The anchor line thing caused his death, his head wound?" Punt asked.

"That's the Marine Patrol's opinion." Detective Curry jingled some change in his pocket. "The police aren't questioning the patrol officer's word. Over many months, the police department's had complaints about Jude's reckless handling of his boat."

"As a kid in a powerboat safety class, I learned to tether the anchor line to a cleat only when I cast the anchor," Punt said. "I learned to untie the line once I hauled the anchor back aboard, but I don't remember the why behind the rule."

"The Marine Patrol officer said Jude must have been traveling at such a high speed that waves caught his tethered anchor line, yanking it and the anchor into the sea. They speculate the fifteen-pounder smacked the water surface so hard and in such a way that it ricocheted and struck Jude's head. Instant death—that's what the medical examiner said. The Marine Patrol officer guessed that without Jude at the wheel, the boat ran untended until the gasoline tank emptied."

Tears suddenly streamed down my cheeks and I made no move to stop them or to dry them. Tears of relief. My worries about Jude were over.

"You still have feelings for Jude Cardell?" Detective Curry eyed my tears.

I didn't respond. Any words of sorrow would have been lies. Any words of glee might turn out to be incriminating. I kept my silence as I found a tissue and dried my eyes. Let Detective Curry think what he liked. Let him draw his own conclusions.

"I dance the habanera on his grave," Gram muttered.

"Count me in as her partner." Punt eased closer to me, slipping his arm around my waist and pulling me close.

Detective Curry shrugged and turned toward the door. "I'll leave you people alone with your thoughts for now, but I felt sure you'd be, perhaps, more than interested in the news about Jude."

What did he mean *more than interested?* Detective Curry

might represent our police department, he might represent our tax dollars at work, but I didn't trust him to have my best interest at heart. No way.

Nobody said thank you to Curry. Nobody saw him to the door. I didn't even worry about what he might be thinking.

"Maybe we all need a cup of espresso," Punt said after Detective Curry left.

"Agreed." I spoke just as the phone rang again and another patient cancelled. I sighed. At least my patients had the courtesy to call me rather than to let me sit waiting for them.

I left the CLOSED sign in my office window, left the drapery drawn. I might as well close my office as long as the Ashford case dominated the news, or until the court vindicated me. I started to follow Gram and Punt to the coffee shop when I saw Mr. Moore hurrying along the sidewalk toward us.

The word "round" bounced in my mind whenever I saw Mr. Moore. His moon-like smiley face blended into a pudgy neck and a beach ball figure, and his black walking shorts accented his pasty white skin in a way that shouted TOURIST.

I straightened my shoulders and lifted my chin as if by towering over him I could calm the jittery feeling in my stomach. What could I say if he blamed that fire on my negligence? At least he hadn't brought his wife with him. Facing one person would be easier than facing two.

"Am I interrupting something?" he asked, stepping into my office and seeing everyone preparing to leave.

"You're not interrupting a thing," I fibbed. "You've already met my grandmother, and this is my friend Punt Ashford." The men shook hands, and then I nodded to Gram and Punt. "I understand Mr. Moore needs to talk to me this morning. If you'll excuse us, please?"

"I'm inviting Keely to breakfast," Mr. Moore said. "Forgive me for not including you all, but Keely and I need to talk about that fire. I have to turn in my rental car and catch a plane for Miami this afternoon. So with your permission . . ."

"No problem," Punt said. "Glad to have met you, sir."

I could tell from the way Gram stood wringing her hands she would have liked to have accompanied us to breakfast. I avoided her gaze. She has a way of getting what she wants, and I wanted my conversation with Mr. Moore to be a private one. My ribs and my jaw still felt battered from yesterday's happenings, and in spite of my relief at hearing of Jude's death, my mind felt battered, too. I guessed it would please Detective Curry to be able to blame Jude's death on me. Perhaps he'd continue working on that angle. A person never knows what goes on in a detective's mind.

Now I had to face Mr. Moore and discuss the fire on Georgia Street.

Chapter 27

On this early Thursday morning few tourists were out and about. Mr. Moore led the way to his car parked close by and helped me inside before he walked to the driver's side and struggled to fit his bulk beneath the wheel.

"Where can we get a good breakfast?" he asked. "Your choice, but I like a hearty meal. No ladies' tea room, please."

"I seldom have the privilege of eating breakfast anywhere except in my own kitchen, but *The Wharf* has a good reputation with both the locals and the tourists. Would you like to give it a try? In addition to good food, there's a special opening display of lavender hibiscus plants scheduled for today."

"Love good food. Love hibiscus no matter what color. Point me to *The Wharf,* please."

"It's a plan." I gave him directions and we drove the short distance to the restaurant. The crowded parking lot warned us we might have to seek breakfast elsewhere, and the fragrance of bacon and pancakes greeted us even before we stepped into the bright interior. While light flooded through the floor-to-ceiling windows that overlooked Hawk Channel, Mr. Moore admired the lavender hibiscus murals a local artist had painted especially for the opening display of Jass's prize-winning plants.

"A lovely spot," he said, smiling.

"Agreed." We both admired the dwarf hibiscus plants set in decorator pots and placed on rattan pedestals around the walls of the dining area.

A glance told me that patrons not only occupied all the

tables with window views, but also most of the other tables as well. It surprised me to see Shandy thread her way through the diners as she approached us.

"Good morning, Keely. I can have a window table for you if you're willing to wait a few minutes."

"Let's wait, shall we?" Mr. Moore asked. "Don't get these sea views in North Dakota."

"Fine with me. Mr. Moore, I'd like you to meet Shandy Koffan, one of my reflexology patients and also Jass Ashford's aide at her greenhouse. Shandy, this's Mr. Moore—my former landlord on Georgia Street." They nodded politely to each other. "I'm surprised to see you here this morning, Shandy. Shandy usually works a night shift," I explained to Mr. Moore.

"I'm pinch-hitting this morning. We're expecting a big crowd today for the first local showing of Jass's plants, so the manager hired a few extra helpers."

We waited only a few moments before Shandy led us to a table for two next to the window, seated us, and placed menus before us. Although the slightly tinted windows diminished the glare of sun against sea, some patrons still wore sunglasses. Others had asked their waitress to lower a scrim of see-through silk between them and the brightness.

In the distance a gray tanker moved across the horizon, and only a bit closer to shore three shrimp boats lay at anchor, their outriggers giving them the look of giant insects silhouetted against the sky. Almost directly below us a windsurfer struggled to remount his board and pull its red sail from the water.

"Would you care for coffee?" Sandy asked, carafe in hand.

We both nodded, then Mr. Moore looked at me. "What would you like to order, Keely? Is there a breakfast specialty of the house?"

"I hear everything's special, but I'd like a toasted bagel to go with my coffee and papaya with lime, please."

Mr. Moore ordered orange juice, bacon, eggs, pancakes, and a double serving of French toast. Somehow that didn't surprise me.

"Well, the fire inspector says no to arson," Mr. Moore said, getting right to the subject of the fire.

"That's good news." I added a bit more sugar to my coffee.

"The wife and I were disappointed to lose the property, but we knew of the home's poor condition when we bought it. That's why we got it at such a good price."

Six hundred thousand didn't seem like much of a bargain to me, but I didn't comment. Tourists and locals frequently see property values from different viewpoints.

"We hoped that by spending another hundred thou or so for remodeling, we could enjoy a comfortable vacation place that offered excellent resale possibilities should we ever decide to sell. The fire inspector said that Hurricane Georges had damaged the roof—that happened only a few years ago, right?"

"Right, but Key West lucked out. The brunt of the storm hit Big Pine Key and Cudjoe. The eye swirled over Key West, and the worst of the winds usually hit to the north of the eye."

"Yes, I suppose Key West did feel lucky—if there is any luck besides bad luck where hurricanes are involved."

We talked for a few moments more before Shandy served our meals. Mr. Moore poured apricot syrup over his French toast and dug in, enjoying several large bites before he spoke again.

"At any rate, the house's former owner chose to sell the place rather than to repair the damage."

"Many property owners feel that way after a hurricane," I

said, "especially if they've suffered through several bad storms."

"I can understand that." Mr. Moore started on his bacon and eggs while I sipped my coffee and tested the papaya. At last he continued. "The fire inspector said that during the passing years, water seeped through the roof every time it rained, dampening the electric wiring. I know nothing about that sort of thing, but his assessment sounds reasonable. He also said that during those years of neglect, the covering on the wires rotted and eventually bare wires made contact with each other, shorted out, and emitted sparks that started the blaze."

I wondered how the inspector could guarantee that as the answer. I felt almost sure Jude had started the fire, but maybe I liked to blame Jude for all the bad happenings in my life.

"I'm sorry Punt and I drove to Key Colony that night, Mr. Moore. If I'd been home, I could have called the fire department and maybe they could have saved the house."

"You needn't apologize. We didn't expect you to keep a round-the-clock vigil. The wife and I are glad you were away, out of danger."

The wife. Mr. Moore irritated me, speaking as if his wife didn't have a name of her own, as if she were merely one of his many possessions. I wondered if *the wife* called him *the husband* when she mentioned him to others. We stopped talking as Shandy refilled our coffee cups, and it surprised me when Mr. Moore stopped her and engaged her in conversation.

"Is Key West your home, Miss?" he asked.

"Yes, it is."

"You lived here a long time?"

"For a few years."

"You like it, right?"

"Very much, sir."

Shandy ducked her head in that shy mannerism she frequently used, and I could tell she wanted to avoid more chit-chat with this stranger. Mr. Moore failed to get her signal.

"Where did you live before you discovered the Keys?" he asked.

"Iowa, sir."

She didn't elaborate on those two terse words, but again Mr. Moore didn't take the hint.

"Guess Iowa has some pretty cold winters, right?"

"Right."

I saw the relief on Shandy's face when a customer at another table signaled for her attention. I felt sorry for anyone so shy she couldn't make a little small talk with customers who might leave generous tips. I also felt a growing irritation at Mr. Moore, who must have noticed Shandy's reluctance to talk.

"Excuse me, please," Shandy said as she hurried to the beckoning customer.

"Certainly." Mr. Moore's gaze followed her for a few moments, then he turned his attention back to me.

"The insurance company's offered a fair settlement for the house, so I'm trying to tie up the legal end of things here today—sign papers and all that."

"I'm so sorry all your wonderful plans turned out this way. Will you look for another property to buy?"

"We're not sure." He sighed. "This's been a blow to the wife. She's always wanted a retirement home where it's warm in the winter. Centerville, North Dakota doesn't offer much along those lines."

"Can't understand why people live in such cold places." I smiled and gave a mock shudder.

"Many times it's because they were born there. That's it in my case. Born and raised in Centerville—near Fargo. My family owned a small TV station and I inherited it."

"A TV station! Wow! That sounds exciting enough to make Centerville an attractive place to live in spite of the cold."

Mr. Moore worked on his pancakes a few moments before he replied. "I've made a good living with the station, but you know . . ."

"What?" I prompted.

"I've always wanted to be a private detective. Never made a big issue of it to my folks—or to the wife. My dad would have been quick to ridicule the idea since I had a going business dropped right into my lap, and the wife would probably have agreed with him."

"I suppose so." I added a squeeze of lime juice to my papaya. I'd dreaded this talk with Mr. Moore, but now I lightened up. Mr. Moore had erased my guilt feelings by sharing the fire inspector's take on the blaze and the insurance company's plan to pay off without argument or lawsuit. Now with Jude dead, I saw no point in mentioning the black sweatshirt.

I felt more relaxed now, and I decided I liked sitting here enjoying a tasty breakfast and talking to Mr. Moore more than I'd like returning to my office to answer cancellation calls. Sooner or later I knew I had to face the fact that Jude's death might narrow our list of murder suspects. On the other hand, just because Jude was dead didn't eliminate him as a suspect. The sweet papaya helped me avoid thinking and wondering about whom else might want to see me blamed for Margaux's death. At least Mr. Moore hadn't mentioned the Ashford murder.

"I did do one thing to pander to my desire to be a detective."

Mr. Moore's voice snapped me back to attention, and I asked the question he obviously expected. "What did you do?"

Chapter 28

Mr. Moore hesitated a few moments before he spoke, almost as if he were reluctant to answer me. I wondered if I had accidentally touched on a sore spot or pried into subject matter he preferred to avoid. Yet his words had invited my question, and I prepared to listen to his answer, full of curiosity by now. He took a long look around the room and then glanced over his shoulder as if he were afraid someone might be trying to overhear our conversation. I let my gaze follow his, but I saw nobody that looked remotely interested in us or our talk.

"Keely, I organized and now direct a local thirty-minute TV program called *Centerville's Most Wanted.* You're right if you've guessed the program's patterned after John Walsh's Saturday night program—*America's Most Wanted.* I've even corresponded with Mr. Walsh, asked his advice on airing my material. Of course, I keep my show in a time slot that doesn't conflict with his program."

I smiled, wondering if John Walsh would consider a local program in Centerville, North Dakota strong competition. I also smiled because I liked Mr. Moore's idea, even liking the butter-ball of a man a bit better than I had a few minutes ago. He showed a lot spunk and creative thinking. I admired that. He'd gone after what he wanted even when his family opposed his idea, and he'd managed to please them as well as himself. We had a few things in common.

"You mean that Centerville, North Dakota has enough major crime to fill a half-hour show once a week?"

He chuckled. "Well, my show featured a murder five years ago, and a kidnapping three years ago, but I have to admit that most of the crimes we highlight involve hit-and-runs, snatch and grabs, missing persons—who usually turn out to be voluntary runaways. I guess the crime my program highlights only seems major to the victims."

"That's usually the case, isn't it? People are most concerned about stuff that involves them personally."

"Right, but the public likes my program. I host it myself and my friends tell me they enjoy that. Also, the police chief has released annual statistics that show crime in Centerville has dropped in the last few years. I find that rewarding in many respects."

"I think that's great. It makes a person feel good to know his work makes a difference. I know how important that is to a person's mental well-being. I speak from experience."

I'd thought my comment might end our conversation. I really had no deep interest in crime, major or minor, in Centerville, North Dakota. I'd finished my bagel and papaya and Mr. Moore had pretty much worked his way through his meal, but he cleared his throat and signaled Shandy, pointing to his coffee cup. This time when she arrived, he looked at her closely, but he didn't try for another conversation. Shandy refilled my cup too. When we thanked her, she went on about her business.

"How long have you known Shandy?" he asked.

"Several years. She's been my reflexology patient for about two years. She's a nice person, a quiet and shy person usually, but she created a bit of a stir on the island when she married Otto Koffan."

"How so?" Mr. Moore leaned forward.

I don't usually engage in idle gossip, but Margaux's murder had pulled the Koffans to the front of my mind. Now that Jude lay dead, Shandy and Otto had moved up on the list of suspects that Punt and I wanted to investigate. Maybe I should re-check Consuela's alibi. Or maybe Nikko's. But no. I couldn't believe Nikko killed Margaux. I didn't realize I'd let my mind wander until Mr. Moore spoke again.

"I sense a reluctance to reply." He smiled, but I knew he wanted to hear about Shandy and Otto.

I made it brief, skirting around Margaux's murder with as few words as possible. "When Beau Ashford lost his first wife to cancer, and began dating Margaux Koffan, she divorced her husband, Otto. He quickly rebounded into Shandy's arms and they married. At first, after Margaux's murder there were only whispers, but the gossip grew. People talk. Even people in Key West who usually take things in stride."

I thought Mr. Moore would ask more about Margaux's murder. His next words surprised me and spared me from having to talk more about Margaux . . .

"What was Shandy's name before she married Otto?"

"Let's see . . . Shandy Mertz. Yes, Mertz, that's it. Why are you so interested in Shandy? I think she's done well as our waitress. Our service this morning's certainly been excellent." I hoped he wasn't going to report Shandy to the manager for some infraction I hadn't noticed.

Mr. Moore reached for his billfold and pulled out a blurred photo of a woman and slid it across the table to me. "Have you ever seen this woman before? Look carefully, now. This's important to me."

I studied the picture. "No, I don't believe I've ever seen this person. I don't recognize her. Should I?"

Now Mr. Moore's gaze bored into mine. "She reminds me a bit of our waitress, Shandy."

I studied the picture more carefully. Then I pushed it back toward him and shook my head. "I can't see it. Can't see any resemblance at all. The woman in the picture has long dark hair and blue eyes. As you can see, Shandy Koffan has short blonde hair and brown eyes. This woman's almost fat. Her cheeks are well filled out. Shandy's slim and her face's almost a perfect oval—thin."

"People can diet. Hair can be bleached. Hair can be cut. Eye color can be changed with contact lenses. Do you notice any similarity at all?"

Again I pulled the picture toward me and scrutinized the woman's features. "I'm sorry, Mr. Moore, but I see no similarity at all. None." I wanted to suggest that he was letting his detective urge get the better of him, but I corked that comment.

"Look right here." He placed his thumbnail on a tiny heart-shaped scar near the woman's right eye. "I consider this a very unusual scar, and Shandy has a scar similar to it."

"I've never noticed such a scar on Shandy's face, and I see her frequently in my office. Are you sure?"

He started to signal Shandy for more coffee, but we both looked all around the dining area and couldn't see her.

"Maybe she's taking a break," he said. "Do you have time to wait 'til she returns?"

"Of course." I turned the conversation to Jass's plants, her blue ribbon. No point in telling him more about Margaux's murder or of my being a suspect. I guessed that Key West crime seldom made headlines in Centerville, North Dakota.

The breakfast hour was drawing to a close and nobody stood in line waiting for our table, so we asked another waitress to refill our cups and we waited.

When Shandy returned to the area, Mr. Moore saw her first and quickly beckoned her to our table.

"Our check, please, Shandy."

We both studied her face carefully as she pulled out her pad and pencil and tallied our bill. I saw no sign of a heart-shaped scar. Mr. Moore said nothing as he left her a generous tip on the table and went to the cash register to pay the bill. Once we were back in his car, he shook his head and sighed.

"I must have been mistaken. Must have been the early morning lighting in the room. I thought I saw a scar when we she first showed us to a table, but I admit there's no sign of a scar now. Of course she could have repaired her makeup while she took a break, could have hidden it under some of that goop on her face."

I smiled, but he had aroused my curiosity. "Is that woman in your picture one of Centerville's most wanted?"

"Right. She most certainly is. We think her name's Sal Mitchell and she's wanted for a capital crime now forgotten by most people—forgotten except by the ones directly involved, directly affected."

"What'd she do?"

"She drove the getaway car for bank robbers when they hit a branch bank in Fargo. The outside surveillance camera caught the woman on film and I had her likeness blown up so I could study it better. I intend to bring that woman to justice sooner or later. She might help us solve that crime. A bank customer lost his life that day—my father."

"Oh. I'm so sorry to hear that." Suddenly I felt a common bond with Mr. Moore. We'd both lost a parent to a gunman. Now I could understand his deep need to detect crime, to run an anti-crime show on his TV station. "Did the police catch any of the robbers?"

"One died on the spot—shot dead by the police. One escaped in the getaway car. Police found the abandoned vehicle later, but the robber and the car's driver are still at large and in hiding. They may have left the country. I know all too well the case's cold, but it's still very much open to investigation."

"If I see any clues, I'll call you up north, but I doubt if Shandy Koffan is the woman you're looking for."

"You remember that promise. Call collect. It would give me great satisfaction to help the police solve this case. I've a feeling they've really shoved it onto a back burner."

Mr. Moore returned me to my office and double-parked long enough for me to get out. Car horns blared, but he paid no attention.

"Thank you for our visit, Keely." He leaned over to call to me through the open window.

"And I thank you for a lovely breakfast." I waved goodbye and he drove off toward the airport, leaving me to think more deeply about Shandy Koffan.

Chapter 29

When I left Mr. Moore's car, Punt beckoned to me from where he sat sipping espresso at Gram's coffee bar. I joined him although my slightly queasy stomach and my shaking hands told me I'd already had more than enough coffee. Gram stood pouring steaming water into the cappuccino machine and I knew she had an ear carefully tuned to our conversation.

"How'd it go?" Punt asked. "Did he want your head on a platter?"

I pulled myself onto a high stool beside Punt's. "No head. No platter. The insurance people have promised payment, and he's satisfied that once the loose ends are tied up, he'll receive adequate compensation."

"He buy another place?" Gram asked. "Another fixer-upper? Market sky high. Fixer-upper help hard to find."

"So what else's new?" I grinned at Gram. "Key West real estate's always sky high. You snagged the only bargain on this island over thirty years ago."

"Fixer-uppers hard to find, and fixer-upper helpers only work no-fishing days," Gram said.

"Right, Celia." Punt grinned and nodded. "Given a bright sun, a smooth sea, and calm winds, red-blooded locals float their boats and bait their hooks." Then Punt looked back at me. "Did Mr. Moore tell you his plans?" Punt's simple question belied the curiosity only partly hidden in his eyes.

"No. He and 'the wife' need to think about the situation at greater length. He didn't blame me for the fire and it relieved him to know I'd escaped injury. He's really an interesting person in spite of his sometimes chauvinistic attitude."

Punt smiled. "He didn't seem like your type to me, Keely. You holding back something we should know?"

"Nothing big, but I found it interesting that he produces a half-hour TV show in North Dakota—*Centerville's Most Wanted.*"

"I suppose they have crime there, too." Punt slid from his bar stool. "Have time for a short ride, Keely? Got something to show you."

"Sure. Where's this something?" I wanted to share Mr. Moore's interest in Shandy with Punt, but not in front of Gram, who'd disliked Shandy from the get-go.

"Car's around back." Punt led the way. "Let's take it. Your office locked?"

I nodded. "Tell me where we're going. You're being very mysterious."

As we slid into the Karmann Ghia, I smiled at my mental picture of Mr. Moore trying to fit himself into Punt's convertible. Surely the man had to reserve large-size rentals. The people at Avis and Hertz probably loved to see him coming. I stopped smiling as Punt hesitated before starting the motor.

"Okay, come clean. Did you talk to Mr. Moore about the sweatshirt?"

"No. He felt satisfied the insurance people planned to treat him fairly and that fire inspectors had proved beyond a doubt the fire started in the attic from faulty wiring. After hearing his take on the situation, I agreed. No point in arguing with the fire inspectors or the insurance company."

"We know Jude had been there."

"Right, but think back, Punt. On the afternoon before the fire, Jude followed us onto Highway 1, ready to give us a bad time. You outsmarted him with your unexpected turn onto Big Pine."

"You're saying he hated being outsmarted, right?"

"Right. I think he returned to Georgia Street planning to scare the bejabbers out of me that night after I got home. I could almost read his mind. He may have discovered the fire much as we did—by surprise."

"You're convinced the fire inspector called it right—faulty wiring?"

"Yes, and so is Mr. Moore. Since Jude's dead, I saw no point in mentioning him."

"You're probably right." Punt started the car and headed west, pausing at a corner when a Conch Train loaded with sunburned tourists rattled onto Whitehead Street. Its driver told his passengers that years ago Key West had offered one free hotel—the county jail. I turned off my ears, refusing to listen to his stale jokes, but the tourists laughed along with him.

"Where you taking me?" Punt had turned onto a side street too narrow even for the Karmann Ghia if we met another car. He parked in a slot that seemed to be waiting for us, a slot too small for larger cars.

"This's my new place of business." Punt pointed to an office with a front barely ten feet wide.

"*Fotopoulos & Ashford,*" I read the bold lettering on the window. "You and Nikko are serious about the P.I. business?"

"Of course we're serious and we want to get started right away. Follow me and I'll show you inside our office." Punt opened the car door for me and I trailed after him into the narrow building, gasping in surprise when Nikko with Moose at his heel came strolling from a back room. The narrow office stretched twenty feet or so to a partition and the air smelled of turpentine and fresh paint.

White walls. Vertical window blinds. Poured terrazzo floors common in Key West twenty or thirty years ago. The austere furnishings consisted of two roll-top desks with captains' chairs, two straight chairs positioned in front of the desks, a four-drawer steel file, and a huge safe bolted to the floor next to the file.

"Good morning," Nikko said, grinning.

"Good morning, Nikko. It looks as if congratulations are in order."

Nikko handed me a business card and pointed to a framed certificate hanging on the wall behind one desk. I read the card and walked closer to the certificate. "Nikko Fotopoulos, Private Investigator." I checked the wall behind the other desk.

"I told you I don't have a license yet," Punt said, "but I've applied for one and Nikko's going to help me meet the requirements necessary to earning it."

"*Fotopoulos & Ashford,* Private Investigators." I let the idea roll around in my mind. "It's wonderful, guys. Really wonderful. How soon will you open for business?"

"We're open as we speak," Punt said. "Have you come to us with a problem, ma'am? We'll expect a retainer, of course." Punt stepped toward me and put his arm around my waist, pulling me close. "This makes me a working man, Keely. A man with a job."

I gave Punt a kiss on the cheek before I eased from him and placed a similar kiss on Nikko's cheek. "This's really exciting. Beau said the other day that he might hire a private detective to investigate Margaux's death. Does he know you two are open for business?"

"No," Punt said. "You and Jass are the first ones we've told."

"I'm honored."

"I think Celia suspects we're up to something," Nikko said.

"Gram always suspects men are up to something. She's uncanny that way. When'll you give her the news?"

"The *Citizen* will carry an official announcement tomorrow," Punt said. "I'd like to tell Celia and a few others before they read it there."

"It'll be announced on local TV and radio tomorrow, too," Nikko said.

"Have you resigned as chef at *The Wharf?*" I asked.

"No way." Nikko grinned. "I love to cook, and a guy hears a lot of talk working at a popular restaurant. We'll need all the contacts we can get. Punt'll keep his eyes and ears open over at Smathers."

I rolled my eyes at that comment, but I had to admit that Punt probably knew all the locals that hung out at the beach. Sometimes the locals picked up information about newcomers. "You do plan to spend some time in your office, I suppose."

"Oh, definitely," Punt said. "Maybe not regular office hours, but at least one of us will be here most of the time."

"And Moose'll be here all of the time," Nikko added. "He's going to be our silent partner."

"Moose has more seniority than I do—for right now at least." Punt leaned to give Moose a scratch behind the ears. "Don't know if I like playing second fiddle to a dog."

"Does Moose still remember all his tricks after being in retirement?" I asked.

"No tricks," Punt said. "Working commands. Yes, Moose remembers. We've been testing him with some potentially dangerous situations, and he's come through for us every time."

"You've never seen Moose at work," Nikko said. "Want a demonstration?"

"I'm not sure." I backed away from Moose. I'd never been

afraid of him, but I'd always considered him a pet, never a working police dog. "I guess I really hate admitting he might attack someone."

"You needn't worry," Nikko said. "Moose won't attack unless I give him the command. For the most part we'll use him for tracking human scent. That's the focus of his primary training, but watch this. Punt and I were putting Moose through his paces yesterday. Punt, slip on that old sweatshirt, okay?"

Punt stepped into the back room and returned wearing a heavy shirt over his tank top.

"Now here's the scene," Nikko said. "I've nabbed a bad guy and I'm about to cuff him."

Punt stood near the window, both hands behind his back. Nikko pretended to start placing handcuffs on his wrists when suddenly Punt turned and began attacking Nikko with his fist.

"Moose!" Nikko called.

I jumped back as Moose sprang at Punt, grabbed the sleeve of his sweatshirt and brought him to the floor. Swift. Final. The attack ended.

Punt lay quietly in Moose's grip, and Moose held him in place without biting until Nikko's next command released him. Once Punt stood, Nikko gave Moose a doggy treat from his pocket.

"Wow!" I could hardly catch my breath, the attack had seemed so realistic. "How long did it take you to train him to do that?"

"Oh, six months or so. A housewife up north who loves working with dogs gave Moose his basic training. Many dogs flunk out before they get to actual police training, but Moose hung in there."

Nikko tried to act nonchalant, but I saw pride and confidence in the way both he and Moose all but strutted around the office following their performance. I examined Punt's arm. It showed only a couple of red marks and no broken skin. The sweatshirt had taken the brunt of the attack.

"Maybe Punt needs a dog, too," I said.

"No." Nikko shook his head. "Dogs so highly trained have big egos. Two big egos seldom tolerate each other. Moose will be our only silent partner. Want to see another bad guy situation?"

"No thanks. Not today." I backed away from the dog.

"Well, don't be afraid of Moose. He's the same dog you've known all along. He's a wonderful house pet in addition to being trained in tracking and attacking. From now on this office will be Moose's home."

"How so?" I eyed Moose warily.

"Give him a pat," Nikko said. "I don't want you to develop a fear of him."

Tentatively, I reached out my hand and Moose raised his head to make contact with me. After giving him a few ear scratches, I relaxed. We were still pals.

"You're going to leave Moose here to guard your office?" I asked. "I suppose a guard's a good idea once you get working on some cases."

"Moose won't be here alone. There's apartment space back of the partition. I plan to move in." Nikko led the way through the doorway to the back of the building where I saw kitchen appliances, a small bathroom with shower, and adequate space for living room furniture.

"An on-the-scene apartment makes sense," I said. "No point in paying two rentals when one's enough. I'll miss you overhead at my place, though, and so will Gram. Your presence on Duval always made us feel safe."

"I'll only be a phone call away," Nikko promised.

When someone knocked on the front door, we all snapped to attention.

"A customer already!" I said. But no. Nikko opened the door to a man wearing a hat with a phone company logo.

"I'm here to install your phone," he said.

"Great." Punt stepped forward. "We'll need private lines to phones on each desk plus one extension to an apartment phone in back. Can you give us a cost estimate?"

I returned to Punt's car, smiling and wondering if it was the first time Punt had ever shown more than a casual interest in the cost of anything. It must have been an effort. When the telephone man left, Punt joined me in the car.

"What do you think? What's your honest opinion of our chances with a P.I. agency?"

"I'm flattered that you think I have the answer to that one. I know nothing about detective agencies."

"Perhaps not, but you started a business from scratch. You know the ropes—the pitfalls."

I grinned at him. "Most of my scratch came from your dad—startup money and all that. It took me a while to repay him."

"We'll have the advantage of my trust fund for startup money, but Nikko's already insisting we watch expenses like misers. He's determined for *Fotopoulos & Ashford* to be a financial success as well as a success in solving crimes. How do you like our location?"

"It's sort of out of the way. Might be hard for customers to find."

"We feel that's an advantage. People who need a private detective will find us. We'll be listed in the phone book. Clients might avoid patronizing a detective agency if they had to approach it from a main street entrance where anyone could notice."

"I suppose that's true. I've never considered hiring a P.I."

"There's one thing very special about our office that you haven't commented on. What do you think?"

"Maybe I need to go back inside and take a second look."

"No, you can see it from here."

"The office window?" I asked. "It only gives your names. It doesn't identify your type of business."

"No, that's not what I had in mind. We're still sort of in disagreement on the window, though. I think we need to add 'Private Detectives,' but Nikko thinks people will have been referred here by someone else. He believes the window with only our names will offer clients more privacy."

"Could be."

"Have you noticed where I've parked?"

"Sure. Right at the side of your business."

"That's a very special thing. We have this slot and two more slots especially reserved for us. That makes easy parking for each of us and also one for a client."

"Hey, that *is* wonderful. Really big time. It's better than I have on Duval Street."

Punt leaned to give me a long kiss and I returned it in kind. "I'm really proud of you, Punt."

"The business brings our lifestyles a little closer together, right?"

"Right. I can't deny it." Punt drew me into another kiss that we held until a kid on a skateboard slapped the trunk of the car, making us jump.

"Way to go, guy," he called over his shoulder as he sped down the street dodging pedestrians and cars.

"I have a favor to ask, Keely."

"Okay. Name it."

"Go with me to Dad's house, will you? Help me break the news about *Fotopoulos & Ashford?*"

"You mean he doesn't know yet?"

"I told you, you and Jass were first to know. I haven't told Dad, and I don't know how he'll take it. It would probably have pleased him if I'd asked his opinion first."

"Yes, it probably would have, but I think he'll be pleased, Punt, and I think he'll realize you've picked a great partner. You and Nikko can do a lot to help each other."

"Yeah. My money. Nikko's brains."

"A business needs both brains and money and you and Nikko can supply those things. That'll please Beau." I didn't add that I thought it'd please Beau to have his son off the beach at least part of the time, and engaged in a meaningful business that'd benefit the community. Yet, I might be wrong. Dogs weren't the only ones with big egos.

"Why not call Beau now? If he's home, we can drive right over." I pulled my new cell phone from my pocket and handed it to Punt.

Punt called and Beau invited us to his home. Slipping the car into gear, Punt headed toward Grinnell Street.

Chapter 30

We parked in front of the house, hurried past the picket fence and onto the porch where Beau met us at the door.

"You were going out?" Punt eyed his dad's black silk shirt, his white walking shorts.

"After a bit," Beau said. "Plenty of time for a visit. What brings you here this morning?" He beckoned us inside, and again he kept his back to the chair where Margaux had died as he started to lead us upstairs to his study.

"We won't delay you if you have a meeting," Punt said, stopping just inside the doorway.

I wondered if Punt was getting cold feet. Would he drive over here and then find an excuse to leave without telling Beau his big news?

"I'm getting ready to go to *The Wharf*. Going to meet Jass for lunch. This's the first Key West showing of her lavender hibiscus. She planned to make our lunch a quiet twosome, but I'm guessing it'll burgeon into something larger. Why don't you two join me? We'll make it a real celebration."

Before Punt could answer, a delivery truck parked behind the Karmann Ghia and a boy strode up the sidewalk carrying a hibiscus plant in full bloom. When he thrust it into Beau's hands, Punt tipped the boy, who pocketed the bill and hurried back to his truck.

Beau opened the card tucked among the lavender blossoms, read it, and then passed it to us. *A first for your garden with all my love, Jass.*

"How gorgeous!" I stepped back onto the porch for a moment, looking around the yard, mentally selecting a place for Beau to plant Jass's gift. I saw hibiscus plants in rainbow colors—all colors except the new lavender. I stepped back inside. "This plant really is a first for you, Beau?"

"Yes, of course. When Jass keeps a secret, she tells nobody. You probably know she kept all her experimental plants under lock and key until she knew for sure her plant had won at Miami. Now I'm guessing people'll be seeing it throughout Key West. Jass has worked and waited a long time for this success."

"She's named it *Scott's Beauty*," Beau said, "honoring her former fiancé."

Nobody said anything for a few moments, then Beau led us on to his study. Papers lay scattered on his desk and a red light glowed from the mouse beside his computer.

"What's on your mind?" Beau looked at Punt.

Punt reached for his billfold, pulled out a business card, and handed it to Beau. I knew what it was although Punt had forgotten to share one with me when we were at his new office.

"*Fotopoulos & Ashford Agency*," Beau read aloud. "Private Detectives."

For a moment Beau said nothing, and we waited. I hardly breathed, wondering what Beau's reaction would be, wondering how Punt would cope if Beau flared in anger. Maybe I shouldn't have come to witness this scene.

"It's something I'd talked Nikko into before Margaux's death," Punt said. "Her murder made us galvanize our plans, get them up and going. Our family needs more help in solving this murder than the police are offering, maybe more than they're *able* to offer. Nikko's wasting his talents at *The Wharf*. Oh, cooking can be a sideline for him, of course, a hobby. He's good at that, too, but he has the know-how to do under-cover detecting. He has Moose to help him, to help us. Key

West needs the three of us to keep the police on their toes. Nikko's going to supervise me while I qualify for my license."

Punt's super-long speech belied his calm exterior, but Beau had listened quietly to the whole thing without interrupting. Now he shook his head as if in amazement and his face lighted up with a smile that included both of us.

"Well how about this!" Beau slapped Punt on the back then shook his hand in a grip that made Punt wince. "What a wonderful surprise, Punt. I think you and Nikko will make a great detective team."

"Key West does need a detective agency," Punt said, as if he hadn't already made his point. "Now you won't have to go to Miami for help."

I wondered what would happen if Beau said he'd rather seek professional help in Miami than to deal with newcomers to the business, but how unfair of me. Nikko and Moose weren't newcomers.

"Are you going to show me your office?" Beau asked.

I could almost feel Punt relaxing, enjoying the moment. "Sure, Dad, but you were leaving to meet Jass."

"Jass doesn't know it, but I've called photographers from several newspapers to meet her and me at *The Wharf*. She can entertain them while I get a first-hand look at your new office. Lead the way and I'll follow."

We hurried back to the car and drove quickly as we could through the heavy traffic to *Fotopoulos & Ashford*. Punt grinned as both he and Beau parked in the reserved slots. Nikko welcomed us at the door, and Moose opened one eye from his napping place beside Nikko's desk.

"Congratulations, Nikko," Beau said. "Punt's told me the good news and invited me in for the grand tour."

"Thank you, sir," Nikko said. "I'll let Punt play tour guide."

I sat in the client's chair beside Nikko's desk while Punt did his thing, and when he and Beau finished talking, Beau sat down near Punt's desk.

"You two will make a go of it," Beau said. "You've got the expertise and the desire and I'm behind you all the way. May I be your first client?"

"That'd be great, Dad. We need to bring everything we know about Margaux's death into the open. Jass, Keely, and I've been discussing murder suspects since last Sunday morning. We can use your input. Right now, my big goal's to keep both you and Keely from having to face more police interrogation. Keely's business is already falling off due to negative publicity."

It seemed ages ago that Jass, Punt, and I had drawn up our list of suspects. Punt now pulled the creased sheet from his desk drawer and pushed it toward Beau. "We've eliminated a few of these people. Jass and I have strong alibis and so do you. We'll keep yours quiet as long as we can, Dad. No point in giving the police or the press any unnecessary information."

Beau flushed. "The police know, but I'd like to keep my diving fiasco out of the newspapers if I can."

"We've met a guy who'll vouch for Consuela's whereabouts last Saturday night," I said, trying to change the subject and lessen Beau's embarrassment about the diving accident.

"Is he the sort of person who'll be believed in court if he has to testify?" Beau asked.

"He's a shrimper," Punt said. "They're not the dressy kind, but maybe with a haircut, a clean shirt . . ."

"Nobody expects a working seaman to show up in a business suit, shirt, and tie." Nikko smiled at the thought. "If the guy should have to appear before a jury, we'd better let him look natural. It's the dressing up that'd alert a jury to phoniness."

"It'd help Consuela's cause if she'd stop telling everyone who'll listen how much she hated Margaux due to their unfortunate writer/editor association." Punt shook his head in frustration.

Beau nodded. "That's Consuela's way of attracting attention."

"One of her many ways," Punt added.

"Not much anyone can do to hush Consuela," Beau said. "She's out to win fame and fortune one way or another."

"If she's not careful she might win it on the witness stand," Nikko said.

"Who else's on this list?" Beau smoothed the tally of names on the desk top and pinpointed each entry with his thumbnail as he ran down the list. "Let's forget about Jude for the moment. Harley Hubble phoned me with the news about Jude earlier this morning. At least we know he's no longer a danger to anyone. Street people? You think a stranger may have shot Margaux? With Keely's gun? I think that's a stretch."

"You're probably right," Punt agreed. "At the time I thought that might be a possibility, we didn't know the murder weapon belonged to Keely."

"So that leaves Otto and Shandy Koffan." Beau refused to meet anyone's gaze. "I suppose Otto might think he had good reason to get even with Margaux."

"Jurors might think that, too," Punt said.

"I don't want to discuss Otto Koffan," Beau said. "At least if I have to discuss him, I'll do it with my lawyer beside me. I suppose it looks to the world as if I whisked Margaux from his loving arms, but it didn't happen quite like that."

"What about Shandy?" I tried to change the subject from

Otto. "She told me she went strolling on Saturday night. Even told me some of the things she saw, but so far I haven't had time to check them out." Mr. Moore's thoughts about Shandy played through my mind, but I said nothing about them.

"We need to check her alibi," Nikko said.

Beau glanced at his watch. "Listen, people. I do have to get to *The Wharf* and meet Jass." He leaned forward. "Before I go, I want to hire you two to handle this case for me. I'll help you all I can, of course, but I want you to really dig into alibis, maybe investigate people the police may overlook."

"Sure, Dad," Punt said. "That's what we hoped you'd say."

"So what's your fee?" Beau pulled a ballpoint from his pocket. "I want to sign a retainer before someone else snaps you up."

"This one's on the house, Dad. If we solve the case, the advertising will be great for our new business. Nikko and I have already talked this over."

"Giving out freebies doesn't mark the pathway to business success," Beau said. "What's your fee? You have discussed fees, haven't you? Come on, Nikko, give me the word."

Without looking to Punt for approval, Nikko said, "Our fee's five hundred dollars a day plus expenses."

"Sounds reasonable." Beau clicked his ballpoint. "Where's your business form? I'll sign it and back it up with enough cash to cover a week or so."

Nikko pulled a form from his desk drawer, filled in some names and dates, and handed it to Beau who read it, filled in a blank, and signed a check for an amount I couldn't read, but an amount that made both Punt and Nikko smile.

"This'll be day one," Beau said. "I want to know you two are hard at work while I'm dining with my beautiful daughter."

Beau stood, shook hands with Nikko, then offered his hand to Punt. As they shook hands, Beau pulled Punt to him in a warm embrace that left them both blinking back moisture.

"In the movies, they'd call that an embrace of reconciliation," Punt said.

"In real life, that's what I'd call it too." Beau gave Punt a pat on the back as Nikko pocketed the retainer and smiled. The *Fotopoulos & Ashford Agency* was off to a strong start.

Beau had his hand on the doorknob, ready to leave when the door opened, revealing Detective Curry ready to enter. The same low-level dread I felt every time I saw him washed over me. This time it pleased me to see his car parked in a tow-away zone even though nobody seemed at hand to perform an immediate tow-away.

"Good afternoon, Detective," Punt said. "How may we help you?"

"Please excuse me," Beau said, looking at Curry. "With your permission, of course. I'm leaving for a previous appointment."

Curry nodded to Beau, then his gaze cut to Nikko and Punt. "My business here today concerns these two men."

Beau headed toward his car and Punt offered Detective Curry a seat, repeating his question. "How may we help you, Detective?"

"I've heard about your new business and I'd like to see your licenses."

Nikko pointed to the framed license hanging on the wall behind his desk. "It's authentic. You can check it out."

"What about you, Mr. Ashford? You have a license?"

To hear Punt called Mr. Ashford surprised me so I almost missed Nikko's reply. "Punt's my assistant for the time being, sir."

"Consider me Nikko's secretary, if you will," Punt added. "I'm learning the ropes, but I've applied for a license and I have all confidence that in due time it'll be forthcoming."

"Miss Moreno, I hadn't expected to find you here," Detective Curry said. "I'd intended to stop by your place of business as soon as I left here, but since you're present, you've saved me a trip."

Nobody said anything as we waited for him to continue. I didn't want to hear whatever he intended to say next.

"Miss Moreno, tomorrow the media will carry the news that the murder weapon in the Ashford case's registered to you."

I'd been expecting this. One shoe had fallen when I'd been identified as the person finding the body. Now the second shoe had fallen. I said nothing and Detective Curry continued.

"This revelation may have far-reaching repercussions. The police department's asking the public for help. We're asking anyone who knows anything about this gun to contact police headquarters immediately."

"Who could possibly know anything about my gun?" I asked. "I thought it lay hidden in my desk drawer."

"So you've told us," Curry said. "Tomorrow we'd like to ask you more questions about that. We're requesting that you report to headquarters at five o'clock tomorrow afternoon. That'll give the public the whole day to respond to our urgent request for help. If you don't have transportation to my office, I'll be glad to send a driver for you."

"I'll drive Miss Moreno there," Punt said. "Miss Moreno and her lawyer."

Chapter 31

After Curry left us we sat there without speaking, and I could feel a dragnet closing in on me. Shandy and Otto still loomed large on our list of logical suspects. Had we overlooked someone? Did the police have more evidence that might link me to Margaux's murder? I sighed. What evidence could be more damning than to have found the body and to own the murder weapon? If I hoped to prove my innocence I'd have to act quickly, but I had no idea of what to do next.

"I'd say Otto might be the logical person to approach next," Punt said.

"Suppose he'll talk to us willingly?" Nikko asked. "Remember, we're professionals now. That may scare him into silence."

"If I went with you, it might help put Otto at ease," I said. "He comes to me for therapy. He's used to talking with me. You two could ask the questions, but I think seeing me with you would help keep him calm." I didn't add that being with them would help keep me calm as I faced a man who might welcome seeing me take a murder rap for him.

"You'd have a fit if we went without you." Nikko smiled and I nodded in agreement.

"Otto lives on Fleming Street," Nikko said, "but I'm not sure of the house."

"I've scribbled it right on this suspect list." Punt checked the address.

"Should we telephone him first?" Nikko asked.

"No way." Punt stuffed the list in his pocket. "Private eyes simply appear on the scene—tough guys demanding answers."

"Works for me." Nikko grinned and jingled his car keys.

"Will you take Moose?" Moose pricked up his ears at the sound of his name.

"Not this time." Nikko tossed Moose a doggie treat. "Otto finds Moose very intimidating. Remember the memorial service? We'll leave Moose here to guard the office."

In view of possible parking problems, we left the Karmann Ghia at the office and rode with Nikko in his old Ford. The Fleming Street address turned out to be only a couple of blocks from the public library where there's a small parking lot for patrons. However, we resisted the temptation to infringe on library property.

"Gotta be law abiding now that we're in the P.I. business," Nikko said.

We drove on until Punt nodded toward Otto's address. "There's his house, and there's enough space to park in his driveway. We'll be leaving soon."

"It's worth a try. If someone arrives demanding the space, we can move."

"Want me to go to the door first?" I sounded braver than I felt.

"It's a plan." Nikko killed the motor and we filed along a narrow sidewalk and then up the porch steps. I lifted an antique brass knocker and let it fall. No response. I knocked again. Still no response. We were about to turn and leave when Shandy called to us from behind the fence at the side of the house, finger combing her hair and clutching a swimsuit cover-up to her wet body.

"Over here, Keely. I was in the pool."

"Sorry to interrupt your swim," I said. "Got the afternoon off?"

"Yeah, I'm free until the dinner hour. What can I do for you?"

"We're here to talk to Otto," Punt said.

Punt continued to explain our mission, but I stared at Shandy's face. Mr. Moore had a keen eye. Now that the pool water had washed away some of her makeup, I saw the barely visible scar near her left eye. Could it be possible? Could this shy woman be the bank robber wanted in North Dakota? Highly unlikely, I thought. I tried to remember how long she'd lived in Key West, but I couldn't pinpoint a date.

"Come on, Keely." Punt reached for my hand, tugging me toward the car. "Didn't you hear what she said? Otto's out right now."

"Thanks, Shandy," Nikko called as we left.

"Where is he?" I wanted to blurt Mr. Moore's suspicions about Shandy, but I held back, not quite knowing why. Maybe I was thinking of my own plight, wanting to find a murder suspect with no alibi, someone to divert police attention.

"I think Otto may be at *The Wharf*." Nikko started the Ford and backed from the driveway. "He hangs out there at the bar. A regular. Sometimes when I finish up in the kitchen I drive him home if he's had too many gins. He doesn't want Shandy to know he's been drinking. Booze sets poorly with his medications."

"How can she help knowing?" I asked.

"Maybe she knows and pretends to look the other way," Punt said. "Wives have been known to do that."

I wondered if Punt was alluding to the way I'd suffered Jude's indignities, preferring to look the other way rather than to take action on my own behalf. Nobody elaborated on Punt's comment and we drove on. Nikko grinned as he pulled boldly into the parking slot marked CHEF.

"This's going to be hard to give up."

"You're not giving it up, remember? *Fotopoulos & Ashford*

need you here to keep up on the chatter."

"Yeah. Right. I keep forgetting."

Even at mid-afternoon *The Wharf* dining room and bar served many customers. In the time since Mr. Moore and I had eaten breakfast here early this morning, someone had hung a lavender banner bearing the words: "CONGRATULATIONS JASS" above the doorway. Jass's blue ribbon from the Miami show now hung under the banner. Beneath it a small sign read: "Hibiscus Plants courtesy of Ashford Greenhouse, Jass Ashford, proprietor."

I smiled and waved to Beau and Jass sitting with a group of friends casually lingering over coffee. Beautiful. I silently mouthed the word to Jass as I motioned to the plants that ringed the room on their rattan pedestals. She beckoned us to her table, but Nikko led us directly to the bar where Otto perched on a leather-padded bar stool sipping a drink and looking forlorn.

"We need to talk with you, Otto." Nikko pulled up a barstool and sat beside Otto. Punt and I stood in silence, waiting.

"Talk what about?" Otto asked.

Nikko showed Otto his new business card. "Punt and I are investigating Margaux Ashford's murder. We'd like to ask you a few questions."

Otto squinted more carefully at the business card. "This something new?"

"Very new," Punt said.

"Want no part of your questions." Otto hunched closer to his drink.

"You need to talk with us." Nikko pushed Otto's drink out of his reach. "We're trying to help you."

"Help me to prison? Ha!" Otto retrieved his drink and took another sip.

"Help keep you out of prison," Punt said. "What were you doing last Saturday night?"

"Don't remember. Don't remember anything about last Saturday night. Your questions won't help me remember something I can't remember."

"Maybe we should go someplace else to discuss this," Nikko said. "Will you come with us to our new office?"

"No. I'm staying right here."

"How about coming to my office?" I asked, remembering Otto's fear of Moose. "You wouldn't mind talking to us there, would you?"

Otto looked at me for the first time and gave me a tentative smile. "Hello, Keely. What're you doing with these two guys?"

"They're my friends, Otto. They're your friends, too. Please come with us and let us try to help you."

"You always help me, Keely." Otto slipped from the bar stool and took my arm. Nikko and Punt exchanged pleased glances as they led the way to Nikko's car. We drove quickly to my office, parking in back and entering through the rear door.

"You give me a foot treatment now?" Otto asked.

I started to say no, but Punt signaled me to agree to the treatment. Why not? The treatments relaxed Otto, made him feel better. Maybe in his relaxed state he would tell us what we needed to know. I had mixed feelings about this talk with Otto. I couldn't help hoping he had no alibi, hoping he couldn't remember a thing about Saturday night. That would make two of us who couldn't prove what we were doing at the time of Margaux's murder. If Otto did come up with a provable alibi, that'd focus more police attention on me—unless Shandy's alibi turned out to be a lie.

I thought more about Shandy's alibi. Was walking on the pier and seeing the lights at *Ashford Mansion* really an alibi that'd protect her? Nobody saw her on that pier. The lights on the widow's walk invited anybody's gaze. Shandy had no way of proving she'd been looking at them. Maybe there'd be three suspects with no alibis.

I prepared a footbath for Otto, adding the relaxing scent of lime as the warm water swished around his feet. Once he seemed comfortable, I hurried to my apartment, grabbed my tape recorder, and clicked it on as I dropped it into my pocket. Moments later I offered Otto a lavender-scented towel to dry his feet and then helped him into the contour chair. He settled in comfortably, and I eased a pillow beneath his head so he'd be looking directly at me as I worked. Before I could say anything, Punt spoke.

"Otto, please try to remember last Saturday night. Maybe it'd help to try to focus on what you'd been doing during the day."

"Don't want to talk to you." Otto jerked his foot from my grasp as I tried to massage it with scented oil. "Keely's giving me a reflexology treatment. This session's between Keely and me. Private."

Punt shrugged and backed away, but Nikko spoke up. "We're here to help you, Otto. Please cooperate with us."

"Why should I? Give me reasons why I should. No, don't bother to give reasons. Leave me alone until Keely finishes, then I'll go home. Don't need you two guys pestering me with questions."

Now both Punt and Nikko backed off.

"Would you like a cup of coffee?" I asked.

"No. Can't drink anything lying in this chair."

I rolled my eyes toward Gram's shop and Nikko took the hint. In moments he returned with two cups of espresso. I laid Otto's foot aside, stepped behind the chair, and took the cups from Nikko. Then facing Otto again, I showed him the espresso and handed him a cup. With my free hand I raised the chair in a way that let him sit upright.

"Let's both try some espresso, Otto. It's Gram's special. Let's relax and enjoy it for a few minutes, then I'll return to the reflexology treatment." I burnt my tongue on the first sip of the brew, but I didn't let on. "How have you been feeling lately? Are your shoulders and back still giving you pain?"

"Some days are better than others."

Otto sipped his espresso quickly, although I could still see it steaming, between sips. I set mine aside and went to my apartment for an ice cube to cool my mouth. When I returned, Otto wanted to resume the treatment so I readjusted his chair. I could feel the crystalline deposits break up between his toes, but he didn't jerk away.

"Otto, I want you to talk to me about last Saturday night. You'll be helping me. You know I'm a suspect in the Ashford case, too."

"All right. If I can, I'll answer questions to help us both, right?"

"Right. Do you own a gun, Otto?"

"Yes. I own a gun and it's registered in my name. It's legal. No way anyone can say my gun is illegal."

"Do you know how to shoot it?"

"Yes. Back east I went to target practice. People called me a good shot."

"Have you ever been in my office alone?"

Otto thought for a moment before he answered. "No. You've always been present when I've been here. How else would I get a treatment?"

"Did you know I had a gun in my bottom desk drawer?"

"You're kidding me. What would a nice girl like you be doing with a gun?"

"Nikko thought I needed one for protection."

"Oh. Protection from that Cardell fellow, I suppose."

"Right. Gram thought I needed the gun, too. So I bought one and I learned to shoot it. Otto, do you remember taking your medication, your pills, on Saturday?"

"Can't remember. Shandy lays them out for me each day. I take what she lays out."

"Were they gone on Saturday?"

"They were, but pills and booze don't mix. I can't remember anything about Saturday night."

I finished Otto's foot treatment and released him from the chair. He started to pay me, but I shook my head.

"This one's on me, Otto." I doubted that any of Otto's recorded words would be of use to us, but before we left my office I removed the tape and dropped it into my desk drawer, then I installed a fresh tape and dropped the recorder back into my pocket.

We drove Otto home, and as we pulled up, Shandy came outside, ready to get into her car. "Thanks for bringing him home, people. I appreciate it."

"You're welcome, Shandy." Punt pulled a business card from his pocket and handed it to her.

Shandy looked at the card and took a quick step away from us. "What's this supposed to mean?"

"Just what it says," Punt said. "Nikko and I have opened a detective agency and we've been hired to investigate Margaux's murder."

"Hired to investigate me?" Shandy took another step back.

"Hired to investigate anyone who had motive and opportunity to kill Margaux. You're one of the suspects we need to talk to, Shandy."

"I don't understand why. Don't understand it at all."

"Will you talk to us about it?" Nikko stepped forward.

"It'll be easier talking to us than talking to the police. You heard the points the lawyer brought out concerning Margaux's will. We all benefit from her will—all of us."

"She didn't leave me a thing." Bitterness tinged Shandy's voice and I wondered if she thought Margaux should have left her a bequest, and if so, why.

"Once the lawyers settle the estate, you'll benefit as Otto's wife," Punt said.

Shandy gave us a weak smile and her attitude changed. She pocketed Punt's business card and started to walk on toward her car. "When would you like to talk to me? I'm working tonight, but I'll be free tomorrow morning."

"That'll be soon enough," Nikko said. "Will you come to our office? Around nine o'clock?"

"I'll be there," Shandy promised.

Would she? I wondered. Did she think her flimsy alibi would hold up in a court of law? I searched her face again. The heart-shaped scar had disappeared, and I remembered my promise to Mr. Moore to call him if I discovered anything new about Shandy. I'd keep that promise. As soon as Punt drove me home, I'd give Mr. Moore a call. The news might mean nothing to him. Or again, it might mean a lot.

Chapter 32

Once Shandy drove away, Punt, Nikko, and I drove toward their new office and I told them both about Mr. Moore's suspicions concerning Shandy.

"I didn't see any scar," Punt said.

"Me either." Nikko honked his horn, narrowly missing a moped rider.

"You didn't notice it because you had no reason to be looking for it," I said. "I saw it when Shandy greeted us, coming straight from the pool, but by the time we brought Otto home, she'd repaired her makeup. The scar didn't show. Guys, I think we've found the person who shot Margaux. We're all in danger. Shouldn't we go to the police?"

"Not yet," Nikko said. "The police can't arrest Shandy because she happens to have a facial scar. They could pull her in for questioning, yes? But arrest? No. They like to feel sure they have a case that'll stand up in court before they make an arrest."

"They need to be able to prove that she was at the scene of the crime," Punt said, "that she had stolen your gun, then used it as the murder weapon. We need to think this through carefully, Keely. So far, any evidence we have against Shandy is purely circumstantial."

"In addition to that, it's flimsy," Nikko added.

"I made a promise to Mr. Moore—promised to call him if I had any more evidence that might link Shandy to the bank robbery and murder in North Dakota. I'm going to call him; he needs to know what I've seen."

"I wish you wouldn't call him yet," Nikko said.

"Why not? What can it hurt?"

"Who knows what he might do with that information? Even though he has this TV show you mentioned, he's an amateur detective at best. He funnels all his info to the police and he might do something that'd accidentally alert Shandy to the fact that she's wanted for questioning in North Dakota. If she's guilty, she may feel cornered. Who knows how she might react?"

Punt nodded in agreement. "Moore's working a cold case. We'll be smart to let it stay cold a few days longer. No harm'll come of that."

"Okay, if you say so. You guys are the professionals. I'd like to hear what she has to say when you question her in the morning."

Neither Punt nor Nikko commented on that, and back at *Fotopoulos & Ashford,* Punt and I left Nikko's car and got into the Karmann Ghia.

"I need to go home, Punt. It's been a long day and I'm exhausted."

"Too exhausted to have dinner with me tonight?"

I hesitated and smiled. "No, not that exhausted. But I do need to rest a bit and I've a favor to ask."

"As usual, your wish's my command." Punt took my hand and I smiled as I eased it from his grasp.

"Ha! If that were true, we'd be on the phone right now calling Mr. Moore."

"Okay. Revision. Your second wish's my command." He took my hand again. "What's the favor?"

This time I didn't pull away. "I want to check out Shandy's alibi. I haven't found time to do that yet and I wish you'd go with me."

"Afraid?"

278

"Uneasy. I don't like the idea of walking alone on the pier after dark. That's a dumb thing to do under any circumstances, but especially now with a killer at large. But we can't see those widow's walk lights clearly in the daylight. It scares me to think Shandy may be feeling the dragnet closing in on her, as I feel it closing in on me."

"Trapped people are dangerous people," Punt agreed.

"I don't feel dangerous. Vulnerable is a more accurate word. I've the feeling that Shandy's watching me, waiting to see what I'll do next."

"I'd like to think that what you'll do next is to have dinner with me, a wonderful delicious dinner—perhaps under the stars with a steel band playing in the background as we dance."

"Not too many steel bands around here, Punt. That's a Caribbean thing. Check in the Bahamas."

"I read that there's one playing at *Mallory* tonight. Musicians came in on the cruise ship and they're setting up at sunset."

"Cruise ships are supposed to leave at five. Before sunset."

"You're trying to change the subject."

"Right. I am and so are you. How can you be thinking about dinner and dancing and steel bands when there's a murderer at large?"

"Okay, then here's plan B. I'll take you home now and pick you up again around seven. How's that?"

"So far, so good. Then we'll go to the pier?"

"Right. It'll be dark by then. We'll walk the whole length of the pier and see if we see what Shandy says she saw last Saturday."

"If we don't?"

"Then Nikko and I'll have a few more questions to ask her

279

when she comes to our office tomorrow morning."

"I'll worry about you and Nikko. You can't be sure what Shandy might do. Why not let the police deal with her?"

"Because Beau hired us to investigate this case and we agreed to do that. You wouldn't want us to blow our first big job, would you?"

"If it meant keeping you safe, I would, but thanks for humoring me. We'll check out Shandy's alibi and then we'll have dinner."

"One more thing," Punt said. "I want to stop at Jass's shop and buy some of her new hibiscus plants. After her lunch with Beau, I want her to arrive home and find that people are already stopping by to make purchases. That'll be an upper for her. She needn't know I'm the buyer."

"Will the shop be open for business today?"

Punt nodded. "Consuela agreed to play saleslady for the afternoon and I sent Dad a note, asking him to detain Jass until I had a chance to buy some plants."

"So let's go. In fact, I could use a plant for my office and one for Gram's shop."

We headed for *Ashford Mansion* and parked near the service door at the greenhouse. Sunlight glinted off the glass roof and I imagined I could hear the plants growing. After we walked to the front porch of the mansion, Consuela appeared in the doorway, wearing a dress that matched the hibiscus blossoms. As usual, she swished and jangled and we could hear her before we entered.

"You have a problem?" she asked.

"No problem." Punt entered the shop without invitation and chose five plants and set them aside. I tried to set more plants aside, but Punt stopped me. "I'll take care of it, Keely. My pleasure."

"You raid Jass's stock of plants?" Consuela stood between

280

Punt and the pots as if to protect them.

Punt pulled out his billfold and extracted some bills. "I'm a paying customer, Consuela, and I want you to keep my identity a secret when Jass asks." He slipped her an extra twenty in exchange for her silence.

"It's a deal, Punt."

Once back outside, Punt crowded the plants into the small space behind the bucket seats in his car then pulled me to him for a brief kiss before he drove me home. Perhaps the kiss would have been longer had Consuela not been watching.

"Where will you put your three plants?" I asked.

"My office desk. Nikko's office desk. My apartment."

We drove straight to my office, and Punt helped me carry two plants inside, setting them both on my office desk before he left.

"I'll pick you up at seven, okay?"

"Right. I'll be ready."

I hadn't been inside for five minutes before Gram dropped in, wanting a complete update on my day. I gave it willingly.

"Don't like detective agency idea, Keely. Will miss Nikko upstairs. And Moose. Duval Street no be the same."

"Right, we'll miss them, but we'll be okay here. Nobody's ever bothered us. The police keep a close watch on Duval Street."

"Don't like idea. Don't like idea. You be in danger. Someone try to put blame on you—blame for Margaux death."

"That person wants me to live, to take a murder rap. I'm safe here, Gram. Believe me. We're both safe here."

Gram scowled. "You thought gun safe here. You wrong. Gun gone. Stolen. Don't like idea."

I gave her one of the hibiscus plants. "Souvenir of Jass's success, Gram." Then, while she stood admiring the plant, I nodded toward her shop. "You've got customers. I'll talk to you later."

Gram left with earrings bobbing and I knew her scowl had turned into a welcoming smile when she faced her customers and began showing off her new plant.

The fragrance of lime and lavender still hung in my office, but it felt stuffy and hot. I opened the front windows and pulled back the drapery behind the CLOSED sign before I hurried to open the rear windows. The fresh air revived me and I stretched out on my bed for a few moments before I closed the front windows again and drew the drapery.

It seemed ages since I'd taken any time to do personal chores. I shampooed my hair and showered before slipping into a terrycloth robe and drying my hair. Pouring myself a glass of iced tea, I made mental notes on what to do first before I began my chores. Laundry. Picking up used towels, I put them in the washer with plenty of detergent and hot water.

I dusted the furniture while the towels swished. After I centered the new hibiscus plant Punt had given me on my desk, I carried a dish with a withered blossom to the kitchen, setting it on the countertop, when someone knocked at my door.

"Sorry, but my office's closed today," I said to the woman standing outside.

"When will you be open? I've heard a lot about foot reflexology and I want to give it a try."

"If you'll give me your name, I call you later in the week."

"We're leaving Key West tomorrow, but we'll be back and I'll stop by then."

"Please do that. I'm sorry I can't help you today."

The woman left and I knew I needed to get on with my cleaning. I pulled the vacuum cleaner from the closet and began to attach the hose, a floor brush. My heart's never totally into cleaning, but I gave the floor a good going-over before returning the vacuum to its closet. As I reviewed the day's happenings, uneasiness began to gnaw at my mind.

I'd promised Mr. Moore to call him if I noticed anything unusual about Shandy. I hadn't promised Nikko and Punt I wouldn't call him. I'd merely gone along with their negative suggestion at the time. Maybe they were right. Maybe they weren't right, but a promise is a promise.

I found Mr. Moore's business card and dialed his number before I changed my mind. I heard the phone ringing. Ringing. Ringing. Nobody answered, so I checked his card again. Yes, I'd dialed his business number. I hung up and dialed again. Perhaps I'd made a mistake. No answer. Strange. His office should be open. North Dakota's time was an hour behind Key West time.

I lifted the receiver again and this time I dialed the operator.

"Yes. How may I help you?"

I stated my problem. "Can you check to see if the line to Centerville, North Dakota's TV station is operable?"

"Sorry, Miss. An ice storm followed by a blizzard has closed most lines in North Dakota. They may be open tomorrow. Can't say for sure."

"Thank you." I hung up, wondering if fate had saved me from myself. I felt somewhat better. At least I'd tried to keep my promise.

I stretched out on my bed again, and this time I dozed, waking only in time to dress for dinner. Again I faced the what-to-wear decision. It wasn't a hard one considering I only had the green silk and an all-purpose white sleeveless. But there's a lot a person can do with basic white. I added a tiny green scarf at the neck, a rope of pearls to match my pearl earrings, and green sandals. I'd be lying to myself if I said I wasn't aware that the green accents emphasized my green eyes. I hoped Punt would be aware, too.

When Punt arrived, I met him at the door.

"Better grab a sweater. There's always a breeze on that pier."

"Right." It pleased me that he'd remembered our plans, not that I'd have let him forget, but it's nice to be able to avoid nagging.

True night covered the island, and Punt pulled me to him for a warm kiss and I welcomed the touch of his lips, lingering over the moment, prolonging it until I sensed Gram watching from her doorway.

"Have good time," she called after us.

We slipped into the car and once we were into the traffic stream, Punt held my hand until we reached the park near the pier. "It's good to be with you, Keely. I miss you when you're not around."

"Thanks." I smiled. "It's good to be missed."

Punt sighed as we left the car. "You might go so far as to say you missed me, too."

"Of course I missed you." I squeezed his hand to give emphasis to my words.

We waited for a break in traffic before we hurried across the street and onto the pier, now closed to vehicles, but open to pedestrians.

"Let's walk quickly to the end of the pier," Punt said. "Then we can look at the widow's walk lights as we return to the car."

"Works for me." The wind had picked up. It always blew a gale out on any pier unprotected by nearby buildings or trees.

"Cold?" Punt asked.

"No. I'm fine."

"I'll have to drill you on more appropriate lines. You're supposed to say you're freezing, then I have an obligation to put my arm around your waist and pull you close for warmth. Even though you didn't say the right lines, I'll do it anyway."

I snuggled into his embrace. The pier scares me at night. It's been closed to traffic for several years, but now many pedestrians walk its length after pausing as we did to view and reflect on the AIDS Memorial. Its polished granite slabs are embedded into the concrete and etched with the names of over a thousand AIDS victims. Tonight the memorial glowed with ground-level lights and bouquets of roses and hibiscus.

We walked slowly to the darker end of the pier, at one spot pausing to study a jagged gap where the retaining wall had broken away. Officials had placed wooden barricades around the spot, but tonight high waves crashed through the opening. Punt guided us to the other side of the wetness.

Several men we couldn't see until we were almost upon them stood at the retaining wall on our right, dropping baited hooks into the sea. Some fishermen never give up. Punt steadied me when I tripped on an empty stringer lying at one man's feet. An old woman stood next to him, flinging a net into the water trying to catch bait. The sea foamed and roared and none of them were having much success. Under other circumstances I would never have ventured out here.

We stood in a corner at the end of the pier and I wondered if Punt felt as reluctant as I to turn, to look at the faraway lights, to learn for sure if Shandy had lied about her alibi. While we stood there gazing at the dim lights of a freighter moving slowly across the horizon in the distance, a huge wave closer to shore slapped against the pier, spraying us with cold water.

We both jumped back and brushed ourselves off a bit, laughing at our foolishness. I tasted salt spray on my tongue,

but in a moment that taste vanished in the sweeter taste of
Punt's lips. With great reluctance I eased from his embrace.

"Punt, this place scares me. Let's remember why we came
here."

"I came here to kiss you."

"You know what I mean. First things first."

"Oh, you mean we look for the lights, then I can kiss you
later, right?"

I wanted to agree with him and my laugh gave me away.
"Right now, we're here to look at the lights."

So we looked. We counted. *Ashford Mansion* stood far
from the White Street Pier, yet its great height made it visible.
"I see only the five lights on one side of the widow's walk.
Think about it, Punt. You can't see two sides of that tower
from this angle. There's no way Shandy could have seen
Jass's one green light because it's on the side away from us."

"So she made the whole story up." Punt sighed and pulled
me closer. "Somehow that doesn't surprise me."

"You think Shandy's the guilty one?"

"I can't say that. I don't think anyone can prove guilt
based on the fact that she lied about seeing the lights, or the
fact that she may have a scar beside her eye."

"I know she has the scar. I saw it. Mr. Moore saw it."

"Nikko and I didn't notice it. I'll be looking for it tomorrow when she comes to our office."

"She'll be expecting you to be looking for it. She'll have it
well hidden under makeup."

"You women are a tricky bunch. Let's forget about
Shandy tonight. Nikko and I'll deal with her in the morning.
You promised to have dinner with me tonight, and I've promised you a romantic setting. But there's been a change in
plans. I have a surprise for you."

Chapter 33

Punt drove us back to *Ashford Mansion* and parked in his carport. Only a few dim lights glowed from the main house.

"Forget something?" I asked, settling more comfortably in my seat.

"This's the surprise. We're dining here tonight and I'll be the chef—the chief cook and bottle washer."

"Nikko's been giving you lessons?"

"No way. No grape leaves, Greek truffles, or ouzo this evening. We're having Punt Ashford specials, but I have to admit that Jass pulled the dessert from her freezer. Pastries are beyond me."

Punt led the way up the stairs to his apartment and I inhaled the mingled fragrance of herbs and spices and sauces I couldn't identify. Chili? Garlic? My mouth began to water immediately. Once inside, I noticed he had slanted the window louvers upward to insure privacy and I liked that. My accents of green fit in well with the green jewel-toned cushions on his couch and chairs, and now I noticed his green silk shirt. Maybe he'd done some color planning as he dressed, too.

"All this looks like a picture from *Better Homes and Gardens*, Punt. I'm overwhelmed."

"As I'd hoped you'd be. And you haven't even tasted the food yet." Punt grinned and I knew my reaction had pleased him. "Sit down and relax while I play both waiter and chef. What would you like for an appetizer? I hope you'll like Yellow Birds and baked brie with almonds and chutney."

I smiled at the delicious choices. "Sounds wonderful."

After a few moments in the kitchen Punt set a plate of baked brie on the coffee table, along with a shallow bowl of sesame seed crackers, then he brought us each a cocktail glass of Yellow Birds served over ice. I tried the crackers and brie first, savoring the exotic flavor before sipping my drink. The blend of orange and pineapple juice offered a perfect chaser for the brie and chutney.

"Delicious, Punt. Really outstanding."

"In case you're worrying, I've mixed the Yellow Birds without rum and with only a smidgen of crème de banane."

"I wasn't worried." We enjoyed our drinks until we emptied our glasses and demolished the plate of brie and most of the crackers. "Wonderful fare, Punt."

"Enjoy another drink while I put the finishing touches on our meal."

"Anything I can do to help?"

"No. Relax and enjoy being my guest of honor."

That's what I did, and one Yellow Bird later Punt invited me to the dining area. An overhead lamp dazzled me as it gleamed against the glass-top table, the gold-rimmed china, and the crystal bowl bearing a single lavender hibiscus blossom.

"Beautiful. You have an artist's eye for color and design."

Punt took my compliments in stride as he served shrimp scampi and new potato and walnut salad laced with a vinaigrette dressing. The meal looked beautiful and, if tastes can be beautiful, it tasted beautiful.

"Where did you learn to cook? You've surely had lessons."

"Mom used to let me mess around in the kitchen. Jass never showed any interest in cooking and I reveled in Mom's attention."

"It paid off well. I had no idea you indulged in such a secret hobby."

"I could show you other secrets, too." Punt winked and offered me more shrimp.

When neither of us could eat another bite, I eased my chair from the table. "Could we save the dessert for later? I know it'll be delicious, but I'm already operating on overload right now."

Punt stood and bowed dramatically. "As you wish, Madam."

In spite of his protests I helped Punt clear the table.

"Take care with the china, please. It's antique and it's been in the family for generations. One of my sea captain ancestors salvaged it from a galleon that went down on the reef. Jass has an account of the wreck written up in the ship's log."

"I'd like to read about it sometime."

"You probably have. I think Dad copied the excerpt and presented it in one of his columns. Family history. Key West history."

I insisted that we do the dishes by hand rather than entrusting them to the dishwasher with its harsh detergent. I washed and Punt dried.

"I like this scene, Keely. We work well together. Think about it for future reference, okay?"

I enjoyed working with Punt in the kitchen, but I wasn't ready to admit it so easily. When we had returned the dishes to their cupboards, Punt tuned in some easy listening music and we sat on the couch to talk. Of course the conversation zeroed in on the new detective agency and on Otto and Shandy.

"One minute I think Otto's guilty," I said. "Inheriting ten million with the pull of a trigger must have played through his mind, but the next minute all the clues seem to point to Shandy."

"Maybe they were in it together."

"Sometimes I think I can sense Shandy following me."

"Big imagination, Keely. Big imagination."

"I'm not convinced it's my imagination. I know how it feels to be followed and spied upon, but I thought that feeling would disappear once Jude . . ."

"We don't have enough evidence to pinpoint Shandy's guilt."

"Why would she give me a false alibi if she didn't have something to hide?"

Punt pulled me closer. "She could have lots of reasons. We'll have to find out what they are before we point a finger of guilt at her. What about Otto? Only presidents can get by with the 'can't remember' line."

"Shandy's scar," I said, trying to pull the conversation back to Shandy. "I remember that scar."

"The scar only you and Mr. Moore have noticed. Nikko and I haven't seen it—and believe me we've been looking carefully ever since you mentioned it."

I let my head rest on Punt's shoulder before I spoke again. "There's another thing to consider. You may say I've been reading too many mystery novels, but I've read that a person choosing an alias frequently selects a name with the same initials as his real name."

"What's that supposed to mean?"

"Mr. Moore said the bank robber's name is Sally Mitchell. Shandy's name was Mertz before she married Otto. Shandy Mertz. Sally Mitchell. It fits."

Punt didn't laugh this time. "That's a bit of a coincidence, isn't it?"

"I say it's more than a coincidence. The more I think about it, the more Shandy scares me. A person who kills once . . ."

"I know, I know." Punt kissed me lightly on the forehead.

"Don't remind me. Maybe we do have strong reason to suspect Shandy."

"And another thing . . ."

"How many more another things can you come up with?"

"This one may upset you, Punt. I didn't mean to go behind your back—or Nikko's, but I couldn't resist trying to telephone Mr. Moore. I promised him. I promised him a call if I noticed anything suspicious about Shandy. I did notice something and I did call."

"What'd he say? Will he fly back down here and check her out—maybe bring his hometown investigators with him?"

"We've been too distracted by Margaux's death to notice national news broadcasts—especially on the weather channel. I couldn't get in touch with Mr. Moore because a blizzard's howling in North Dakota. All phone lines are down and no calls are going through. At least that was true this afternoon."

"So let's try again. Got his number handy?"

"No. We'll have to dial directory assistance." It irritated me that I didn't have Mr. Moore's phone number at hand, but it pleased me that Punt now wanted to call him, to talk to him. When we had his phone number, Punt dialed and we waited.

At last the operator responded. "Sorry. Phone lines in both South and North Dakota are down."

"Any chance of them opening up any time soon?" Punt asked.

"Sorry, but I haven't got that information to give out officially," the operator said, "but I do have relatives in North Dakota and I hear there's a slight possibility of the lines being open late today or tomorrow."

"Guess we'll just have to watch the weather channel," Punt said. "Thanks for the info."

We settled back into a loose embrace on the sofa. "So that's that as far as calling Mr. Moore's concerned." We sat quietly for sometime before Punt spoke again.

"Keely, think carefully. Think back to that terrible Sunday morning when you found Margaux's body. Do you remember anything, any small thing, you haven't told me or the police about? Your mind must have been in a whirl, but think back to that morning. Try to forget about Margaux and think about details."

I rose and began to pace the room as I thought back to that day. At last I shook my head and I'd started to say no when I glanced again at Punt's dinner table. We'd cleared away all the dishes except the centerpiece, the crystal bowl holding the hibiscus blossom. In that moment I remembered, remembered something that might be important. Or it might be nothing.

"What is it? I can see in your eyes that you've recalled something."

"Yes, but . . ." At first I hesitated, then the words came tumbling out. "That Sunday morning I was running late. As I hurried up the steps to Margaux's door, I noticed a hibiscus blossom lying on the top step. I love flowers and I hated to see the blossom lying where it might be destroyed by a footstep, so I picked it up and tucked it into a buttonhole of my jumpsuit."

"What color blossom?" Punt stood facing me, his eyes boring into mine. "What color?"

"A lavender blossom. Lavender hibiscus."

"Dad had no lavender plants at that time. Jass's hibiscus experiment was still top secret—a secret from everyone except the judges at the Miami show."

"A secret between Jass and Shandy. They were the only two people who had access to Jass's greenhouse, and Jass has an alibi for Saturday night. Punt, Shandy dropped that blossom on the porch."

"Hmmm." Punt turned and walked to the window. "Hmmm."

"I know it, Punt. I know it. In Shandy's haste to leave the murder scene, the blossom fell unnoticed. Maybe she'd been wearing it in her hair. She does that sometimes—wears a blossom. She could have tucked that blossom into her hair as she helped Jass prepare plants for the show—tucked it in and forgotten about it. Shandy visited Margaux's home on Saturday night."

"We can't prove that," Punt said. "We know someone came there and that someone dropped a lavender blossom. Beau had no lavender plants in his yard or his house, but we can't say Shandy visited Beau's house on Saturday night, that Shandy dropped the blossom. We've only circumstantial evidence. We've no witness who actually saw it happen."

"Aren't cases sometimes brought to court and killers found guilty on the strength of circumstantial evidence?"

"Sometimes. I suppose it's possible in Florida. Do you still have that blossom? Or did you toss it?"

"You know my housekeeping reputation. I think the blossom's still there. On Sunday morning Curry came to my office—unexpected. I tried to neaten my desk in a hurry, and I removed a withered red blossom from a crystal dish, exchanging it for the blossom I'd picked up at Margaux's. Today I set the plant you gave me on my desk and I carried the blossom dish to the kitchen. I intended to drop it into the wastebasket, but just then someone came to my door."

"Then that lavender blossom has to be in your kitchen." Punt grabbed my hand and started pulling me toward the door. "We have to get that blossom before . . ."

My stomach lurched. ". . . before Shandy remembers

seeing it on my desk when she came in for her foot treatment on Tuesday. If she remembers the blossom, she'll wonder where it came from since I had no access to Jass's plants at that time. Then she may remember she wore it on Saturday night, that she lost it. Punt, we have to find that blossom."

"Right." Now Punt followed me as I raced down the steps and to his car. "Please don't get your hopes up too high. Hibiscus blossoms are fragile. On the plant they may last several days, but picked and placed in water they may last only a day or two. Seldom more."

"Even after they wilt, you can identify color—in this case, their special color."

Punt parked behind my office and we entered quietly before I snapped on the overhead light. It was past eleven and I hoped Gram would be in bed with her ear plugs in place. I headed straight for the kitchen. Yes. The blossom lay in the dish on the countertop near the sink. I snapped on another lamp and placed the dish directly under it.

"It's a lavender all right," Punt agreed. "It's withered, but the petals are still wide and there's no mistaking the special color."

"So now we know Shandy's the killer."

"*We* know," Punt agreed, "but we still have no way of proving it to the police. Besides that, the police really hate accepting help or ideas from private investigators."

Chapter 34

"Do you have an envelope, Keely? I want to take this blossom to my office and put it in my safe."

I brought an envelope from my desk and Punt carefully placed the blossom inside it and tucked it into his shirt pocket.

"Keely, what was it you wanted to do before you face the police in the morning?"

"I need to go back to Beau's home again. Should we call him first? I don't want to bother him, but I hate barging in unannounced."

"Going to reveal the nature of this mission?"

"Not yet. Humor me, okay?"

Punt used my desk phone to dial Beau's number and I heard the phone ringing. After six rings, he replaced the receiver. "Nobody home. Or maybe he's not answering."

"He does that sometimes? Ignores the ring?" I couldn't imagine anyone with such a lack of curiosity. When my phone rings, it's like a command performance. I rush to answer.

Punt nodded. "Beau's always said that telephones are for his convenience, not his inconvenience."

"He doesn't have an answering machine?"

"No—says if it's important the caller will call back. Sometimes if he's writing, or trying to sleep, he turns the phone off. I think his column's due tomorrow. He may be home writing. Or he may be out for the evening."

"I need to go there now. We don't need to bother him. Don't need to go inside, but I need to check one more important thing. Probably another circumstantial evidence thing, but if we come with enough of them, maybe they'll catch Shandy in their web."

"Okay. We'll go there, but first let's put this blossom in the agency safe."

We drove down the alley to Whitehead Street and then along narrow streets until we reached *Fotopoulos & Ashford*. Vandals had broken the street light and total darkness surrounded the parking slots.

"Be back in a sec, Keely."

"No way am I waiting here alone." I slid from the car.

"Shandy really has you spooked, right?" Punt took my hand. "Or are you making excuses for more togetherness?"

"Maybe both. You got a problem with that?"

"No problem. No problem at all. You don't have to make excuses for togetherness. I'd like it to be our way of life."

When Punt locked his car, I knew he felt as uneasy as I did in the blackness surrounding us. Keeping a firm grip on his hand, I followed him as we made our way across the broken concrete sidewalk to his door.

I screamed as I sensed a movement at our feet and heard a guttural voice muttering unintelligible words. Punt jumped back, pulling me with him, and I felt a bone-crushing tension in his hand before he relaxed.

"Okay, buddy. Move on. Now. Move on."

My eyes were growing used to the darkness, and I could make out a long-haired and shaggy-whiskered man huddled in the doorway. He managed to haul himself to his feet, sending the odor of stale beer into the air.

"Who are you?" He looked at us through bleary eyes. "Getting so a guy can't get no sleep anymore. Gonna report you to the cops. Disturbin' the peace."

"You do that, buddy. Let me know what they say."

We waited while the drunk stumbled off into the night.

Punt fumbled with his keys for a few seconds before he managed to unlock the door and turn on the lights.

I squinted into the sudden brightness, realizing immediately that the light made us targets for anyone who might be watching. Shandy? Did Shandy ever skulk around this area? I felt someone watching us, or maybe it was my imagination.

"This place scares the bejabbers out of me at night, Punt."

"I'll call City Electric about getting that street light fixed tomorrow."

Punt hurried to the safe, turned the knob until the door opened, then laid the blossom in the safe's green interior and relocked the door.

"Let's get out of here," he said. "This'll be a safer place once Nikko and Moose move in."

I agreed. We returned to the car and drove back to the bright lights of Duval Street.

"I'll give Dad another ring." Punt keyed in Beau's number, but the ringing went unanswered. "Well, we'll drive there anyway. How long will your mission take once we get there?"

"A very few minutes. A few important minutes."

We drove to Grinnell, parked in front of the house, and hurried to the porch. Although no car sat in the carport, Punt knocked on the door to announce our presence. No answer. I knocked again to make sure nobody was home.

"Now what?" Punt asked.

I turned and stood at the top of the porch steps. "Stand here beside me and look toward *Ashford Mansion*, the widow's walk. From this cattycorner angle, I see five white lights on one side and five on the other side—one of them being green."

"Right," Punt said. "That's what Shandy said she saw last Saturday night."

"Only she said she saw the lights from the pier. Here's where she saw them. Right here—after she shot Margaux and had started to leave the porch. You know Shandy's compulsion for counting. Even after killing another human being, she couldn't help taking time to count the widow's walk lights, to notice that one of them glowed green."

"I believe your theory." Punt squeezed my hand. "Again, it's circumstantial evidence. We have no witnesses."

Just then Beau pulled into the carport and a moment later joined us on the porch. "What's up, people? Anything I can help you with?"

Beau invited us inside and again he avoided the sitting room and led us to his study. We sat around his desk while he listened to our story, nodding at appropriate moments, shaking his head at others.

"I think your theories are right, Keely," Beau said. "I believe Shandy's the killer." For a moment he rested his head in his hands, then he looked up, and when he spoke again, his voice seemed to come from a great distance and through a heavy veil of weariness. "As you realize, you/we have no witnesses to prove a case against her."

"So what do we do now?" Punt asked.

"You're the detective," Beau said. "Maybe you and Nikko need to talk. Sometimes four heads are better than three. Nikko may have some good ideas."

"I wish you and Nikko would be with me when I face Detective Curry's questions tomorrow morning, Punt," I said.

"That might be unwise," Punt said. "The police hate to accept P.I. help. They'd see our presence as interference."

"Maybe you need a lawyer," Beau said. "I could get someone from *Hubble & Hubble* to represent you."

"At one time Detective Curry said his questions were informal, that unless they placed me under arrest, I didn't need a lawyer. Maybe if I appeared with a lawyer, Curry would see it as an admission of guilt."

"I don't know," Beau said, "but if Curry should place you under arrest, don't say another word. From that time on, you can bet the police are trying to trip you up, to make you say something incriminating. That's the time to call me, or better yet, call *Hubble & Hubble* and ask them to send someone to represent you. I'll phone Harley first thing in the morning and alert him to the possibility of a summons from you."

Beau's words helped ease my fears. I didn't want to dial his number only to find I'd chosen a time when he'd turned his phone off.

"Thanks, Beau. I really appreciate your concern. It gives me confidence to know I have your backing."

"We'd better be going, Dad. I'm glad you're on our side and sorry we don't have some witnesses to back up our suspicions."

"Maybe Shandy'll do or say something that'll tip her hand," Beau said.

"I'm not counting on it," Punt said. "But Nikko and I'll keep her under surveillance starting tonight. We'll take turns. We'll know every move she makes, every place she goes. We'll be on her like paint on a wall. I wish we could get permission to tap her phone."

"I'm fairly sure that's illegal," Beau said, "but maybe with just cause it might be possible. Want me to check with Hubble?"

Punt nodded. "Sure. See what he says. Right now, I need to get Keely home, need to talk to Nikko and put a surveillance plan in motion."

I sensed an urgency in the way Punt drove to Duval Street and pulled up in front of my office. I made no motion to open the car door or to get out and neither did he. He leaned toward me, taking my hand in both of his.

"This isn't the way I wanted our evening to end, Keely. I dreamed of a quiet, undisturbed time at my place. Key lime pie. Coffee. Soft music. And you in my arms—and maybe in my bed."

"Me and a piece of Key lime pie?"

"Don't make jokes. I'm very serious. I lost you once and I don't want that to happen again."

"I'm not making jokes. I'm sorry Shandy's intruded in our lives. She's a killer. We can't really enjoy ourselves until she's been brought to justice."

"I like what you're saying."

"About bringing Shandy to justice? Well, I should hope so."

"My thinking goes beyond Shandy. I like the part about us enjoying ourselves. I like hearing those words from your lips. Once this case is behind us, I wish we could start a new relationship from square one. We do have a relationship, Keely, a tentative relationship, perhaps, but definitely a relationship."

"Yes, we do have a relationship of sorts—maybe one based more on business than pleasure."

"So my next step will be to get it based more on pleasure than on business. That's my goal."

"I don't know. We're different people now than we were at square one. Very different. We're both carrying a lot of excess baggage involving a horror of a marriage for me, drug and alcohol addiction for you. We've both been through bad times that'll be hard to forget."

"Maybe we shouldn't try to forget." Punt tightened his grip on my hand. "Maybe we should put all our baggage right out front, look at it carefully, and try to learn from it as we move on. We've both changed. We've known good times.

We've known bad times. Maybe we're back to facing good times again."

"You may be right. I hope so."

"Do you really?" He pulled me to him and began a kiss that threatened to turn into something we couldn't handle within the confines of the Karmann Ghia. After a long time, I reluctantly pulled myself from his embrace.

"I love you, Keely. I've always loved you."

"And I love you, too, Punt." Warmth flooded over me as I said those words, a warmth I hoped would last forever.

"That's all we need to know for now. All we need is each other."

"I must go in now, Punt. It's been a strange evening, a scary evening, a wonderful evening."

"I vote for wonderful." Punt helped me from the car and waited until I was safely inside before we shared a farewell kiss that left us both trembling and reluctant to part.

"I'm going up to Nikko's apartment now to talk to him about Shandy. We'll see to it that she's brought to justice and that she doesn't harm you before that time. Remember, you have any trouble with Curry tomorrow, you call *Hubble & Hubble*."

"Right. I'll remember." I hated ending our evening on that grim note. I admitted to myself that I'd have rather seen it end in Punt's bed—without the Key lime pie.

Chapter 35

After Punt left, I double-checked both my office and apartment doors, making sure they were locked. A long shower helped relax me and I was about to crawl into bed when I heard a knock at my door. I sighed. I thought I'd managed to come home without waking Gram, but no. I slipped on my robe as I hurried to the door.

"Gram?"

"Keely. Need to talk."

I never doubted the voice was Gram's until I opened the door and faced Shandy holding a gun pointed at my heart. Surprise and fear left me open-mouthed and speechless. No matter. Shandy controlled the conversation—and my life. So much for Punt and Nikko's surveillance. Maybe they hadn't had time to form a plan. Maybe they'd gone to their office.

"Come with me. Come quietly. Now." Shandy had lost her little-girl voice and her tone held authority—authority backed with a gun.

"Where're we going?" My voice rasped with fear, anger, terror.

"Shut up and come. Now."

As I stalled, my mind began to function. "Let me get dressed, Shandy. People'll wonder why I'm outside barefoot, wearing nothing but this flimsy robe."

"It's late. Nobody's going to see us. If you think Punt's going to save you, forget that. He left Nikko's place ten minutes ago. My car's nearby. Come."

I clutched at straws. "You know Gram's probably watching. She doesn't miss much in this neighborhood. If you want things to look natural, you'll let me slip into a jump-suit. People'd think nothing of seeing us together if we both were dressed and I wore my regular working outfit."

"I could shoot you this minute." She raised the gun a bit.

I forced calmness into my voice. "Right, Shandy. You could do that, but a shot would alert lots of people. Even in Key West, folks notice a gunshot, especially one late at night. Please let me get dressed."

Shandy lowered the gun a fraction of an inch and I thought I saw her hand trembling. What if the gun went off acciden-tally?

"All right. When the cops find your body, the circum-stances of your death'll seem more probable if you're wearing clothes. Who'd accidentally fall into the sea wearing only a robe? Dress, but be quick about it. Turn on no more lights."

She followed me back to my apartment and in the dim-ness, I stood at my closet for a moment before I reached for the jumpsuit I'd worn all day. I stepped into it, wiggled it up and over my shoulders.

"Need shoes." I stalled a few moments longer. With my back to her, I stooped and fumbled through the sandals and boat shoes on the closet floor. In those moments I managed to reach into my upper pocket and thumb the tape recorder on, praying she wouldn't notice, praying she wouldn't re-member that I recorded every work session, praying the bat-tery was up.

When I stood again to face her, I could think of no more ways to delay her plans. She nudged me toward the front door.

"Open the door. Turn off the light. Get into my car."

I followed her orders, wondering if I might be able to grab the gun away from her while she drove. I soon nixed that idea. She held the gun in her right hand, guided the car with her left. With her head turned slightly to the right, she looked ahead at the road, but I knew that through peripheral vision she could see any movement I might make.

"Where're we going?"

"Wait. Soon all will be revealed to you."

I hated her smart-ass answer, but I said no more while she drove us to the *White Street Pier* and parked in a spot where shadows hid her car. Pulling the keys from the ignition, she dropped them into her pocket, her gaze never leaving me.

"Stay where you are." She opened her door and walked behind the car, coming up on my side and opening the passenger door. In those few moments I managed to thumb Punt's number into the cell phone I'd dropped in my pocket after we called Beau earlier in the evening, but I'd no time to call for help.

"Get out." Shandy motioned with the gun.

"Where're we going?"

Her gun spoke for her as she nudged me toward the pier. Cold terror rose inside me until I felt like an ice bag, frozen and immobile. I stopped walking, but her gun nudged me forward until we were on the pier, heading toward the far end of it. Only a few dim lights on shore lit our way. The wind had freshened until it was blowing a gale and thrashing raging waters to a foamy froth.

"Feel like a swim tonight?"

"Shandy, you've lost your mind. Take me home and I'll say nothing about this to anyone."

"You enjoy the water, Keely. So enjoy tonight. It'll be your last chance for a midnight swim." Shandy's gun prodded me toward the broken retaining wall.

"You won't get by with this. People will be looking for me. Punt. Nikko."

"Punt and Nikko may look, but it'll be Coast Guard or

Marine Patrol boys who'll find you. They'll think you're some dumb broad who walked where she shouldn't have walked and accidentally fell into the sea. Sharks feed at night, you know. They can smell blood for miles—and there'll be lots of blood. If the sharks and 'cudas don't get you, you'll die of contusions as the waves ram you into the rocks and the pier pilings. This's it, Keely Moreno. You and your alternative healing! Maybe you can give the sharks a little foot reflexology."

Shandy's voice grew more inane and frenzied as she talked, and now we had reached the broken retaining wall. The wind had come up even stronger, and waves crashed onto the pier as Shandy pushed me toward the opening. Water soaked my shoes, and the wet legs of my pantsuit clung to me like a second skin.

"You won't get by with this, Shandy." I sounded like a broken record, but I had to keep her talking. "I called Mr. Moore. He spotted you at *The Wharf.* He knows you were in on the bank robbery in North Dakota."

"You may have called him, but you didn't get him. I know about the blizzard, the ice storm. No messages going through. I tried, too. With you dead, I'll be safe again. Key West is a nice place to hide out. Too many freaky characters for anyone to notice a plain little barmaid just doing her job, and now I'll be a rich little barmaid."

"That's why you shot Margaux, isn't it?"

"Yes, I shot her. Easy pickings. She deserved to die."

"You killed her so you'd be rich. And you tried to make it look as if I killed her. Thanks a lot, Shandy. Tell me, how did you get my gun?"

"Easy, easy. One day I pretended to be in a hurry after you finished my session in the chair. I gave you a dollar bill and asked for parking meter change. You didn't have any quarters, so you ran to Celia's shop to get some. While you were away, I took the gun."

"How did you know it was there?"

"I overheard you talking to Nikko about it. Arguing about your using it. About where you kept it. Dumb broad."

"So now you'll be rich—as soon as the courts probate Margaux's will. A rich barmaid. Don't you think people'll think it strange if you continue working? Having all that money may blow your cover. People will be noticing you, speculating about you. You can't get by with murdering me, Shandy. Punt knows you're guilty. He and Nikko will find the proof they need. You're getting yourself in deeper and deeper." I felt myself talking in circles, making no real sense, but I had to keep talking.

"One murder. Two murders. Three murders. The penalty's much the same. Anyway, I won't get caught. You're bluffing about Punt and Nikko."

Keep her talking. I had to keep her talking. I had thumbed in Punt's number on the cell although I wasn't able to talk to him. Maybe he was searching for me right this minute. I had a chance if I could only keep Shandy talking.

"How does it feel to be a rebound wife, Shandy? You feel good knowing Otto married you because Margaux dumped him? That's what your marriage is. A rebound affair. He couldn't care less about you. Everyone in Key West knows that."

When Shandy spoke, I heard the fury escalate in her voice.

"That's another reason Margaux had to die. She made a fool of me. She gets the rich Beau Ashford. I get the poor Otto Koffan. All my life I've been cheated. In the bank robbery, one guy escapes with the money. I get none. Instead, I get a lifetime of hiding. When I kill Margaux, money begins to come my way through Otto, a druggie on his way out. I may help him along to the next world, too—after he makes the proper bequests in my behalf."

"It'll never work, Shandy. Never. Never."

Shandy peered into the raging waves before she looked at me again. "I'm curious. How'd you know I shot Margaux? I hid my tracks well."

"Not well enough." I told her about the dropped blossom. I told her about Mr. Moore noticing her scar. Then I had an idea. "Shandy, you used a walk on this pier as part of your alibi. That was your downfall. You miscounted the widow's walk lights."

At the word "miscounted," Shandy turned to recount the lights. In that moment I gave a chop to her wrist and the gun flew from her hand and dropped at our feet.

Chapter 36

Startled, we both stared at the gun for an instant before we scrambled for it. I stooped to grab it, slipped, and crashed onto one knee, but I felt the gun's wet coldness beneath my fingers. My hand closed around the butt, and as I tried to get my finger on the trigger, Shandy shouted.

"Drop it. Drop it now." Ramming into my left side, she knocked me off balance, giving my hand a kick that sent the gun skittering away from me—and also away from her. She had the advantage of being on her feet while I still struggled to get up.

The gun rattled past the pedestrians' safety barrier and stopped dangerously close to the gaping hole in the retaining wall. I regained my balance, leaped up, and dove on top of the pistol seconds before it dropped into the sea. Again I lay sprawled on wet concrete, but this time, as Shandy rushed toward me, I clutched the gun with my finger on the trigger.

"Stop where you are." I pointed the pistol at Shandy. "One move and you're dead."

Could she hear the shake in my voice? See the tremble in my hand? I rose to my feet ever mindful of the slick concrete, the thrashing sea. My mind whirled, searching for some bit of wisdom that would tell me what to do next. I'd never expected to be thrust into the role of captor, but I liked it a whole lot better than the role of prisoner.

"You don't know how to use a gun." Shandy's words taunted me. "You'll end up shooting yourself, you dummy."

I tried to block her words from my mind—and failed.

"Don't push the envelope, Shandy. Of course I know how to use a gun."

"Maybe—on the target range. Bet you never practiced on a moving person."

"Move at your own risk."

Why talk to this woman? I needed to think, needed to keep focused on getting help. Maybe I could force her to walk back to the car, to drive us to police headquarters. Or maybe I could do the driving. *Move away from the broken wall.* My mind shouted orders, but my body refused to obey. Terror froze me to the spot.

What if I ordered Shandy to walk toward the car and she refused? Could I bear to shoot her? Could I bear the guilt of snuffing out a human life? I had no answers. I only knew I didn't dare shout an order I couldn't back up with a bullet.

Cell phone. My thoughts began to focus as I remembered the cell phone in my pocket. I clutched the gun in my right hand. Through wet fabric clinging to my legs, I felt the cell phone in my right-hand pants pocket. The awkwardness of the situation scared me, but I managed to keep the gun trained on Sandy while I thrust my left hand into my right-hand pocket and pulled out the cell.

I didn't dare lose eye contract with Shandy by looking down at the phone, so working by touch, I managed to push the power button to break whatever connection I might have had to Punt's phone, then I pushed "power" again and keyed in nine-one-one.

"Phone's probably dead or too wet to work," Shandy taunted. "Must be soaked from all those waves. You'll get no help from the Key West's finest tonight. You're on your own."

Shandy's words reinforced my worst fears, but working left-handed, I pressed the phone to my ear and waited. Good!

It lived! I could hear the rings.

"Police dispatcher. Your name, please?"

"Keely Moreno calling." Once I spoke, once I knew help lay only a phone line away, words poured out. "I'm on White Street. At the end of the pier. I'm holding Shandy Koffan at gunpoint. Need help. Now. I'm holding Shandy's gun. She used it to kidnap me from my apartment, drive me to the pier, and try to drown me. Hurry. Please hurry."

"Stay where you are, Miss Moreno. Help's on its way. Keep talking to me. I'll hold this line open. Keep talking to let me know you're still okay."

I forced myself to keep talking. I talked. And talked. In my terror, I gave up any thought of moving or of ordering Shandy to move. The police were coming. Let them give Shandy orders. I kept talking and talking until the howling wind crashed another wave onto the pier, a wave so strong it knocked us both to the concrete, drenching us as it swept both the cell phone and the gun into the sea.

Shandy attacked me in the next instant, pounding my head with her fists, kicking my shins and legs. I tried to focus on the dim lights on shore, but a world of blackness whirled around me. *Fight back.* I wanted to fight back, but all stamina left me and I concentrated on protecting myself from Shandy's onslaught. She kicked the barrier blocking the hole in the retaining wall and the heavy sawhorse fell across the small of my back. Pain shot through my body and I gasped for breath as I felt her kicking me and then tugging me toward the hole where the sea came crashing through.

"Tell the world goodbye, Keely," Shandy shouted in my ear as she pushed the sawhorse from my back. "This's it. Over you go. Over and out. I'll tell the police you attacked me and you won't be around to deny it. They'll think about Margaux. They'll think about Jude. They'll think I held the number three spot on the list of a madwoman—a serial killer who killed without motive."

In my mind, that future scene played out as Shandy described it. The police had suspected me of murder all along, but with my last bit of strength, I clutched a protruding chunk of concrete and hung on. There's a universal force within a human being that'd rather live than die. Shandy kicked my hands, my fingers. I held on. Waves kept me so wet I couldn't feel my blood spurting from my body, but I could smell its rust-like odor as it leaked into the sea.

Sirens wailed in the distance, but so what? Crazy things flashed through my mind while I clung there dying. I thought of books and articles I'd read about people near death seeing a bright light at the end of a tunnel, seeing loved ones waiting to welcome them. I saw none of those things, and that fact gave me strength. If I saw no tunnel, no bright light, no deceased friends waiting, maybe I wasn't dying. I clung to the life remaining in me.

The next thing I knew I woke up in a dimly lit room. Where? I peeked through slitted eyes, wondering if Shandy still waited, ready to attack again.

"Keely? Keely?"

Punt's voice. I opened my eyes wider.

"Keely, can you hear me?"

"Of course I can hear you. Where am I? Why are these mittens on my hands?"

Someone turned on a brighter light and I bolted upright in bed in spite of muscles that screamed in protest. "Where's Shandy? She's after me. She's going to kill me. Watch out, Punt! She's dangerous!"

Punt gently eased me back onto my pillow. "You're in the hospital, Keely. Relax. Everything's going to be okay."

Before Punt could say more, a nurse entered the room. "Good morning, Miss Moreno. How are we feeling today?"

The nurse raised the window shade and sunlight flooded the room. I didn't know how she felt, but I felt really rotten, and the medicinal smell that traveled with her increased my nausea.

"It's Friday morning?" I whispered, remembering Thursday night's horror as I tried to relate to this calm world.

"It's Saturday afternoon," Punt said. "You've lost a few hours, but you'll never miss them."

"I want out of here. When can I go home?"

"That's up to the doctor," the nurse said. "He'll be in later to see you. Right now you need to rest."

"Seems to me I've been resting for a day or so. Where's Gram?"

"She's been here a lot. Would still be here now, but Nikko and I insisted she go home."

"I want you to rest now," the nurse insisted. "I'll bring you some tea and toast. Mr. Ashford, I'll have to ask you to leave, please."

"No way." I sat up again and forced strength into my voice, if not into my body. "If Punt goes, I go, too. We need to talk."

The nurse eased me back onto my pillow, but she raised the head of the bed. "All right. You may talk for a few minutes while I get you something to eat." She left the room, closing the door.

"Where's Shandy?" I demanded.

Punt hesitated before he gave me a kiss. "I'd take your hand if I could, but I hate holding bandages."

"Where's Shandy?"

Punt sighed, but he looked me in the eye. "She's dead. As she tried to shove you into the sea, she slipped—and fell into the waves."

312

"Nobody rescued her?"

"Impossible. We called the Coast Guard, the Marine Patrol. Water near the pier too shallow for their boats. They launched a dingy, but it sank before rescuers could board it. Her body washed to shore Friday afternoon."

My heart thudded against my rising panic. "Police saying I murdered her?"

"Of course not. Forget that thought immediately."

"We had enough circumstantial evidence against her to clear me of Margaux's death?" I asked.

"Yes, we had that. We also found your tape recorder turned on in your pocket."

"The tape survived? I can't believe it. Water everywhere. Drenching everything."

"That's true, but Detective Curry dried the tape. Water destroyed much of it, but some of it played—enough of it to convict Shandy of Margaux's murder and your attempted murder, had she lived. Detective Curry asked me to give you a message."

I scowled. I wanted Detective Curry out of my life forever. "What did he say?"

Punt smiled. "He's afraid you won't feel like giving him a foot treatment today. Said you had scheduled him for Saturday afternoon. He wants to reschedule."

I managed to smile. I even found I could laugh—weakly. "What can I say? Business is business."

"Curry thinks you're a hero, Keely. So do I, and Keely, I want to talk to you about our lifestyles. They're quite well matched these days. We're both detectives."

"Wrong. You and Nikko are detectives. I'm a foot reflexologist."

Punt leaned to give me a deep kiss. "I love you, Keely. Once you get out of here, I want you to give my heart some alternative healing. It's been badly bruised."

Sudden exhaustion almost overwhelmed me as I relaxed and smiled and muttered some words I could hardly hear.

"I feel sure I can help you, Punt. I never turn a needy patient away."

About the Author

Award winning author Dorothy Francis works from her home studios in Iowa and Florida, writing books and short stories for adults and children. She is a member of Mystery Writers of America, Sisters in Crime, Short Mystery Fiction Society, and the Society for Children's Book Writers and Illustrators. Her first novel for adults, *Conch Shell Murder*, received critical acclaim from *Book List*, *Publisher's Weekly*, and *Crime Scene Magazine*. She lives with her husband, Richard, a jazz musician and avid fisherman. For more information, visit her website: www.dorothyfrancis.com, or send her an email: rdfran@attglobal.net.